YOUR
PERFECT
LIFE

BOOKS BY VICTORIA JENKINS

YOUR
PERFECT
LIFE

VICTORIA JENKINS

bookouture

Published by Bookouture in 2023

An imprint of Storyfire Ltd.
Carmelite House
50 Victoria Embankment
London EC4Y 0DZ

www.bookouture.com

ISBN: 978-1-83790-507-2
eBook ISBN: 978-1-83790-506-5

For Mia, Emily and Hettie – the best of cousin love

PROLOGUE

In front of me, a piece of furniture is dragged across the room. It is dropped, hitting the stone floor with a thud that echoes. I should be able to see what's happening more clearly, but the darkness swallows the details, making the outlines of shapes barely visible. There is silence for a moment that stretches far too long, then the gentle hiss as a cap is unscrewed. My body stiffens at the sound. Then comes the liquid, slopped over the floor. The smell of petrol as it fills the dampened air.

Everything happens so quickly. The argument... the accusations; the blame for everything that is now beyond all of our control. Petrol fumes and vitriol fill the room. In the darkness, there is a flash of the blade. It all happens so quickly. I wait for the scream, but there is none.

Next there comes the click of a lighter: a tiny dancing spark that lights the darkness of this cold and dank room. No one makes a sound as the flickering flame catches the fuel and bursts alight. The fire spreads quickly, crackling and blazing, a rope of flame that snakes around the room as it follows the thread of petrol.

For all these months of planning, I should know what to do.

But I wasn't prepared for this. I shouldn't be here. And above the raging noise of the fire and the klaxon of my fear, a single thought screams louder than any other: I should never have trusted her.

The smell of the petrol and the smoke is already overpowering. If we don't get out of here soon, the smoke alone will kill us. She hasn't listened to my instructions. She writhes on the floor, her back arched, her feet moving like a drunk cyclist's as she tries to push through the pain, until eventually she falls still. I say her name, again and again, over and over. I nudge her, begging her to stay awake. To stay with me. The fire has circled us now. There's only one way to get out of here. We're going to have to go through it.

She has fallen unconscious. I don't know whether it's blood loss or the shock of the pain, or perhaps it's smoke inhalation. Whichever way, we are running out of time. She can't die here. This isn't how it's supposed to happen. Ignoring the pain that flares up my arm, I stand and feel the blood run back through my numb limbs. I stoop and lift her, fighting the pain in my hip and in my head as I heave her up and over my shoulder.

I have to walk through the fire. This must be what it means to go out in a blaze of glory. I take a deep breath, readying myself to push through the flames, feeling now that perhaps everything that has led up to tonight was all training for this; like this evening was, in fact, meant for me.

ONE

ANNA

When I come face to face with Siobhan Docherty for the first time in nearly two decades, she looks exactly as I remember her: pale-faced and faraway; somehow other-worldly. If she was a celebrity, and I was one of those freelance journalists who describes every female using the verb 'flaunting', I might describe her as ethereal. And yet she is so different to how she was all those years ago: thinner, sharper-edged; her hair darkened and shorter than she used to wear it.

She stands in the non-fiction section of the library, fingers I imagine to be beautifully manicured caressing the pages of a book she hasn't appeared to really look at, because her focus lies on the back of the room somewhere, lost to thoughts I can only guess at. I wonder where she is in this moment. I wonder whether it's a place where I was with her.

I watch her return the book to the shelf before picking up another, flicking through its contents with the same glazed disinterest she afforded its predecessor. Her head moves from side to side, eyes darting to take in the details of the room. I'm so close to her that there's no way she can't see me, so I wait for her to turn, for her gaze to eventually land upon me. And then it does. She looks right at me. And just as she always did, she looks through me before turning away.

I return my focus to the computer screen, trying to ignore the sting of her ignorance. Do I look that different? Half a lifetime has passed, but not everybody changes beyond recognition as they slide through adulthood. Siobhan is thinner than she was as a teenager, but she isn't altered to the extent that someone might not know her. And of course, I would know her anywhere. She is still as familiar to me as my own reflection in the mirror.

When we were younger, Siobhan never saw me. I was there, in the background, an inanimate feature that was neither beautiful nor functional. She paid me little attention, not unless she wanted something. Not unless I could be of some use to her. Whenever an opportunity arose where I might serve a purpose that would be recognised, I jumped at the chance. Sometimes she noticed my efforts. Sometimes she didn't. Yet every time I was grateful that I'd somehow, in one way or another, managed to get a little closer.

'Excuse me, please,' I hear her say, waving for the attention of a curiously formal tie-wearing library assistant who's reshelving returned books from a trolley. 'Do you know if you stock the rest of this series?'

He says something in reply that I don't catch, some mumbled response made with little eye contact. I watch him scuttle off to the front desk and tap something into a computer as he searches for her request. Siobhan still has the same effect on young men that she did all those years ago, apparently. She is still capable of reducing them to stammering idiots. Still capable of getting them to do whatever she asks of them. Whatever she doesn't ask. Although in this case, it is his job, I suppose.

I always used to wonder what it would be like to be Siobhan. She resembled me in some ways: we were always close in height despite the three-year age gap, same sort of build; we had the same murky-puddle-coloured eyes. But she was better than I was. She had a way of carrying herself, of making other people want to be around her, an invisible magnetic force field pulling them towards her. Every girl wanted to be her friend. All the boys wanted to be her boyfriend. She nailed exams with seemingly little effort. I longed for all those things, and I believed that one day, with the right set of circumstances, I could have them. Siobhan was me, if I'd been an improved version of myself.

I know that despite how popular she always was with the opposite sex, she has never married. I imagine this is a conscious choice, and not through a lack of offers. Looking at her now, it's easy to see just how well single life suits her. She looks glowing. Happy. And I know neither of those things should bother me like they do. Unlike me, Siobhan has been sensible. She's never made the mistake of tying her life to someone else's. She's retained an emotional freedom. I admire her for everything she is. But there's more to it than that. There always has been.

A flame flickers through me. I think of that night two years ago, still so raw that it burns me as though they're in front of me now, the scene replayed on the library floor. I got home early from work. I was exhausted, still unwell; I'd been carrying a headache around with me for days, and in the end I'd caved and told my boss I couldn't function. Looking back, I think I must have already known. Some kind of sixth sense sent me home early that day, knowing what I'd find when I got there.

I knew Dean was home, because our bedroom light was on. I was expecting him to be there – he never worked Wednesdays – though usually when I got back I'd find him sprawled on the sofa watching whatever Netflix series he was currently bingeing. I'd moan about the state of the place, resentful that there were dirty dishes in the sink or a pile of wet washing left to fester in the machine, and then I'd set about righting things, preferring to do it myself anyway because at least then I'd know that it had been done correctly.

Neither of them could have heard me. Not until I'd reached the landing, at least. There was music coming from the bedroom, the television on, the sound turned down low. And then there was laughter. A woman's. He pulled the duvet over her as I went through the door, and when I look back upon that moment – which I do too many times, torturing myself with all the ways I wish I'd reacted – it was this that seemed to hurt me more than anything else. This simple act stung like a deliberate betrayal; even though he'd been having sex with another woman, the attempt to preserve at least an element of her dignity was the thing that sliced through to my core. I could have killed them both.

My attention is yanked back to the present when I see Siobhan follow tie-man to the other side of the library. They disappear for a few moments behind a bookshelf, and when they emerge again, she's carrying the book she asked for. I wonder what it is. They're in the biographies section now, so I wonder whether it's something work-related. The man gestures to a self-service machine in the far corner. She's going to take out the book. She's going to leave.

I gather my things up quickly from the desk, and throw my coat over my arm.

Because I can't *not* speak to her. I've let her go too many times before, when I wasn't ready to face her. I've always been too scared of rejection, the thought that she might not want anything to do with me after all this time apart holding me back from speaking to her. I know there's still a chance she may try to shun me. I just need to make it as difficult as possible for her to be able to.

She's already walking towards the lift when I catch up with her.

'Siobhan.'

When she turns to me, the first thing that strikes me is how clear her skin is. It's almost too perfect, as though she's managed to filter herself in real life, every blemish and line erased. Her make-up is immaculate, the winged eyeliner applied with precision. Her hair, once dirty blonde, is now a shade of chocolate brown so rich that even the poorly lit library corner manages to catch its highlights. I find myself feeling everything I used to feel, as though I'm thirteen years old all over again, inferior and invisible in her presence.

'Hi,' she says, but it's obvious she has no idea who I am. She is looking at someone she thinks is a stranger. And perhaps, despite everything, that's what I am. Because blood might be thicker than water, but it's no more adhesive.

'It's Anna,' I tell her.

I watch her face change as the realisation reaches her. I wonder if the same wave of memories that knocked me sideways just a few minutes ago has now crashed over her.

'Anna. Oh my gosh, I'm so sorry, I didn't recognise you. You look so different.'

I don't look any different. Older, obviously, but no different really. I have the same mousy brown hair, still worn in the same styleless way. I'm not much taller than I was at thirteen, and despite the amount of comfort eating I've done over the past year or so, I've somehow managed to stay near the weight I was at twenty.

'How are things?' she asks.

'Oh, you know. Same old.'

In some ways, this is true. In other ways, everything is different. Either way, I'm already lying to her.

'I didn't know you were living in London.'

'Been here for a while now,' I tell her. Since getting married seven years ago. And since separating last year, I've still not moved on. I came here with Dean. *For* Dean. Now, there's nothing left for me here. Or so I'd thought. 'And you?'

'Greenwich. But I work not far from here.'

'Are you still in radio?'

Already I've said too much. I haven't seen her since she was sixteen and I was thirteen, so I've no reason to know what she does for a living. I can't even use the excuse of social media: her online presence barely exists, offering few clues to her life.

'Yes,' she says, nothing in her tone to suggest she's seen anything suspicious in my question. 'I'm at City Sounds now. I've been there a few years.'

There's an awkward silence in which neither of us knows what to say next. Time's a funny thing, really. Enough should have passed by now that this mightn't happen; we've had years for old tensions to dissipate, and yet here we are, both transported back to a time now consigned to history, both regressed to a former self we'd probably prefer to forget existed.

'How's your mum?' she asks.

'She's fine. I don't really see her much these days, not since I've been living in London. What about yours?'

'Same as ever.' She glances at her watch. 'I'd better be getting back. It was good to see you.'

She adjusts the bag strap on her shoulder.

'We should have a proper catch-up,' I say, too quickly. Too keen. 'I mean... it's been so long, hasn't it? I'd love to hear everything I've missed.'

She jolts as the lift door opens suddenly. A woman pushing a sleeping baby in a pram exits and walks past us. 'Um... yeah. Of course. That would be lovely.' She reaches into her pocket for her phone. 'Let me take your number.'

I recite it and watch as she taps it in, wondering whether she's even noting it down correctly.

'If you call me, I'll have yours,' I suggest casually.

'Of course.'

A moment later, my mobile starts to ring. I cut the call; I'll save the number under her name later. At least now I know it's really hers, and she hasn't tried to fob me off.

'Thanks,' I say. 'Let me know when you're free to catch up. I imagine you're busier than I am.'

She says goodbye and I watch her get into the lift. I wait for the door to slide shut before I take out my phone again and stare at the lit screen, my mind filled with the possibilities of what has just happened.

I've got her number now. I can contact her whenever I want to.

She left me once. I won't let her do it again.

TWO

SIOBHAN

After leaving the library, I wish there was someone I could call to speak to about what's just happened. But talking to anyone about Anna means explaining things I can't go into. Our lives have been separate from one another's for over eighteen years. No one from my life in London knows her or knows who she is. And no one here knows about the things that altered us all those years ago. No one would understand what makes our relationship so complex.

My thoughts drift to my mother and what she'd make of our encounter. To my knowledge, she hasn't seen Anna since I last did, and I'm not sure she's had any contact with my aunt Claire for a while either. Neither of them has come up in conversation for years now, though I realise that not talking about them doesn't necessarily mean my mother hasn't wanted to. Perhaps she's been too hesitant to bring it up with me, scared that she'll open old wounds and resurrect too many ghosts. We were all bound by the same tragedy, all too scared to scar each other further. For whatever reason, I already know my mother would be less than impressed to find out Anna has made a reappearance in my life.

The radio station isn't too far from the library, just a ten-minute walk or so across to the South Bank. It's usually a lovely walk, but today it's raining, a driving wind making any attempt at the use of an umbrella a pointless effort. I pull up my hood and raise my scarf closer to my face, bracing myself against the wet and the cold. The pavements swarm with people, a crowd of office workers and sightseers bustling to their business like an army of ants. Even when dulled by a reluctant mid-March day, the city is alive with culture and activity, and it's at times like this, when I feel displaced, that I remember the reasons I came here. I wanted to make something of my life – something more than what I'd left behind. As I wait at the crossing, I realise how much I love everything about this part of the city. I can be surrounded by strangers but never feel alone. I can immerse myself in its vibrancy when I want to. I can disappear in its chaos whenever I choose.

The lights change, and I step from the pavement, a crush of people moving with me, the weather heightening their urgency. I'm halfway across the road when I feel a shove from behind, someone stumbling into me as they lose their footing. My right shoulder is knocked forward and my bag flips from my arm. In the rush of pedestrians, it gets trampled underfoot. I swear loudly, my love for the city quickly squashed by frustration. This is the downside of the place: everyone is in a rush, always, no matter what.

When there's a gap in footfall, I make a grab for my bag. But someone else gets there before I can. He's wearing his hood pulled up, his face half hidden. At first, I think he's going to do a runner. Instinct tells me to react, but my brain sends a signal that he could be dangerous. Armed, even. My fears are quickly allayed. Instead of fleeing, he hands me the bag.

'Thank you,' I mumble, noticing behind him that the lights have turned to amber and we're about to get mown down if we don't move.

He says something, but against the downpour of rain and the hood that blocks my ears, I can't make out what it is. A car horn blares, and we go our separate ways.

City Sounds is based on the fourth floor of a sprawling glass-fronted building that overlooks the Thames. I use my ID card to gain access past reception, and when I get to the studio, Carrie is already there, always the first at work. As I tend to most days, I planned today's features yesterday, meaning most of the prep is already done. I hate anything being left until the last minute, particularly since things in radio can change so quickly. We've got a guest coming in later to talk about his rise from a childhood in the care system to BAFTA-nominated actor. Before that, we have our usual Tuesday feature of 'You Pick the Theme', which involves a listener call-in, and this for me is always one of the highlights of the week.

The afternoon show with Carrie Adams started with a small but loyal fan base and now attracts over three million listeners every week. Carrie is popular on social media, with a big following on TikTok and Instagram. I imagine that at some point she might want to branch out into television, and I don't think she'd have any issue making the transition. She's still only thirty-one, and with a Norwegian mother she has a Scandinavian beauty that's garnered her a lucrative modelling contract with a large online fashion retailer.

'Those arrived for you,' she says as I'm taking off my coat. She nods to the corner, where a large cardboard box sits waiting. The company name, *Blooming Lovely*, is printed in fancy lettering along the side. 'Please tell me I haven't forgotten your birthday.'

'Not till September,' I remind her.

I take the box to my desk and get a pair of scissors from the drawer. Carrie's gaze rests on me expectantly as she waits to see what I've been sent. I feel her eyes warming my skin like spotlights, and will myself not to flush beneath the attention. I don't want her to see my reaction. And I don't really want to see what's inside this box. I already know that whatever it is, it wasn't sent with best wishes.

It's a huge bouquet of black roses. Two dozen, at a quick scan. I lift them out and put them on the desk; there's no point in trying to hide them from Carrie, who'll only nag me for the rest of the day if I don't show her. Besides that, I'll make myself look suspicious if it appears I'm trying to hide something.

'Oh,' she says. 'Wow. They're... different.'

I suppose they may be beautiful in a dark kind of way. If you like that sort of thing. Their petals are glossy, like black velvet. Yet they send a shiver down my spine.

I don't really know why I do what I do next, but without thinking, I reach into the box and pretend to read a card. The truth is, there's nothing in there. I could see that when I first opened it. No small envelope clipped within the flowers. No note beneath the bouquet. The silence seems to speak more than words might have.

'Ah,' I say, with a knowing laugh, as if I've just read an in-joke delivered by a mate.

'Well... are you going to share?'

'Old school friend,' I tell her. 'Long-running joke.'

She eyes me questioningly but makes no further comment. I motion as though I'm pushing the non-existent card down into the box before returning the bouquet and closing the lid. Flynn, the production assistant on the show, comes into the studio just as I'm shoving the box beneath the desk in the far corner. He slips off his sports jacket and hangs it over the back of his chair.

'Morning,' he says, with his east London twang. 'I come bearing gifts.' He reaches into a paper bag and pulls out two takeaway coffees followed by two double chocolate chip muffins. I recognise the logo on the bag; he's made a point of going to one of the best bakeries around.

'One decaf,' he says, passing a cardboard cup to Carrie. 'One fully caffeinated.'

'You're a star,' I tell him, taking the drink. 'Thank you.'

'You're going to make us fat,' Carrie jokes.

Flynn rolls his eyes at me and smiles. 'Men can't win, can they? This is why I'm single.'

He pulls a chair alongside mine and together we start discussing the schedule for the afternoon's show. The next couple of hours pass smoothly. 'Anti-Hero' plays as we head towards the listener call-in, today's subject being embarrassing first dates. The topic for the Tuesday feature is always suggested by one of the previous week's callers. Last week's was text messages sent to the wrong person, the responses ranging from someone who'd pulled a sickie and then accidentally messaged their boss to ask if he fancied meeting in the pub at lunchtime, to a young man who'd sent an explicit text to his girl-friend's mum. Today's subject is likely to garner some amusing anecdotes, and Flynn gets the job of listening to them all before the callers go live on air.

'It's two forty-five,' Carrie says as the track ends, 'and we all know what that means.' She's interrupted by the cheesy 1970s game show-esque jingle we use every week. 'It's "You Pick the Theme". Big thanks to Lara from last week, who suggested embarrassing first dates as this week's topic. We've had a lot of messages about this one, all with suitably cringey tales of dates gone horribly wrong. There are so many good ones, I wish we had longer. But let's go to the phone, where we've got Ella waiting to share her story with us... Ella, are you still there?'

There's a crackle on the line, but no one responds.

'Ella?' Carrie tries again.

'I'm still here,' a voice says, distorted and barely audible. 'Time is up, you lying little bitch.'

Carrie's reactions are quick, and she cuts the caller off before either Flynn or I get a chance to intervene.

'Okay,' she says, businesslike as ever. 'Apologies to those of you who heard that, and to anyone on the school run who may have children listening in the car. This is live radio... unfortunately these things sometimes happen. Let's play some music.'

She puts on the next song on the schedule, cuts off her microphone and turns to me to roll her eyes. 'What the hell was that all about?'

'She was telling me about a date with someone she found out was one of her best friend's uncles,' Flynn says, flustered. 'I'm so sorry... I don't get why that just happened.'

'It's not your fault,' I reassure him.

'It was very specific, though,' Carrie says. 'Don't you think?' Despite her professionalism, she appears unsettled by the incident.

'You dealt with it really well,' I tell her. 'Well done. Are you okay?'

'Fine. It's annoyed me, that's all. Where do some people get off, thinking they can just behave like that?'

I shake my head and turn my attention to the schedule, pretending to focus on what's coming up next: whether we should go to the next waiting caller or scrap the feature for this week. When I look up, our boss, Dylan, is at the door, gesturing to let us know that our guest has arrived. Flynn goes over to welcome him into the studio. I find my bag and pull out a bottle of water, trying to steady my thoughts as I take a sip. The caller's words repeat in my head, a broken record spun on an endless loop. *You lying little bitch... you lying little bitch... you lying little bitch.* I watch Flynn offer Carrie a silent reassurance as he introduces the actor who's come in to be interviewed; he has a hand on her shoulder while he speaks words I don't hear over the noise of my thoughts. I could do the same; I could usher her from the room as the next song plays and tell her not to worry about what just happened. I could give her a guarantee that the words spoken weren't intended for her, and it would be true, all of it.

I know they weren't meant for Carrie. They were meant for me.

THREE

ANNA

Siobhan Docherty. Thirty-four. Radio producer. It's funny, isn't it, that our lives can be condensed to a few simple facts. Name. Age. Occupation. All the other things – the important things – are left for the few to ascertain, the intricacies of who a person really is consigned to the deduction of those who choose to stay around long enough to find out. And let's be honest, not many people even know their own partners that well. You can live with someone for a lifetime and only ever really scratch the surface of what makes them tick.

When we die, these will be the things that are known to others: name, age, occupation. The best we can hope for in the end – the *most* we can hope for – is that we achieve enough during our allotted time within this mortal coil to leave something that's worth remembering. Some sort of legacy, I suppose. Even if we don't invent a cure for a deadly disease, or design tools to revolutionise the way people live, surely we're all capable of something memorable to someone. There's that saying, isn't there, that we won't always recall what people said or did, but we'll remember the way they made us feel. That's what Siobhan did for me, back when we were kids. She made me feel all kinds of shit.

A fly on the inside of the bus window pulls me from my thoughts. There's something wrong with one of its wings. It looks as though it's trying to take off but can't, its impairment condemning it to a frustrating circular journey of getting nowhere. I feel myself relate. Then I squash it against the glass with my phone cover, putting it out of its misery. A teenage boy wearing headphones over a beanie hat glances at me from the row of seats opposite. I give him a thumbs-up, which works in turning his attention away again.

The bus pulls up to a stop and the doors hiss open to spit a couple of passengers out onto the pavement. I watch a young woman wearing a headscarf struggle to pull a buggy up the steps. The kid sitting in it starts wailing as though he's just got whiplash. No one near the front offers her any help. Perhaps I should, but I don't. Instead, I return my attention to my phone: to the photograph of Siobhan on the screen in my hand. It was taken at some sort of radio awards ceremony. There's three of them in the photograph: Siobhan, standing left, wearing a deep blue off-the-shoulder dress, her lobbed hair framing her face like a set of brackets; a blonde woman in the middle, clutching an award that at first glance looks like a gold-plated dildo but on closer inspection I realise is supposed to be a microphone; next to her, a young black man with cropped hair and the grinning enthusiasm of an overly excited puppy. All three of them look happy: the sort of happiness that easily irritates a person who hates their job with the kind of enthusiasm usually reserved for traffic wardens.

My journey to work is monotonous, and for weeks now I have filled the boredom with internet searches of Siobhan's name. Despite my time and efforts, I've never been able to find too much about her, only what she does and where she works – a vague LinkedIn profile that doesn't even have a photograph, and a few social media accounts that are mostly set to private. It's the opposite for her colleague, Carrie Adams, whose face is splashed wherever she seems able to get it, her desire for publicity apparently far keener than Siobhan's. I understand why Siobhan prefers to remain out of the limelight, though it doesn't seem right that someone like her should have to do so.

I know Siobhan. I know her better than she realises. There are two types of people in the world: those who watch, and those who want to be watched. I'm a watcher. I prefer to blend into the background and fade among the shadows, somewhere hard to see but easy to see from. For all her online secrecy, Siobhan is someone who wants to be watched. For as long as I've known her, she has been the kind of person to check over her shoulder to see who might be looking at her, hoping for the kind of attention that fortunately for her she always seemed able to attract easily. It was only circumstances that changed that, forcing her to feel she had to hide.

Siobhan is the flip side of the family coin. We're all just a fluke of nature and timing – a chance sperm meets a chance egg, leaving the less fortunate squirming towards a fruitless end. It's easier to think of things this way because it involves far less personal responsibility. The coin landed head up, and the world was blessed with the arrival of Siobhan. If it had flipped the other way, Aunt Sarah and Uncle Garrett might have been cursed with a child whose nature more resembled mine. Nurture can only account for so much. Siobhan and I share some genetic make-up, though beyond that our lives were in many ways different. Our mothers are sisters, and neither moved far from the home where they'd grown up. Aunt Sarah married an Irishman and settled down to a quiet suburban exis-tence, the perfect life until a freak accident changed everything when Siobhan was just twelve years old. I remember little about Uncle Garrett now. I know he used to call me Anna Banana, and I've a vague memory of being carried on his shoulders on a beach somewhere, but beyond that there's nothing much before the night he died.

When we were kids, Siobhan and I were more like sisters than cousins. I spent evenings after school over at her house whenever my mother worked late; she'd been a single parent all my life, only ever referring to my father as 'the donor'. According to Aunt Sarah (who I relied upon to get a greater level of information than my mother was prepared to share), he'd been a one-night stand. She'd tried to dress it up in words that sounded prettier, but I'd got what she meant, even at a young age. I appreciated her honesty. I liked being around Aunt Sarah. I liked being at their house. It felt like an extension of my own, but nicer. Everything was nice. Familiar. Until it wasn't.

Now, Siobhan lives in Greenwich, in a huge and beautiful three-storey Victorian red-brick terraced house that's divided into two flats. I went there once, not long after Dean and I split up, just to see what her life looked like now; just to feel a bit closer to her after years of separation. I realised then how much I'd missed her, and I suppose that's where my interest in her life resurfaced. I'd like to see the inside of her home, to see if it looks like the photographs I've browsed online: the open-plan living area with the windows overlooking the park; the mezzanine bedroom floor with the sloping ceilings and ornate coving. I pay attention to details. I like details.

Siobhan would probably wipe her feet after leaving my flat. The place is a shithole, previously occupied by a couple who seemed to have let their kid and their pet defecate wherever the need took them. It took two months to get rid of the smell of dog shit, and I've given up on trying to get the felt-tipped pen marks off the wall. The whole place needs redecorating, but if the landlord can't be bothered to cover the expense, I'm certainly not going to pay for it.

I'm not sure whether Siobhan owns her flat or rents it. I can't imagine ever owning anything more than the clothes in my

wardrobe and the box of sentimental crap that's followed me
from my mother's house to every flat share, hostel and terrace
I've lived in since. Dean and I rented the house we lived in, and
when I look back now, I realise this was probably a deliberate
decision on his part. The conversation about buying somewhere
together reared its head on several occasions, but he was always
quick to dismiss the idea. According to him, property ownership
is a British obsession that in other parts of Europe is mocked by
people who enjoy having a greater amount of disposable
income. Most Swiss and Italians and Germans rent, he told me.
I said that was nice for them. But we weren't in Switzerland or
Italy or Germany – we were in London, and we were being
shafted for a monthly rental that would have paid a mortgage
twice over. In hindsight, I realise it was all an excuse. He never
really wanted to commit, and I suppose a marriage was easier to
get out of than a joint mortgage would have been.

Thank fuck we never had a kid together.

Now, I'm stuck in a shitty one-bed flat in Hounslow, with a
view of the recycling bins at the back of some fancy council
offices. It comes to something when the council's reception area
is bigger than an entire floor of the tower blocks that house the
flats they offer to people struggling to find accommodation. For
anyone yet to find out, 'studio apartment' translates as poky
hellhole. My cleaning job at the hospital involves over an hour's
commute each way until I find somewhere closer that comes in
at what I'm paying here, and the chances of finding that nearer
central London are next to zero.

You could spend twenty-four hours cleaning a hospital and
the work still wouldn't be done. The place never closes, and
because it never closes, the traffic passing through it never stops,
and the illnesses keep on coming and the germs keep on
spreading and the whole act of trying to maintain some kind of
infection control becomes a thankless and near-impossible task,
like trying to keep an umbrella held up against a force 10 hurri-

cane on a dinghy in the middle of the Atlantic Ocean. The cleaners are the lowest paid, the easy pickings at the bottom of the food chain, and when things don't go to plan, which they invariably don't, we're the first people to have accusatory fingers pointed in our weary faces.

When I get to work, I keep my head down and just get on with things, as I do every shift. I speak to patients occasionally, if I'm in the right mood and they seem the right kind of person, but any exchanges with the other staff are brief and kept to the necessities. Thankfully, the day passes without incident and, for once, surprisingly quickly, though I'm sure that it's the thought of Siobhan that spurs me along and makes things more manageable.

At the end of my shift, I sign out before getting changed. My heart sinks when I see one of the porters, Billy Chapman, waiting at the lift doors. The patient with him – a skinny octogenarian in a pair of blue and grey striped pyjamas that make him look as though he's just been released from a prisoner-of-war camp – is hunched so far forward in his wheelchair he's practically at a right angle.

'Anna.' Billy acknowledges me with a smile I don't believe.

I say nothing, just wait for the doors to close again.

'All okay?' he asks, as though an exchange of pleasantries is standard day-to-day behaviour between us.

'Fine, thanks.'

He takes a step closer to me, and I edge towards the corner of the lift.

'We're probably due a chat.'

'About what?'

'Your little side hustle.'

I can see a tuft of dark hair hanging from his left nostril that moves back and forth in the breeze of each heavy exhalation.

'I don't know what you're talking about,' I lie, keeping my voice even. The last thing I want is for this prick to think he has some kind of hold over me, but when I glance at the old man, who's now somehow managed to fall asleep with his chin on his chest, I realise I'm very much on my own here, and the thought unsettles me.

'Is it earning you much?' he asks.

And then he puts a hand on my waist. I freeze with the shock of the touch, hating myself for the reaction.

'Don't, Billy. Please.'

He pulls a face, as though I've hurt his feelings. 'Don't what?'

I glance at the light above the lift door, still moving down past floors where no one's waiting. Why is it taking so long?

Billy presses himself closer and squeezes my waist.

Behind him, the lift finally pings. We've reached our floor. I look past him, though the door hasn't yet opened, and when he moves away a fraction, put off by the possibility of someone catching a glimpse of what he's doing, I take my chance.

'I asked politely,' I tell him, and then the heel of my right hand connects with his nose, a swift but effective self-defence move that I learned years ago and hoped I'd never have to use again. Blood bursts from his face in a colourful spray just as the lift doors slide open, and he staggers back, clutching his broken nose and moaning like a wounded pig.

There are six people waiting for our lift. There would be, wouldn't there. And I can appreciate how bad it looks when the sight they're greeted with is an injured man wiping blood from his nose, an apparently unharmed woman nursing her stained palm, and a sleeping pensioner in a wheelchair who's now so silent and inert that I wonder for a moment if he might have died on our descent and neither Billy nor I noticed.

'She's a fucking lunatic,' Billy screeches, launching himself into full victim mode, keen to get himself some eyewitnesses who've witnessed nothing yet other than his hysteria. 'She just went for me!'

A nurse I don't recognise rushes to his aid, while another goes to assist the man in the wheelchair. I see the old man stir. He isn't dead. Thank God. The last thing I need is the blame for that as well.

I wonder for a moment why no one else is getting in the lift before realising it's because I'm still in it. No one wants to get too close to the crazy woman with the bloodstained palm. The thought makes bile rise in the back of my throat. I need to get this bastard's blood off me. When I step out into the corridor, everyone moves aside, eyeing me as though I might at any second decide to lash out at one of them as well.

'He just tried to sexually assault me,' I say calmly.

Perhaps my voice is wrong – not teary or shaky enough. Maybe I don't look enough like a victim to convince them I'm telling the truth. Victims are beautiful and fragile and vulnerable. I caught sight of myself in the mirror before I left the lift, so I know I look more like Kathy Bates's character from *Misery*. Whatever, our audience's sympathy still seemingly lies with Billy, who's now being led to a chair at the other side of the corridor. Two of the waiting patients get into the lift. Two hang around, not wanting to miss the end of the free show that's brought unexpected entertainment to their otherwise quiet afternoon.

'Stay there,' the nurse with the wheelchair instructs me brusquely.

I shrug; I hadn't planned to go anywhere anyway. Why would I run? I'm not the one in the wrong.

Someone's already called security. An impressively unintimidating guard appears at the double doors that lead to the car park, his cigarette break presumably cut short. He couldn't look less interested if he pulled a doughnut from his pocket.

'He assaulted me,' I tell him quickly, before anyone else gets a chance to speak. 'Just now, in the lift.'

The security guard glances from me to Billy and then back again. 'He's the one with the bust-up face.'

'It was self-defence. I'm not running anywhere, am I? If I was in the wrong, don't you think I'd have pissed off by now?'

He shrugs nonchalantly before calling for unneeded backup. Billy glares at me while leeringly lapping up at the attentions of the nurse who's still pandering to him. The nosy patients who'd hung about for drama give up on their pursuit and get into the next lift, and it's just as the doors shut that, whether from a surge of adrenaline or not having eaten anything since breakfast, I pass out.

FOUR

SIOBHAN

When I get to the studio late on Friday morning, Carrie isn't there yet. She usually arrives before I do so she can spend an hour catching up with the show's social media. There's probably a delay on the Underground again. Strikes seem to be a monthly event now. With just me here, I set about my usual pre-show routine of checking through the schedule, making sure everything's in place for the day's features. But it's hard to concentrate when my mind keeps wandering off track.

I'm still unsettled about the caller on Tuesday's show. The voice was distorted, which only occurred to me much later; I was so distracted by the erratic jumping of my thoughts in the moments that followed that the only thing I was able to focus on was the fact that the words were meant for me. That night, back at home, I found the clip shared on social media and played it back. I paused it. I played it again. I repeated. I realised it was impossible even to tell whether the caller was male or female, though Flynn had said he'd spoken with a woman when they were off air prior to the call-in.

After I left the studio on Tuesday evening, I shoved the box of black roses I'd received into an industrial bin at the side of a newsagent's once I was far enough away from the building for no one to see me. I felt sick at the thought that someone was somewhere close by, watching me dispose of their 'gift'. Because someone *is* watching me; I've no doubt about that. I feel it like a sixth sense, like something brushing against my skin when my face is turned the other way. Like a ghost, I suppose.

I don't hear anyone at the door, so when there's a movement behind me, I nearly fall off my seat.

'Jesus... don't creep up on people like that.'

'I just walked in,' Flynn says casually, taking off his jacket. 'Like I do every day.'

'It's sort of normal for people to say hello or something,' I tell him a little too abruptly.

'Sorry.' He pulls his shoulder bag over his head and puts it on the desk. 'Are you okay?'

No, I want to say. Not really. I think I might have a stalker. But I can't tell Flynn this. He's worked at the studio for less than a year; I don't know him well enough to confide in him. If I tell him, he's likely to jump straight to what happened on Tuesday, and I don't want anyone here to think I'm bringing trouble to the show.

I realise now, for the first time, that I've never used the word 'stalker' before, not even in my own mind. Until recently, I'd considered the possibility of a secret admirer, as laughable as the thought was. I don't think I've used that term since I was in Year 8. I toyed with the idea that the nuisance phone calls I'd been receiving – always a 'number unknown', always shallow breathing at the other end of the line – had been intended for someone else. That feeling of being watched, I've tried to dismiss as paranoia. But I know it's more serious than that – more sinister – and I feel the threat moving closer to me.

'I'm fine.'

'Where's Carrie?'

Good question. 'Probably got held up on the Tube.'

'Never known her to be late.'

I don't tell Flynn that the same thought has already occurred to me, but I get out my phone to send her a message on WhatsApp. I wait to see it double tick, but it doesn't. She may not have signal if she's still on the Tube, though.

Together Flynn and I prepare for our Friday feature, 'TGIF'. By midday, Carrie still isn't here. The show starts in an hour. She's never arrived this close to a show's start, not even when there's been a strike on public transport. Something's happened.

'I'll call her,' I tell Flynn, and I take my phone to the window, waiting for the call to connect as I watch the world move outside, streams of people pushing along the pavements either side of the Thames in a wash of colourful raincoats and unruly umbrellas.

'Hi, you're through to Carrie. I'm sorry I can't take your call right now, but leave a message and I might get back to you, depending on who you are.'

I hang up before the answerphone can connect. Carrie always has her phone on. Always. It's never more than a couple of metres away from her. I've joked on countless occasions about her addiction to social media, offering to pay for surgical attachment to her mobile as a thirtieth birthday gift.

'Everything okay?'

I turn back to Flynn. 'I hope so.'

In the event of spontaneous illness, we've made arrangements for another presenter to always be available as backup, though we've never had to make use of the plan. Today, Mila Green is on the schedule. Mila has been working at the station for a couple of years now, co-hosting the breakfast show with another presenter who's been here longer than anyone else. When I call her, she tells me she's nearby. She's never made any secret of the fact that she hopes to have her own show one day, so I know she'll jump at the chance to take Carrie's place and present solo.

I try Carrie's phone again, but again it goes straight to voicemail. An icy cold settles on my skin, working its way through to my bones. If she was unwell, she'd have let one of us know. She would have called or messaged me. Behind me, Flynn says something, but I don't hear his words. The noise of my thoughts is too loud, and the pain in my chest tightens like a fist. Because I know in my heart that something is very, very wrong.

FIVE

ANNA

Two days after my unfortunate run-in with Billy Chapman, I get a call from my line manager. I saw her briefly on Wednesday; I came around from fainting to find myself propped like a rag doll on one of the plastic chairs in the corridor, the ones bolted to the floor in case a drug-addled patient was to decide to use one like a battering ram against a member of staff. Billy was gone – my left ear burned with the thought of what he may have been saying about me at that moment – and only the disinterested security guard was still with me. Moments later, Sheena arrived. I don't mind Sheena. She's always seemed a fair enough woman, not prone to tyrannical demands and unrealistic expectations like some of my former bosses, and she's never acted as though she's better than the rest of us on the cleaning team. But I've a feeling as I answer the call that all that might be about to change.

'Anna,' she says, pleasantly enough, though there's an underlying edge to her tone. 'How are you feeling?'

'Fine, thanks.'

'You obviously know what this call's about. We need to talk about what happened on Wednesday.'

'I told you on Wednesday what happened on Wednesday.' I can't keep the hard edge out of my voice. No one believes me, not even the woman who I'd thought in this situation might be my closest ally.

'I just need you to tell me again. This is likely to go to a hearing, you know that, don't you?'

'For Billy?' I say, the words dunked in sarcasm.

'Mr Chapman may need reconstructive surgery to realign his nose.'

'Oh dear. Well poor Mr Chapman should learn to keep his hands to himself then, shouldn't he?' There's an awkward silence. 'You must know Billy,' I say. 'I bet you've been on the receiving end of his interest at some point.'

I hear her sigh, as though the suggestion alone is an inconvenience to her. Whatever happened to sisterhood? I wonder. I know how this is going to go. There's no CCTV in the lift. That's exactly why he approached me there rather than in one of the corridors or the wards. He may be perverted, but he isn't stupid.

'You're lucky he's not pressing charges.'

'He's lucky *I'm* not pressing charges, you mean.'

I'm going to report him. Soon. Just not yet. He knows too much, and besides, there are other, more important things that need my attention first. Billy can sweat it out while he wonders what my next move might be.

'What are you accusing him of, Anna?'

I sigh. 'Let me rephrase that for you. I'm not "accusing" him of anything. What I can tell you, categorically and without any doubt, is that two days ago in that lift, when there was no one there to witness it, that fucking pervert tried to grope me.'

'Please, Anna, I know you're upset, but could we try not to have the language.'

'Fuck. Really? I've just told you, *again*, that he assaulted me, but it's my swearing that concerns you? Fuck this shit.'

I hang up on her. I know I'm probably fired now, but it'll save them the hassle of arranging a disciplinary hearing. I expect a few paper-pushers higher up in the NHS food chain will lament the loss of a free buffet lunch, but if they want to side with sewer rats like Billy Chapman, then they can stick their job. Perhaps it's for the best. I suppose it was only a matter of time before he started talking.

I turn my phone off. If Sheena calls back, I'm currently unavailable, no longer giving a shit. I go into the bedroom and pull a pair of leggings and a hoodie out of the wardrobe. I wonder what Siobhan would do in a situation like this. Would she even have allowed that piece of crap to get so close to her? The thought throws me off balance, and I sit on the edge of the bed. Was what happened in that lift my fault? Maybe I should have done something sooner than I did. I think of the way my body just froze, hating myself for my involuntary, instinctive reaction. If I looked different, would people take me more seriously? If I was someone else, would Sheena believe me?

If I was more like Siobhan, would people start to listen?

I strip off the clothes I'm wearing and stand in front of the chipped floor-length mirror that was left fixed to the bedroom wall when I moved into the flat. For someone who doesn't do much to look after herself, I'm not too bad. I've got a bit wider around the hips than I used to be, and the lithe gymnast limbs I had as a kid have given way to a less toned set of thighs. But I'm not a lost cause just yet. These imperfections could be improved upon, I think. I know from experience how quickly changes can be made, with the right attitude and a bit of determination.

After I change into the leggings and hoodie, I dig out a pair of trainers I haven't worn in as long as I can remember and leave the building, breathing in the outside air, purging my lungs of the stale stench of the flat. Once I turn the corner at the end of the road, I start to run. I haven't run in years – I'm not really built for physical exertion, more for drinking tea and reading autobiographies – and by the time I get to the top end of Inwood Park, my heart is thumping so hard it threatens to burst from my chest. I pause at a railing near the children's playground to catch my breath. The stitch in my side burns like a bitch. But I keep my thoughts on Siobhan and push off again, willing my body to do better. To remember why we're here.

The park stretches into a mini forest once I'm past the playground; an artificially constructed woodland amid the cityscape that stands beyond it. I pass dog walkers and people glued to their mobiles, so distracted by their digital existence that a couple almost stumble straight into me. I keep going over what happened with Billy Chapman and whether I should have done things differently. But there was no room or time for an alternative. He deserved what he got. It's not what he got that bothers me, though. It's what he *didn't* get. He deserved so much more. But now I'm the bad guy. I'm the one who appears violent and unhinged; I'm the person people will be wary of. Justice rarely comes to people like Billy Chapman, but for someone like me, one black mark and you're tattooed with your indiscretion for life.

When I get home, I strip off all my clothes again and stand on the scales. I'm 136 lb. Siobhan is near enough the same height as I am, and she must weigh at least 10 lb less. After showering, I sit on the bed with my wet hair wrapped in a towel and google the fastest ways to lose weight. Intermittent fasting... keto... Atkins... cabbage soup diet. None of them sound appealing. I knew this wasn't going to be easy. But then anything worth having is worth the effort in getting it, I suppose.

The stitch in my side has been replaced by a burning ambition, something I know will keep me going through the days and weeks of uncertainty ahead. I set myself a time goal. In six weeks, I must drop 10 lb. It seems realistic. Doable. I wonder how different I'll feel. How much more capable. Just the thought of it is all the motivation I need. In six weeks, I will become more like Siobhan than I am myself.

SIX

SIOBHAN

It takes me just over half an hour to get from the South Bank to Shoreditch. I've been to Carrie's flat on plenty of occasions; she's infamous for her hosting abilities and for the parties that have often continued into the following morning, but I prefer to visit when she's home alone, just to drink coffee and chat while I browse her impressive vinyl collection. We bonded over a love of music, even though our listening tastes couldn't be more different. She likes deep house music, while my escape is classic Motown. I don't know why the thought hits me in the chest as I'm exiting Shoreditch High Street station, but for some reason it does, and it shakes me to my core.

Her flat is a ten-minute walk from the station, in a sprawling block called Hanover House. I press the buzzer for the intercom at the main doors. No response. I try again, but there's nothing. I wait, wondering whether there's another entrance to the building somewhere; I presume there must be, though it'll be equally secure. I try Carrie's mobile again. Once again, it goes straight to answerphone. She must have switched it off. Either that or the battery's dead.

As I'm staring at her name on my phone screen and

wondering what I should do next, a man comes down the stairs and approaches the door. He presses a button to let himself out. Now's my chance. I go to hold the door and slip inside, but he stands in the doorway, not allowing me room to pass.

'Who are you here for?'

'Number eight. Carrie Adams.'

'But she hasn't let you in?'

'I don't know that she's there. I'm worried about her. She isn't answering her phone. Do you know her?'

The man nods, but eyes me suspiciously. I suppose the rest of the building should be appreciative of having such a safety-conscious neighbour, but at the moment he's in my way, and the thought that Carrie might be in need of help keeps gnawing away at me, making me conscious of time.

I show him my ID for the station and explain that I'm the producer on Carrie's radio show. I tell him she's just missed her own show and that it's something she's never done before. I explain that her phone is never usually turned off.

'I'll come with you,' he says, still suspicious of me.

He allows me to go first, presumably checking that I'm telling the truth about having been here before by making me lead the way. We get up to the first floor and I go to Carrie's door. I knock a few times, but there's no answer.

'Maybe she doesn't want to be bothered,' her neighbour suggests.

'Something's wrong. I know it. She would never just not turn up for work like that, not unless something's happened. She loves her job.'

His expression changes; for the first time, he's taking me seriously.

'Do you know anyone who's got a spare key?' I ask.

'Maybe next door. I mean, I don't know how close they are, but people usually leave one with someone in case of an emergency.'

'This *is* an emergency.'

I go to the flat next door, praying someone will be in. The door is answered by a woman in her forties who's dressed as though she's only recently got home from work. The man explains what's happened, and once again I retrieve my ID to prove I am who I say I am. She goes to get the spare key she tells us Carrie gave her after an incident with a burst pipe, and I feel my body sag with relief.

'Thank you,' I say to the man.

When the neighbour returns, she leads us to Carrie's door. 'Let's hope she's not got anyone in there,' she says with a raised eyebrow, 'or this is going to be embarrassing.'

I bite my tongue. Carrie isn't seeing anyone, and she's so committed to her job that she'd never skip work to spend an afternoon in bed, not even for Tom Hardy.

'Carrie!' I call. Her shoes are lined up in a rack in the hallway. On the coat stand in the corner, all her favourite jackets, the ones she wears most frequently, are hanging up. When I look into the living room, I see her handbag on the end of the sofa. I know she's home, and the air is sucked from my lungs as I wonder why she doesn't respond to her name when I call her again.

The man and woman from the neighbouring flats hang back in the hallway as I go through to the living room. There are wine glasses on the table, two of them. A plate sits empty, a few crumbs left scattered on its surface. By the sideboard, a stack of vinyl sleeves are propped against the cupboard door.

'Carrie,' I say again, but my voice sounds weaker this time, as though I'm being dragged underwater and my lungs are already half filled. I see an empty wine bottle by the draining board as I glance into the kitchen. Carrie hasn't been alone. I go to her bedroom. The door is ajar. It's dark inside, so the curtains must still be closed. I step into the room, my eyes adjusting to the gloom.

That's where I find her. She's in bed, the curve of her hips beneath the floral duvet cover, her long blonde hair spread on the pillow. She's topless. She's sleeping. It's gone six in the evening and she's fast asleep, as though she hasn't yet got up today. I say her name. I step closer. And then I see her face. Pallid. Eerily translucent. The colour drained. The life inside her gone.

A sob escapes me and echoes around the high-ceilinged bedroom. I feel hands on my shoulders, the stranger I met at the front door pulling me back, telling me not to look. But it's too late. I've seen everything. I've seen the dark marks around her throat. I've seen her naked breasts pale and pimpled with the cold, the flesh around her nipples peppered with bruises. But worse than that, I've seen her eyes, wide and terrified, her face frozen with a look of horror as she silently pleaded with whoever has done this to her.

SEVEN

ANNA

My alarm goes off at 6 a.m. on Saturday, waking me up to the realisation that I am divorced, poor and now unemployed. The thought hits me like a hangover, which would be preferable. At least if my sore head was the result of a night of overindulgence, some fun would have preceded it. I reach an arm out from the duvet and swipe off the sound, knocking the phone to the carpet in the process. Sunlight pushes through the thin bedroom curtains. The day looms ahead of me, empty and pointless. Then I remember my promise to myself. My new purpose.

I get up and dress in the clothes I wore to go running yesterday, then drink two pints of water and wait till I need to use the toilet, which doesn't take long. I tie my hair back, put on my trainers and force myself through the front door, knowing I'll need a greater level of enthusiasm if I'm going to hit my six-week goal.

My chest feels tight by the time I'm just three streets away. My jobs have always been ones where I've been on my feet, active and busy, and I'd mistakenly assumed this to mean I had at least a modicum of fitness to boast of. Turns out I'm just as breathless as I probably would be if I'd spent the last decade sitting at a laptop doing an office job, which seems an injustice really: all that ugly labour for minimum wage and my body can't even reward me with a decent lung capacity.

My pace has slowed to little more than a crawl by the time I turn onto the main road. I pass a couple of charity shops and a butcher's, where the door is open and the smell of blood and raw flesh makes my stomach flip beneath the Lycra. A few shops ahead, I see newspaper stands lining the edge of the pavement, and a headline screamed in bold red stalls my pace from a crawl to a stop.

RADIO PRESENTER MURDERED IN HOME

I stop outside the newsagent to take a closer look at the front page. Carrie Adams' photograph dominates. It's a good photo. She's sitting at her desk, her head tilted to one side, a pair of headphones hanging around her neck. If I was dead, it's the kind of photo I'd like people to remember me by. I try to catch my breath. My heart is pounding so hard it feels as though it might spontaneously stop. I'm not built for running, especially not after being starved of carbohydrates for twenty-four hours. I opted for the Atkins diet in the end, just for the promise of rapid results. I'll probably end up with breath that smells like a yak's, but that's a small price to pay for the end result.

'Shame, isn't it?'

I turn to the voice beside me. An elderly man with a dog on a lead is looking at the rack of newspapers and shaking his head solemnly. You didn't know her, I feel tempted to point out, but instead I say, 'Hmmm,' seemingly too cut up by the tragedy to find the right words for a more detailed response.

'More than likely the boyfriend,' he adds, pulling his dog back from the kerb. 'Nine times out of ten, it's the partner that's done it.'

He tuts and turns, mumbling something to his dog before

continuing on his way. I put my hands on my lower back and tilt my spine. There's a pain in my kidneys that doesn't feel healthy. I can't be dehydrated, not after the two pints of water I necked. When I bend forward, Carrie Adams is looking right at me, her eyes following mine like a creepy painting, suddenly more sinister than beautiful.

I pick up a copy and take it into the shop, paying for it with the bank card that's been tucked into the pocket of my leggings. My legs are begging not to run any further, so I dutifully listen to their needs and instead walk the rest of the loop back home.

I think about calling Siobhan to see if she's okay. To offer my condolences. But then I remember I'm not supposed to know who she works with. I shouldn't be aware of just how much of an impact Carrie's death will have on her.

I check the time on my phone. Siobhan would usually be heading to her favourite coffee shop soon; the same one she visits every Saturday morning, only ever deviating from her routine when she's away for the weekend somewhere. Surely she won't go this morning, though, not under the shadow of what's just happened?

Despite my doubt that she'll be there this morning, I get on the Underground at Hounslow East, getting off at London Bridge to catch the train. I haven't been to the coffee shop every week, obviously. That would be too much. Some Saturdays I've been working, and that was supposed to be the case today, until Billy Chapman lost me my job. I suppose, in the strangest kind of ways, I should be grateful to him. If he hadn't done what he did on Wednesday, I wouldn't be here now.

I put my earbuds in as the train rattles through the city. It's just gone 9.30: if she's going to be there, it'll be within the next hour or so. Luckily for me, the weather is good this morning, so when I get to Greenwich and reach the street where Coffee Corner is, I'm able to wait outside on one of the benches on the opposite side of the road. I open the newspaper I bought earlier and feign interest in its contents, raising it high enough so that if she should pass by, she wouldn't see me.

Almost forty minutes later, I'm ready to head home. I've read the entire article on Carrie's murder, as well as the sports page and my horoscope, which has optimistically informed me that better times are around the corner while at the same time heeding the warning that I should be wary of a stranger delivering good news. That's when I see her, turning onto the pavement further up the road.

Even though she's wearing sunglasses, I can tell that she's exhausted. She's dressed in leggings, a pair of boots, and a baggy coat that swallows her small frame. Her shoulder-length hair is pulled back in a messy bun at the nape of her neck, and her posture is rounded, her pace slowed with fatigue. Did she find out about Carrie's death in the same way I did? Did she check her social media this morning to be assaulted with a hashtag using her colleague's name, or did someone call her to tell her what had happened?

I'm surprised to see her at all, but I'm grateful that she's made it here. There's comfort in the familiarity of her routine, which is probably the reason she's managed to leave her flat this morning. Maybe she doesn't want to be alone. None of us wants to be alone really, especially not at times like this.

I watch her go into Coffee Corner. I expect her to stay in there for a little while, twenty minutes at least, so I stretch my legs for a moment, my bum numb from sitting on the metal bench for so long. Movement from the coffee shop catches my eye, but when I look, there's just a man leaving through the front door. I go to return to the bench, but moments later, Siobhan also leaves. She's holding a cardboard takeaway cup in one hand, her bag slung over the other shoulder. She's still wearing the sunglasses. I watch as she walks away, unsettled by the change in her routine, then I wait for a gap in the traffic so I can cross the road to follow her.

She heads into Greenwich Park, and once there stops to sit on a bench. I hang back near the trees at the park's edge, finding a spot at the boundary wall where I can stand and pretend to take a call, my phone pressed to my ear, listening to silence. It's a lovely morning, so I suppose it makes sense that she's ventured outside rather than staying in the coffee shop as she usually does. Perhaps she needs the fresh air to clear her head. I wonder what's going on in there; what thoughts are trailing circles in her brain. I wish I could sit beside her, rub her arm to make it better. Hold her like I did when we were children, to make the pain go away.

She keeps her head lowered, occasionally looking up from her phone and her coffee, but never enough to show her face. I wonder whether she's keeping herself hidden to conceal her grief-stricken features, or if there's another reason she hopes to fade into the background.

A man passes her and drops something into a nearby bin before heading out of the park. Siobhan looks up. Her gaze follows him. Moments after he has disappeared from sight, she gets up. She takes her coat from the back of the bench and puts it on before picking up her probably now empty cardboard cup. She walks to the bin and disposes of the cup, but almost immediately changes her mind and takes it back out again, slipping it into her bag. She looks around shiftily, checking whether anyone might be watching, but the few people nearby are absorbed with their dogs or their phones, no one paying sufficient attention to notice what she's doing. I wonder just how much Carrie's death has affected her. More than I realised, if her odd behaviour is anything to go by.

She begins to walk again, reassured that she's not being observed. The idea sparks a pleasure in me that I know isn't normal, but I'm used to it. These small triumphs. My little victories. I am always here, at a distance. I see most things, and now I wonder as I watch her walk away whether her behaviour this morning has been caused by Carrie's death alone.

I follow her through the park and out onto the main road, staying close enough that I can keep up with her but far enough away that I won't be spotted should she sense she's being followed. We turn off, and she heads up the steps at the back of a supermarket. I stop and stand at the railings, pretending to check my phone as I turn my back to her. I can't follow her any further. She's heading towards the police station.

EIGHT

SIOBHAN

I've never been in a police station before. This one seems impressively clinical, either kept purposely minimalist in an effort to make sure everyone inside the place is calm and subdued, or else the product of a bored desk sergeant prone to decluttering when there's a quiet day on the capital's crime front. That day is not today. News of Carrie's murder hasn't so much rippled across the city as collapsed in a tidal wave upon it, and the headlines this morning were a reminder of a nightmare it feels like I'll never escape.

As I wait in the reception area, I try to fight the image that keeps returning: Carrie lying on her side, her throat ringed with dark bruises like some macabre choker. The memory of it brings bile to my throat. She was so young. So brilliant. She was one of my closest friends, and I can't yet begin to process what life will look like without her in it. But more than all these things, there's another thought that won't leave me alone. Her eyes. That they were open. That they saw everything.

'Ms Docherty?'

My name pulls me from the nightmare. A plain-clothes officer is standing in front of me.

'If you'd like to follow me.'

I get up and go with her through the double doors at the end of the corridor. Yesterday, at Carrie's flat, I was too shaken to give a statement. I was barely able to speak, my words choked with the horror of what I'd seen. There were police. A forensics team. People everywhere, swarms of them, their faces all a blur. Someone kept asking me if I was okay, but I've no idea who it was. All other voices were muffled beyond the one I could hear the loudest and the clearest: the anonymous voice that had spoken to us just a few days earlier during the phone-in. *Time is up, you lying little bitch.*

Once I was near-functioning again, an officer told me I could come to the local station this morning to give a statement. It all feels very formal, as though I'm considered a suspect, but I suppose it's just procedure.

'Ms Docherty? Would you like to take a seat?'

I sit at the desk, and the woman asks if I'd like a cup of tea. I tell her white, no sugar. When she leaves to get it, I check my phone. There's a message from a number I don't recognise.

Hi Siobhan. So lovely to see you on Tuesday! When are you free for that catch-up? I'm off on Thursdays and Fridays, so let me know when's good for you. Anna x

I realise I never saved her number, so I do so now. I start a reply, but before I'm midway through, the officer returns. She passes me tea in a cardboard cup and eyes me with sympathy as she takes the seat opposite.

'How are you doing?' she asks. 'This must be so difficult for you to process.'

'I'm fine,' I say, an automatic response that once aired sounds ludicrously out of place. It occurs to me now that she must have told me her name at some point, but I haven't heard it. I'm still existing in a fog of shock. 'Do you know who did it?'

'We're following a couple of lines of inquiry at the moment.'

I know that's my cue to not ask any more. Whatever they may or may not think they know, it isn't to be shared with me or anyone else. The truth is, they may know nothing. Regardless, I keep on.

'There must be CCTV at the building?' I press. 'Whoever did this, he was in the flat with her. It must have been someone she knew.'

I close my eyes for a moment, but immediately regret doing so. All I see is Carrie's pale throat and the bruising that ran in a chain around it.

'As I say,' the officer says kindly but firmly, her eyes meeting mine as I open them from the nightmare, 'we're looking into a few things.'

I bite the inside of my cheek, frustrated, and take a sip of tea. It's so hot it burns the tip of my tongue, but it's a welcome pain, a reminder that I'm still alive.

At the officer's prompting, I go through everything that happened yesterday, from getting to work and Carrie not being there to finding her in the bed and then blanking out. Throughout my account, the woman watches me with a disconcerting intensity.

'Thank you,' she says when my statement is completed. 'I appreciate this can't have been easy for you.'

I ask her to keep me informed about any developments, although why would the police do this? As far as they're concerned, everyone is a suspect, and I suppose that includes me. It's only a matter of time before they begin to investigate that phone call to the radio station, and once they do that, it won't take them long to realise I'm inadvertently linked to all this, even if no one, including me, yet knows how.

After leaving the police station, I make my way back towards the park. I put my headphones on and find the track I've listened to twenty times or more already this morning: an early noughties dance track that was one of Carrie's favourites. It came on in a bar one night when we were out with some of the other staff from the radio station, and I recall so vividly now how she looked: the floral skater dress that skimmed her thighs, her blonde hair piled high on her head; I can picture how she danced without caring what anyone might have thought of her. I envied her that abandon, that ability to remove any shred of self-consciousness to just live in the sound of the moment.

And now she's gone. Just like that, everything stolen from her.

A hand grips my shoulder and my arm swipes back instinctively, my elbow ramming into the chest of the person behind me. I turn sharply, bracing myself for an assault that doesn't come. It's Flynn. He looks fraught and sleep-deprived, dark rings circling his eyes.

'What the fuck, Flynn,' I say, pulling my earphones from my head. 'What are you playing at?'

'I need to talk to you, Siobhan. Can we go somewhere?'

I feel as though ice has just been injected into my bloodstream. The chill starts at my shoulder where he touched me and snakes through my body like a parasite, quick and relentless.

'This is about Carrie, isn't it?'

He doesn't answer me. But he doesn't need to. His eyes fill with tears and his face is stamped with panic.

'Jesus, Flynn.'

I step back and he grabs me by the arm. 'Please. I need your help. I need to explain everything to you.'

'Get off me,' I tell him. His fingertips are digging through my jacket, pressing into my skin. I think of the bruising on Carrie's neck. The marks around her breasts. An intrusive image fills my head: Flynn straddling Carrie on her bed, his hands squeezing the life from her.

He lets go. Instinct tells me I should run, but I can't. My feet are pinned to the ground, my body too weighted to move.

'I didn't hurt her,' he says quietly, his eyes darting to the people passing us. 'I loved her.'

I don't know what I'm supposed to make of this, or what the hell is going on. Flynn has been an assistant on the show for little less than a year. Neither Carrie nor I expected him to hang about for very long; he's young and ambitious and the station is a stepping stone to lead him to bigger things. Never over the past twelve months has there been anything to suggest that the relationship he had with Carrie was anything other than professional, for either of them.

'Can we go somewhere? Please.'

I deliberate. He's panicked me with the uncertainty of who and what he is, yet this is Flynn: the man who arrives at work with coffee and muffins for everyone, who always asks how people are in a way that suggests a genuine concern for their well-being, a man who holds doors open with old-fashioned gentlemanly manners; he is a *gentle* man, in the true sense of the word.

There's a café just around the corner from the train station. We go in and take the table in the far corner, suitably removed from other customers but public enough that should anything happen, there are other people about to help me. We wait until a young woman comes over to take our order before continuing the conversation that was started on the street.

'I was there,' Flynn says, his voice broken with panic. 'I was at her flat.'

'When? What do you mean?'

I don't think Flynn's a killer. I may not have known him long, but I just don't believe it. But then... how would I know, really? He might be capable of anything. We're all capable of anything under the right circumstances. Or the wrong ones.

'We went out together on Thursday night. I went back to

her flat. I left early the next morning. She was fine, Siobhan. I promise you, when I left there, she was fine. She was happy.'

I put my hands to my face and try to press out the headache that's twitching at my temples. 'Can we go back a bit? You and Carrie... when did it start?'

'About eight months ago. Remember that night we all went to the comedy club? There was this thing between us then. She was flirting with me all night, rubbing her leg against mine while we were having dinner, making suggestive comments when we went up to the bar together. We ended up in a hotel.'

I remember that night well. There were six of us: me, Carrie, Flynn, Mila, Dylan and his wife. I got a taxi back to Greenwich with Mila, who was living not too far from me at the time. Carrie told me she was going home. She texted me when she got there, as she always did when we'd been out anywhere together, to let me know she was back safely. Except apparently she hadn't made it home. If Flynn's telling the truth, she must have texted me from the hotel.

'Why the big secret?' I ask, not really understanding why they hadn't wanted anyone to know. There's the small fact of Flynn being a good few years younger than Carrie, but they were both adults and both single: they weren't hurting anyone.

Flynn shrugs. He's about to answer when the young woman comes back with our drinks. He sits silently as she puts two lattes on the table, waiting until she's gone before he speaks.

'It was exciting. She loved the sense of danger. I mean, so did I, I suppose. She was out of my league, you know that. I didn't expect it to last. She made it clear it was just sex.'

'But you wanted more?'

'Not at first. But then... yeah, after a couple of months, I did.' He pushes his drink away. 'Siobhan. Look at me. Please. I didn't hurt her. I promise you, I never laid a finger on her. Not like that.'

I think back on the conversation I just had with the detective at the police station. CCTV cameras. The fact that any visitors would have been picked up coming and going. Flynn had been in the flat with her. If the police don't already know that, it won't be long before they find out. They'll see him going in with her on Thursday night and coming out on Friday morning.

It's as though he's able to read my thoughts through the changes in my facial expressions.

'Siobhan,' he says, his eyes pleading with mine. 'I need you to believe me.'

'Because the police aren't going to?'

He laughs bitterly and raises his hands in the air. 'Look at me,' he says, a little too loudly, attracting the attention of a man sitting at a nearby table. 'Black fuck-buddy none of her friends knew about? I'm the easy target.'

He sits back, his jaw tight. I can't pretend to know what Flynn's life has been like, or the challenges he's faced. He talked a bit about his family background when he interviewed for the job of production assistant, and Carrie and I were both drawn to his honesty and humility, to the fact that though he hadn't had an easy upbringing, he'd done everything he could to escape the pattern of destructive behaviour we later found out had mapped the lives of his older brothers.

'Maybe you should be honest about the relationship,' I suggest. 'Tell them now before it comes out? Because it will, somehow, eventually.'

'But as soon as I do, I'll become the prime suspect.'

I can't argue with that. He's right. Perhaps the police will try to claim the murder was motivated by jealousy, or that Flynn had become violent when Carrie tried to end things between them. I can't imagine what he must be going through right now, but it still pales in comparison to the thought of what poor Carrie endured in those final moments leading up to her death.

'I'd been arrested three times by the time I was seventeen,' he admits, staring into the beige surface of his milky coffee. 'The first couple of times it was literally just for being somewhere. Not somewhere I shouldn't have been, or somewhere that suggested I was causing trouble or was about to cause trouble... I was just *there*, in the wrong place at the wrong time. Or the right time, as far as the police were concerned. The third time was a case of mistaken identity. Because all black teenage boys look the same, don't they?'

He tears the end from a sugar packet and empties its contents into his drink.

'I didn't kill her, Siobhan,' he says, still not meeting my eye. 'I loved her.'

He stirs the sugar into his latte. He doesn't look as though he has any intention of drinking it.

'You believe me, don't you?' he says looking up at me, his voice pleading and pitiful. Desperate. 'Please, Siobhan... I didn't do it.'

'I know you didn't.'

This much is true. I don't believe Flynn killed Carrie, because I think I know who was responsible. No... that's not entirely true. I don't know who he is exactly. Not yet, anyway. But I think the person who's persecuting me may also be the person responsible for her murder, because anything else seems too coincidental.

Time's up, you lying little bitch.

NINE

ANNA

It doesn't take long to hunt through my wardrobe for the nicest thing I own. In fact, it's less of a hunt, more a ten-second grab and run. The little black dress laid out on the bed beside me – knee-length, pretty in a plain, unassuming sort of way – has seen me through job interviews, dinner dates and funerals, and based on the disastrous history of all the aforementioned, it's safe to assume it's never likely to bring me much luck. But it'll have to do. Today, it adds reunions to its résumé.

I didn't expect to hear back from Siobhan this quickly, or to be meeting her before the weekend was even out, but I'm guessing this is her way of trying to keep busy. Trying to keep her mind off things. I search for her Instagram account – the only one of her socials not set to private – and browse the limited number of photographs I've already seen countless times. She's not that active on social media; most of the photos she shares are holiday snaps, all in the kind of far-flung places I've only ever been able to dream of visiting. Exotic locations and fancy dinners take the limelight. Never her. No smiling selfies or posed photos by famous landmarks. Siobhan, it seems, prefers to stay hidden.

I message her a couple of hours before we're due to meet.

Are we still okay for 7?

I don't expect to get a reply until later, but there's one within minutes.

Of course. See you there. Looking forward to it.

I wonder if that's really true, or whether simple curiosity is what's bringing her to me today. She must be as nervous as I am about meeting up properly again after all this time. She must worry that the conversation might take us down a path to which she doesn't want to return.

I get to the restaurant first. I've booked under my name, and a good-looking waiter wearing thick-rimmed glasses shows me to the table.

I've not been there long when Siobhan arrives. She looks beautiful in the kind of way that suggests she's made little effort when it probably took her three hours to get ready. She's wearing wide-legged trousers, heeled shoes and a denim jacket over a white blouse with an oversized bow at the neck, and she looks like a model from a fashion blog. If I wore the same outfit, I'd look as though I was auditioning as a circus act. I never managed to be quite as cool as Siobhan was. I swallow the ball of jealousy that sits in a lump at my throat. We're not kids any more, Anna, I remind myself. There's no room for that now.

'Hi,' she says, as she takes her seat. 'Thanks for booking this place. I've never been here before.'

'The food's always good,' I tell her, when the truth is I've never set foot in the place before. I can't even afford to eat out at McDonald's, but I don't want Siobhan knowing that. I went for middle of the road with this restaurant: fancy, but not too extravagant. Tripadvisor made the decision for me, and if the food turns out to be useless, watching the waiter will have been money well spent.

'I'm actually not feeling very hungry,' she says, scanning the menu. 'Typical, isn't it?' She laughs, but there's no humour behind the sound. If anything, she looks sad. Beautiful, but somehow tragic, like one of those paintings of a Tudor queen you know later gets her head chopped off. 'I'll probably just order a starter. You don't mind, do you?'

'Of course not,' I tell her, grateful that this is going to prove a cheaper evening than I'd budgeted for. 'Are you feeling okay?'

'Fine. How are things with you, anyway?'

'Not so bad,' I lie. 'Work, eat, sleep, repeat. Same old.'

'Where are you working?'

'Pinewood Hospital.'

I don't tell her what I do there, and she doesn't ask. I also leave out the detail about getting sacked. She probably assumes I'm a nurse, and I don't correct her.

The waiter returns to take our order. Siobhan orders a starter and I do the same, because at eleven quid for a bowl of soup, I can't afford to even be looking at main courses.

'I hope I've not spoiled your meal,' Siobhan says, once the waiter's left us.

'No, not at all. I'll get something else if I fancy more later.'

I watch her reach for her glass of water and sip it tentatively, wondering whether she lied when she said she was fine. She doesn't look too well, her cheeks a strange shade of grey.

'Are you sure you're okay? You don't seem yourself.'

Not that I'd know, I think. Not that I *should* know. Siobhan should be a mystery to me, unseen and barely spoken of in so many years.

'God,' she says. 'I'm so sorry. I promised myself I wasn't going to do this, but it's so hard to switch my mind off from anything else.'

'What's happened?'

'You may have heard about Carrie Adams?' she says. 'The radio presenter who was...' She trails into silence, watching me expectantly.

'Oh my gosh,' I say. 'Yes, I read about what happened. You work together?'

'I produce her show.'

I feel my mouth contort, eyes widen. 'Siobhan, I am so sorry. It's just awful. Poor woman.'

I wait a moment before asking, 'Do they know what happened to her?'

What I really mean is, do they know who did it? Everyone knows what happened to her, or a version of it at least: the account of her final moments shared in sensationalist detail by a gutter press exploiting someone else's misery to sell pages.

Siobhan shakes her head. She falls silent for a moment, and I watch her pale face flush with discomfort. I can't remember ever seeing her like this before. As a teenager, nothing ever seemed to unsettle her. She was always in control; or at least she liked to think she was. In fact, I'm the only person who knows exactly when that control was lost.

'I found her,' she tells me. 'I was worried about her when she didn't turn up for work, so I went over to her place. She was...'

But again she can't finish her sentence. She reaches for the napkin on the table beside her and presses it to her mouth, as though trying to force the words back down her throat, swallowing them to make them disappear. As though if they can be undone, the truth might somehow be different. Her friend might still be alive.

'Oh my God,' I say. 'That must have been horrific for you.'

The waiter comes over with our food. He eyes Siobhan awkwardly, registering her reddened and wet eyes, unsure whether he should acknowledge them by asking if everything's all right or whether it's best to stay quiet and say nothing. I thank him on behalf of both of us, Siobhan lowering her head to hide her face. When he leaves, she looks up at me with a forced smile.

'This smells delicious,' she says, as though the last five minutes didn't just happen. She picks up her spoon, but it doesn't make contact with the contents of the bowl. I wonder just how much she usually eats, or if grief is currently affecting her appetite. I can't afford for her to lose any more weight. It's going to be difficult enough matching her as she is now.

'You need to keep your strength up,' I say, nodding to her soup. She manages a small, grateful smile before finally taking a sip from the spoon. I do the same. It tastes disgusting. There's some weird flavour in it, strong and off-putting, like aniseed, and I have to put my own napkin to my mouth to disguise my reaction.

Silence settles in stretches between small talk about the weather and the restaurant's art nouveau decor (as if I'm expected to have a clue about that sort of pointless shit), and we manage to avoid any further talk of Carrie. It's only a couple of days since her death. Too soon for Siobhan to have started processing it. Too soon for her to be eating in a fancy restaurant like she's celebrating something, too, but I'll assume it's self-preservation rather than insensitivity: she probably doesn't want to be sitting at home on her own.

'Let me pay for this,' I say, once we've finished our drinks.

'No, honestly, I can't do that.'

'I insist,' I say, putting a hand across the table and resting it lightly on her arm. 'Please. I'd like to. It's been so lovely to catch up with you after all this time. I just wish it had been under better circumstances. I'm so sorry about your friend.'

'Thank you.' She reaches to the back of her chair and puts on her jacket. 'It's my turn next time then,' she says, and my heart swells at the thought that there will be a next time: that she wants to see me again.

'It's a deal.'

We say goodbye awkwardly, neither of us sure whether we should hug or kiss cheeks or neither, and in the end our body language is so stilted that humour breaks the tension and we both end up laughing at our own self-consciousness.

'I'll speak to you soon,' Siobhan says. 'Thanks again.'

I watch her leave before I take my phone from my bag and tap out a message.

Always here if you need someone to talk to. Anna x

I won't send it yet: it's too soon. In an hour or so, maybe. I'll give her time to think back over the evening first, to wonder whether she said the right things at the right times, or if she might have said or done anything to expose the cracks we've so politely and silently papered over since our meeting at the library.

I put on my own jacket before calling the waiter over for the bill, and when he brings it, I pay in cash with the notes I took from Carrie's purse just after I'd squeezed the life from her.

TEN

SIOBHAN

I've tried my best to act normally over the past couple of days, but it's been the hardest thing I've ever had to do. No one expects me to turn up for work on Monday, but the thought of staying home alone terrifies me. That's why I arranged to meet Anna last night, to be anywhere other than in my flat, with only the silence and my thoughts for company.

Flynn hasn't made it in. I'm the only one who knows about him and Carrie, and I'm not saying anything. It isn't my place. My heart tells me he's not responsible, yet before too long the police are going to turn their focus upon him anyway. When that happens, I'll do all I can to help him, though I wonder now whether his absence today will end up making him look more guilty. And I wonder just how likely it is I'd be able to help him without turning too much attention to myself.

'I didn't expect to see you today, after... you know,' Mila says by way of a greeting. 'Dylan told me you were still coming in.'

Mila has temporarily taken Carrie's place, until they find a new presenter and a new name for the show. We've been inundated with messages of support and condolences from listeners, both online and through the post, Carrie's desk currently a shrine adorned with flowers and cards.

I take off my coat and hang my bag on the back of my chair. 'Staying home isn't going to help anything,' I reply, only because she's looking at me and waiting for some kind of response.

'I can't imagine what you're going through. I heard about... you know... what happened when you went to the flat.'

I realise as I look at my desk that we've no schedule for today's show. I usually would have planned for the Monday show after Friday's had ended, but I was too concerned for Carrie's well-being. I couldn't wait to leave the studio as soon as 4 p.m. hit. Now, we're going to have to wing it, something I've never yet experienced in my career. I should care, but I don't. I can't bring myself to, not with Carrie gone and everything hopeless in her absence.

I ask Mila to sit with me while we mock up a rough plan. We're going to have to recycle some old features and hope no one notices, and if they do, I hope our listeners are sensitive enough to understand the reason for the shambles this afternoon is likely to be.

'Dylan wants me to address Carrie's death at the start of the show. Are you okay with that?' she asks.

I don't envy her the task. The coward in me wishes we didn't have to do it, as though by not mentioning it we might undo the truth, but I know it's unavoidable. Everyone already knows; Carrie's face has been smiling from the front page of every newspaper I've seen over the weekend, happy and carefree against the stark and brutal headlines announcing her violent death.

'I don't think we have a choice,' I tell her.

Together we decide what she should say. I suggest a few tracks, music we would never usually play, more suited to a Friday-night late show than a Monday afternoon, but I know they were some of Carrie's favourites. Mila says she'd also like to choose a couple to dedicate to Carrie, and I don't object; I don't have the energy.

By the time the show is due to start, I already feel exhausted. I have a headache that pulses at my temples, and every time Mila opens her mouth, it drives a wave of annoyance through me. I try to swallow the irrational bitterness I feel towards her as I listen to her voice come in after the show's opening record ends. An REM song. It couldn't be further from what Carrie would want.

'Good afternoon,' she says solemnly. I'm Mila Green. It's Monday the twentieth of March 2023. Most of you will already be aware of the terrible news that has shaken City Sounds to its core over the weekend. Needless to say, everyone here at the station is devastated by the news of Carrie Adams' death.'

She speaks slowly and deliberately, with that forced affectedness newsreaders have to quickly adopt when there's breaking news of a tragedy somewhere. It's unfair of me to resent hearing her voice and knowing she's sitting in Carrie's chair. This isn't her fault. She's doing a brilliant job in the circumstances, professional in a near-impossible and last-minute situation. I just wish it didn't have to be so. I want so badly for everything to return to how it was just a few days ago, when we all naïvely believed ourselves to be secure and safe in our routines.

My mind zones out from what's happening around me, enough focus retained to see me through the next three hours. The show is a disaster, but I don't think anyone, including Dylan, is expecting anything more. I leave without saying goodbye, desperate to get home. I barely functioned over the weekend. I moved through the appearance of a routine as a survival method. I met up with Anna because I couldn't bear to be alone. Carrie and I had countless mutual friends, but since her death I've realised that none of these people are the type I can actually call or talk to. Acquaintances would be a fairer word to use than friends. We've drunk together, danced together, shared work-related anecdotes and stories about places we've been. We know *of* each other. That's it. None of us really knows each other at all.

I pick up my phone and look at the message Anna sent me after our dinner. I'm sure that as far as she's concerned, I'm popular and successful. That I have a contacts list full of friends I can call on at any time to help me through my grief. I'm happy for her to continue to believe these things. Despite everything, she always thought I was the grounded one.

I'm stepping into the shared hallway area when Dominic appears at the door of his flat. He's wearing woollen plaid pyjamas that along with his bed head and bleary eyes manage to age him by about twenty years, though he must be only a few years older than I am.

'Found this left on the doorstep earlier,' he says, in his thick Leeds accent. He looks at me awkwardly, embarrassed about something, and when he's close enough for me to get a better look at the box in his hands, I realise why. It isn't addressed to me. There's no flat number; my name appears nowhere on the cardboard. Instead, there's a photograph stuck to the top of the parcel, fixed with multiple layers of Sellotape to presumably protect it in case of rain. Or to make sure it can't be easily removed. Either way, it's me. An old version of myself: the person I was once upon a time, before the life I live now.

Dominic hands me the parcel, doing everything he can to rest his focus on anything other than the photograph. When I take it from him, I find it's surprisingly light despite its size.

'I heard about your colleague. I'm sorry.'

'Thanks,' I say, avoiding eye contact.

'If you need anything, you know where we are. Actually, Freya made a shepherd's pie earlier. She was going to bring some over, but I told her I thought you might be vegetarian. You wouldn't have been in anyway. *Are* you vegetarian?'

I nod.

'I'll let her know. She'll do a cheese and leek pie next time. She makes a really nice one actually, with mozzarella, although she might have to tweak the recipe what with cheese costing what it does now. The prices on everything have gone crazy, haven't they? And I can't remember the last time I saw a leek anywhere, come to think of it.'

He stops abruptly, aware that filling the space between us with talk of his girlfriend's dairy preferences and the rate of inflation is somehow only managing to make it feel more claustrophobic.

'I'll let you get inside. If you need anything... like I said...' and he gestures awkwardly to his door, as though if I do ever happen to think of calling on either Freya or him for assistance of any kind, I'm likely to find them both sitting out here in the hallway patiently awaiting my request.

I wait till he closes his front door before I go through my own. Upstairs, I put the box on the coffee table in the living room, then take off my coat and hang it up before returning to study the photograph. I must be fourteen or fifteen. I'm wearing a bright blue crop top and wide-legged baggy jeans, my pierced belly button on display. My mother told me I couldn't have it done, but I went and did it anyway. I probably thought I looked great at the time. Three months later, the hole got infected. My mother tried not to be smug about it, but failed spectacularly in her efforts.

I'm trying to remember where the photograph might have been taken, but there's so little background to go on, it's hard to tell. It could be someone's living room. It could be the nightclub at the back of the working men's hall that used to hold under-eighteens parties. It could be the school hall. The photo has been cropped so that I'm the only person visible, though there was someone else there with me, so close their hand can be seen resting on my shoulder, their arm amputated from the rest of their body when the image was cropped. I tell myself I don't know who it is. There's so much I don't remember. And there's so much I do remember that I would rather be allowed to forget.

I go to the kitchen for a pair of scissors and return to open the box. My hands are shaking as I slice through the tape that holds its lid closed. The box is filled with bubble wrap, at first glance appearing to contain nothing else, but when I move it aside, I see something within it, navy blue and obscured. I unwrap it. It's a baseball cap. Kappa, with the symbol of two female figures sitting back to back. The kind of cap teenage boys wore back in the 1990s when I was a kid.

I drop it as though it's burned me. I don't know who it belongs to. I've never seen it before. Not this exact one, at least. Maybe something similar, or another just like it. There's a tightening in my chest, like the onset of a heart attack. This cap represents the past, and it's the possibility of the implied time – the month, the day, the moment – that sends fear snaking through me, injected into my veins. Nothing happens by coincidence, not any more. The cap stares at me accusingly from the kitchen table. I push the lid of the box back down so I can see the photograph, my fingertip tracing the arm of the unseen person beside me. I know exactly who it is. I might try to lie to myself, to convince myself sometimes that things were different to how I remember them, but I can only fool myself so far.

Thoughts of Lewis have stayed with me my entire adult life. He was my first proper boyfriend, and in so many ways my first real friend. The first person to show me true loyalty. I saw what he did for me, I recognised it for everything it was – and when he needed me most, I let him down. I could have changed what became of his life, what became of him, but I didn't. I was too scared for myself. And then I was scared of him, too. No matter what I'd believed him to be, his confession painted a different picture.

Nothing has ever been sent to the flat before. Everything

I've received so far has been sent to the station; it's easy enough for anyone to find out where I work. It was unnerving, but it wasn't like this. I feel as though someone could be in the flat right now, watching my every move, and my thoughts are jolted to Carrie, to the notion that she was inadvertently dragged into the mistake I made almost two decades ago. But why would someone hurt her because of what I did? Because of what I didn't do.

The baseball cap continues to taunt me from the table. I should throw it out. Burn it.

The thought scoops a hollow from my stomach. Fire.

I can still smell the smoke; I can still taste its acrid tang on the back of my swollen throat. The memory of its noise fills my ears in a hissing, spitting thrum. What if everything comes back to that night? What if all of this comes down to what we did?

ELEVEN

ANNA

I should probably explain why I did what I did, or at the very least how I came to be in Carrie Adams' flat. I used to be her cleaner, going back nearly a year now. Obviously that was no coincidence: I knew exactly who she was, and I knew her relationship to Siobhan. I knew they worked together and that beyond the studio they were friends – or so Siobhan thought, at least.

When you're friendly to people, it's amazing what you can get them to believe. The right smile, some kind words, a listening ear... they see what they want to see when you wear the right disguise in front of them often enough. If you're suitably skilled at assuming a false persona, you can get people to confide in you with just about almost anything. I've always been a good listener, just not for the reasons people assume. Carrie liked me. I left her home immaculate. Spotless. I've always been good at what I do. Within just a couple of visits to her place, she was making me cups of tea once I'd finished my work. We'd sit on the sofa side by side like friends getting together for a catch-up. It wasn't long before we started chatting about subjects beyond the weather and her work. I got to know details. I like details.

Carrie trusted me. After a couple of months she gave me a spare key to the flat so she wouldn't need to stay home while it was being cleaned. I did extra jobs to help her out, like the ironing she would leave in a pile on the chair in her bedroom, and though she offered to pay me extra for my time, I always made a point of refusing. I needed her trust far more than I ever needed her money.

The truth is, I liked her. She was never the type of woman I would normally choose to spend my time with, but maybe that was the point: she was different, and that was the thing that was appealing about her. It may sound strange now, after my admission that I ended her life, but sometimes bad deeds are done for good reasons, and this is one of those cases. Carrie wasn't the friend Siobhan thought she was; I found out as much when I overheard a telephone conversation one afternoon.

She hadn't realised I was still there. I'd been delayed that day: there'd been a hold-up on the Tube for some reason I don't remember now, and I was over an hour late arriving to the flat. When she got home from work, I was on my hands and knees in the bathroom, scrubbing the base of the shower cubicle. I don't know who she was talking to; I never caught a name. But I heard Siobhan's. *Thinks she's something...* those were the words she used. And I understood. I knew before she'd even said my cousin's name that she was talking about Siobhan, because I'd felt exactly the same way about her. The description was recognisable. *Hopefully she'll move on... everyone knows how ambitious she is... she'd drop us all without a second thought.* I got it.

By the time I came out of the bathroom, the conversation had ended. Carrie's hand flew to her heart at the sound of the door, and I apologised for scaring her, explaining then why I was there so late. I'd put my earbuds in so she'd think I'd been listening to music and would have no clue that I'd overheard what she'd said. Not that it would have mattered. As far as she would have known, I'd have had no idea who she was referring to anyway.

I sent her a message a couple of days later to tell her there'd been a family emergency and I needed to go home to my mother's for a while. She replied to say that she was sorry to be losing me temporarily, and that the job would still be there if I wanted it when I returned to London. The first thing that struck me was that she hadn't asked whether everything was okay or said she was sorry to hear I was having problems; her first thought was for herself, as I imagine it must have been most of the time. It seemed an unfair slight upon Siobhan somehow, though at the time I wasn't sure why.

It was the memory of that telephone conversation and those final texts that drew me to Carrie's home on Thursday afternoon. I knew she wouldn't be in; her show ran between 1 and 4 p.m., and she was rarely home before 7 p.m. on a work day. I planned to wait, to look around a while and see what I could find there. Someone like her was bound to have skeletons lurking about. I just needed to find the right closet.

Before I'd given her back the spare key she'd loaned me, I got a copy cut. I kept it in a safe place, never thinking I would use it. But I had it just in case, and the knowledge alone made me feel secure. It somehow made me feel closer to Siobhan. I never planned to kill Carrie. I realise no one will believe that, but it's the truth. I should have left after a couple of hours – enough time to learn that whatever I'd been hoping to discover was unlikely to be found there – but I got distracted by her books, her vinyl collection; her life. Just being among her things again after all those months of separation felt liberating. For a few stolen hours, I was someone else. I was immersed in another life. But Carrie's life was never the one I wanted.

I was in the bedroom when they got home. I'd left the living room exactly as it had been when I'd arrived, so when they went in, there was nothing to suggest anything was other than normal. Along with Carrie's voice, I heard a male one I didn't recognise.

When they came into the bedroom, I'd had time to move the books I'd been looking at on the bed, but the duvet had been disturbed and there were clothes on the chair that I'd taken from the wardrobe. Neither of these things seemed to matter to her, though, not when she was so absorbed by the man she was with. I was under the bed by the time the door opened. It was so low I was barely able to squeeze beneath, and when the slats began to move with the weight of the couple above me, they were little more than centimetres from my face. Fortunately, I've never suffered from claustrophobia. I was always good at hide-and-seek as a child, mainly a result of being able to contort my small frame into the spaces my opponents wouldn't risk attempting for fear of getting stuck. As children, Siobhan and I spent hours playing hide-and-seek in her parents' enormous garden, and until she'd got accustomed to my favourite hiding spots, I'd managed to outsmart her by folding myself into the tightest of spaces behind the shed and the fence. I'd spent prolonged periods of time hiding and waiting, though admittedly never beneath a bed while two people were having sex above me.

I had no idea who Carrie was with, but an hour or so after they'd got back to the flat – and after thirty minutes of grunting and moaning that refused to be drowned out even with my fingers in my ears – the man swung his legs over the side of the bed and I saw a pair of black feet pad their way across the carpet. I thought of the photograph I'd seen while I was scrolling my phone on the bus on the way to work: the one with Carrie and Siobhan with the production assistant from the radio show. Flynn something. Was this him?

I got a cramp waiting for him to go home, but after a while I realised he wasn't going to. The turn in conversation quickly revealed that this wasn't a one-off between them, and when they started discussing the radio station, my guess at his identify was confirmed.

'I didn't miss what you were doing in front of Siobhan the other day,' I heard Carrie say teasingly.

'When? What do you mean?'

'At work. All that "this is why I'm single" routine when I commented on the chocolate muffins.'

Flynn said nothing, but her words were followed by a horrible sucking noise like someone using their tongue to try to extract a piece of meat from between their back teeth. They were kissing again, and the thought of it happening just inches from my face was enough to make my stomach churn, my earlier hunger pangs soon forgotten.

'I wonder what Siobhan would make of this if she knew,' Carrie said after a while.

'Why would she care?' Flynn said.

'I reckon she'd be jealous. She's so uptight all the time. She probably needs a good shag, let some of that tension out.'

'Carrie,' he mock-scolded, managing to give her name more than two syllables.

'Come on, I'm just messing around. It's still true, though.'

He laughed awkwardly. 'I thought you and Siobhan were friends?'

'We are. Sometimes, I suppose. But I still like to call people out on their bullshit from time to time.' Silence settled between them. I had to hold my breath for so long I started to feel as though I might pass out. 'What?' Carrie said eventually. 'What have I said?'

'Nothing. I just... it doesn't sound like you when you talk like that.'

'You don't really know me, though, do you?'

There was a sharp, acidic edge to her tone, and from the silence that followed, I guessed Flynn had been cut by it. Beautiful, successful Carrie Adams and her adoring lapdog. What a fucking idiot he was.

'Do you want me to go?' he asked, his voice pathetic. I wanted to slide from beneath the bed and confront them both then, mainly to tell him to grow a pair of balls. He was letting this woman talk to him like crap, and instead of standing up to her, he was rolling over and inadvertently begging for more.

'No. Unless you want to.'

She knew he didn't want to leave. What she also knew was that he'd have done anything to stay; he was infatuated with her to the point that a stranger overhearing their awkward exchange could hear the desperation that dripped from his words. Flynn might have almost defended Siobhan, but he'd still joined in with the mean-girls laughter that followed Carrie's nasty assessment of their co-worker.

'I'll be nice about Siobhan,' she said, in an annoyingly overly affected voice, mocking my cousin and this Flynn idiot in one short statement. 'Will that make things better?'

And then they started back at it again. Honestly, I thought I was going to lose a limb by the time they'd finished. My right shoulder was dead and my mouth was dry; I'd lost track of time and my will to live was quickly following.

Once it was eventually all over and they were both asleep, I was able to slide out from under the bed. I needed to pee, so I used the bathroom. That's when I should have left the flat. But I didn't. Instead, I helped myself to a piece of cheese and a couple of cherry tomatoes from the fridge, and I waited. I couldn't get that conversation out of my head, and the more I thought about it – the more it replayed in my brain – the further the mist descended.

I'd seen red before, but this wasn't the time or the place for that, not with two of them in the flat. I've always been confident in my abilities, but I'm not arrogant enough to assume I could fight my way out of a two-to-one situation, no matter how much alcohol had been consumed by the opposing team. Besides that, Flynn hadn't said anything bad about Siobhan. In fact, he'd made a half-hearted defence against Carrie's thinly veiled vitriol – something she hadn't responded to with much grace. I suppose that counted for something.

I slid back under the bed before he woke up. I heard him stirring, then saw his bare feet appear just a couple of feet from my face. He dressed quietly, careful not to disturb her. I hadn't really thought through what I'd do if he didn't leave, so it was a relief when he did. I was alone with her, just the way it needed to be.

Carrie Adams had got under my skin. Something about the pair of them in that room had brought back memories of Dean and that bitch he worked with, and once again I was stung by the regret of not having done anything about it other than divorce him. I'd effectively just handed him over to her, to do with as she pleased. I'd let them both get away with it.

Siobhan deserved better. Those spiteful, hate-filled things Carrie had said about her felt too personal for me to let go, as though in bad-mouthing Siobhan, she had inadvertently insulted me. Neither of us deserved it. But Siobhan is too nice to stand up for herself, and that's where she's always needed my help. That's why I waited a while longer, letting the resentment fester.

I heard her stirring beneath the duvet about an hour after Flynn had gone. I inched slowly across the carpet, sliding out from under the bed on the side he had left. I waited a moment to listen to her breathing, still heavy enough to tell me she wasn't yet fully woken. Pushing onto my knees, I saw that her eyes were closed, her face turned to the space Flynn had left. My fingers reached out to her, meeting her skin. She reciprocated, her hand touching mine. I slid onto the bed. Moved on top of her. Then she opened her eyes.

TWELVE

SIOBHAN

It starts with a strange smell. It's burning, but it's not the kind of charcoal smell that comes from forgetting a piece of bread in a toaster or putting too much food beneath the closed lid of a barbecue. This is something far more overwhelming; something that clings to your clothes and your hair, seeping into your skin and embedding itself in your memory with permanence. This is a chemical smell. Something far more sinister.

The fire is thick and solid; it looks tangible, as though if I reached out to grab it I might be able to hold it while it wriggled for freedom, a slippery snake of flame that would writhe and coil, charring my skin. I look down to the duvet that's pulled over my legs, but it's not my duvet cover: not the one I went to bed with earlier tonight. I recognise it, though. Spots and stars in yellows and pinks. The duvet cover I had when I was a child. It's on fire, melting to my legs as it disintegrates and burns.

I don't feel any pain. I know I should, that I should feel *something*, yet my body is numbed, not really belonging to me. I try to move, but I can't. I panic at the paralysis, but even fear isn't enough to send a jolt of feeling through me. And then my other senses heighten, compensating for the absence of a physical sensation. The noise builds in a crescendo. I try to scream, but my face won't move. My mouth can't make a sound. It's then that I hear his voice, breaking through the cacophony of other noises. One word. My name. So fleeting and brief, it might not have been there at all. *Siobhan.* I hear it so clearly he might be standing at the bed beside me. I try to call back, but I can't. Downstairs, I see him as he might have been. I picture him lifeless at the bottom of the stairs. I smell that smell again and realise it's me, my flesh on fire. Then I hear a scream, shrill and piercing, but I know it only exists within my head.

My eyes snap open. In the darkness, I grope for the duvet on top of me, feeling the familiarity of its embroidered pattern. As my eyes adjust to the darkness, I see the shape of the furniture in my bedroom, and my pounding heart eases slightly, the safety of my home bringing the bad dream to an end. For now, at least. I sink my head back into the pillow and inhale slowly, counting to five. Then I breathe out slowly through my nose, this time counting to ten, exhaling the confusion of memories that have merged into one long nightmare.

And then I hear the scream again, though I understand now that it wasn't a scream that broke through my sleep to rouse me: it was someone ringing the doorbell.

I reach for my phone from the bedside table and press its screen into light. It's just gone 1 a.m. My nerves are shredded, and when the bell goes again, I ignore it: it wouldn't be the first time a passing drunk has pressed it for no reason other than to be annoying. When it rings a fourth time, I check my doorbell app to see who's outside. I can see the doorstep, but there's no one on the grainy image from the camera. Then someone moves into focus: a dark shadow, hood pulled up, face concealed. He looks up, his face framed on the screen in front of me. Flynn.

'What are you doing here?' I say into the phone. 'It's one in the morning, for God's sake.'

'I've just been released from the police station. Please, Siobhan. Can you let me in?'

No chance. I've still only got Flynn's word that he didn't kill Carrie. It means nothing. I might have thought him innocent – harmless, even – but I've no proof of that. My fear that somehow Carrie's death is inadvertently my fault is for the moment just that – a fear. I've no proof to offer any weight to the suspicion, and until I do, I can't trust Flynn, no matter how much I might want to. I can't trust anyone. I can't let him into the flat. There's no one else here. If anything happened, no one would know.

'You need to go home,' I tell him. 'I can't help you. I'm sorry.'

'They think I killed her. My fingerprints are everywhere – I never tried to hide that they would be. I told them all about us, about Carrie and me, but they think we had an argument, that I killed her because she said she was finishing things between us.'

I get out of bed and open a drawer for a sweater. 'But they let you go.'

'They must know it doesn't stand up,' he says, his voice breaking. 'Why would she have let me go back to her flat if she was planning to end things? Why would she even have gone out with me that night?'

It doesn't make sense, but then neither does the fact that there were no signs of a break-in. Whoever killed Carrie had been with her inside that flat – with her because she had let them in. It was someone she knew. Someone she trusted. And Flynn was there, he's made no secret of the fact.

'Do you have a lawyer? I can recommend someone.'

'I don't need a fucking lawyer,' he snaps. 'You told me to tell them the truth, and now I'm totally fucked.'

His tone cuts through the air. I've never heard him speak to anyone like this before. There's another side to him, obviously – one he's managed to keep hidden for the past year.

'And I still think you've done the right thing,' I tell him.

'I'm prime fucking suspect,' he shouts at me through the app.

I step away from his voice, my finger poised over the button that will cut him off. The angrier he gets with me, the stronger the sliver of doubt that has wormed its way into my brain becomes. Because what if he really is guilty? It wouldn't be the first time I've got a person wrong. I was wrong about Lewis all those years ago.

'I'm going to go now, Flynn. I'm sorry. I'll do everything I can to help you, but you need to go home. We can talk tomorrow. I can get you a good lawyer, someone who'll find a way to prove you didn't do this, okay? Trust me.'

But why *should* he trust me? He has no more reason to trust me than I have to trust him.

I hear him swear before I cut him off. The room feels bigger in the silence, its darkness swallowing me. My mind returns to the shadows of my dream. My nightmare. The chemical smell that hung over me when I lay in bed remains as though seeped into my skin, tainting everything I touch. This is the power of memories, I suppose. This is the lingering strength of the senses.

I'm ripped from my thoughts once again when my phone, still in my hand, starts ringing. Withheld number. I swipe the screen, put the phone to my face and blurt a 'hello' that sounds like an accusation. It's meant to.

'Who is this?' I say, when no one responds.

For a moment, there is silence. Then comes the sound of breathing, steady and controlled. In a way, it would be preferable if whoever this is was unhinged and erratic, their breath, along with their actions, rambling and confused. Instead, I know that the person at the other end of the call, silent in their intention, is acting deliberately, every move, every inhalation calculated and planned. For the first time in a long time, I wish I didn't live alone. I wish there was someone else here to reassure me that everything is going to be okay.

THIRTEEN

ANNA

On Thursday, Siobhan invites me over to her flat. She sends me her address, unaware that I already know it. Ignorant of the fact that I've been here before. I dress down, opting for a pair of leggings and an oversized sweater that's got a coffee stain down one sleeve and a hole at the wrist of the other, purposely going for the look of someone with not quite enough energy to care about how she looks. Someone vulnerable. A woman in need of a friend. I press the button with her name next to it at the main door and wait for her to let me in.

'It's good to see you,' she says as I follow her upstairs.

I can't imagine this is how Siobhan's home usually looks. There's laundry in a messy pile on the chair by the window; dirty cups and plates left on the coffee table. She has always been such an organised and precise person, so I can only assume this behaviour is recent – a result of her grieving for her friend.

'How have you been?' I ask, now that my mind's on the subject of Carrie.

'Okay. Well... not great.'

'Are there any updates on what happened? Any news?'

She shakes her head. If she knows anything about Flynn

being there with Carrie the night before she died, she's keeping it to herself, for now at least.

'Would you like a cup of tea?' she asks.

I nod and follow her as she heads to the kitchen area on the right-hand side of the large open-plan living space. The stairs to the mezzanine floor of her bedroom curve in a grand white spiral, the room above them open to the rest of the flat. It's as fashionable as I'd imagined it would be, like something from an Instagram-post. Everything seems to be in order, a place for everything and everything in its place. I have the urge to shove a cushion out of place, just to set things a little off-balance.

She flicks on the kettle and takes a bottle of milk from the fridge. 'How about things with you? Everything okay?'

'Not really,' I tell her. 'I lost my job at the hospital.'

She puts the milk down. 'Oh, Anna, I'm so sorry. What happened?'

'I was sexually assaulted by another member of staff.'

Her mouth forms a small circle. 'God, that's awful.' She pauses, tentative about asking for more details of what happened. 'Was it a doctor? Do you want to talk about it?'

Not really, but I tell her anyway, along with Sheena's response to the incident. It comes with the revelation that I'm a cleaner and not medical staff, though Siobhan gives no reaction to this.

'That's terrible,' she says. 'I still don't understand how you've lost your job over it, though. Surely there's someone else you can go to, someone senior to Sheena?'

'I'm just a cleaner.' I shrug. 'No one cares.'

'I care.'

Those two simple words fill me with a sensation I wasn't expecting. I didn't realise just how much it would mean, even after all this time. All I've ever wanted is for Siobhan to see me. For her to realise my true potential.

The kettle boils and she makes us both tea. She hands me a

cup before apologising that she doesn't have any biscuits to offer. 'I've been a bit disorganised,' she says, by way of explanation, but I suspect the truth is that she never has biscuits in the flat, or much else that involves more calories than an apple.

'Had this already happened when we met at the restaurant on Sunday?' she asks. 'I'm so sorry, Anna – I spent the whole time talking about myself.'

'Yes,' I say, waving a hand to bat it away. 'Look, it was nothing compared to what you've been going through. You've lost a friend. This bloke's just a creep. He'll get what's coming to him.'

I follow her to the living room and we sit at opposite ends of the sofa.

'Will he, though? He's the one who assaulted you, yet you're the one who's lost your job. Doesn't seem like any kind of justice to me.'

'Do you believe in karma?' I ask her.

'I don't know. I suppose I've never given it much thought. Do you?'

I raise an eyebrow and shrug. The truth is, if karma existed, I probably should have died a hundred deaths by now. The universe doesn't know what it's doing to that extent, and the only people who like to think it might are the ones who can't bear to believe that sometimes bad shit happens for no reason and with no consequence.

'I like the idea of it,' I tell her.

'No one should have to rely on it, though. Not where people like that are concerned.'

I start to tear up. I've been able to do this for as long as I can remember, always with the left eye first. Think of something sad and relive the moment – that time my mother refused to buy me the same light-up trainers that Aunt Sarah had bought for Siobhan – then blink hard after about thirty seconds. Wait for the first drop, then blink again quickly, three times, to set the rest in motion. Like a dodgy tap that only works with a certain sequence of turns.

'Are you okay?' She looks at me more intently than anyone has in as long as I can remember. She cares. She cares about me and what happens to me, and the feeling of it warms me, like stepping into sunshine after being housebound through a long and lonely winter.

And then, because I have no intention of making it stop, I allow the floodgates to open.

'Oh, Anna.' She moves beside me and puts a hand on my arm. 'It'll be okay.'

Three simple words. So easy to say. So meaningless. How does she know that? She can't guarantee anything, any more than I can myself.

'It won't be,' I tell her, wiping my eyes with my sleeves. 'I can't afford the flat without my job. And who's going to offer me another job knowing I've been suspended from my last one for assaulting a colleague?'

The word 'colleague' manages to scrape the roof of my mouth on its way out. Billy doesn't deserve even that.

'I haven't got any savings to fall back on. I lost everything in the divorce.'

We've not really spoken much about Dean yet. He was mentioned briefly when we met for dinner, but I didn't want to go into too much detail. I don't want Siobhan to know too much about my life. Knowledge is power, after all.

I apologise for getting upset. She rubs my arm before getting up and going back to the kitchen. In the open-plan living space, I'm able to watch everything she does. While her back is turned to me, I take a look up to the bedroom. If she was in bed, I'd just about be able to see her from where I'm sitting on the sofa. It's the kind of layout that could only suit a single person or a couple, because it affords no privacy to anyone unless you're in the bathroom. Yet there must be a spare bedroom, through the door next to the bathroom behind the staircase.

'I just remembered these,' Siobhan says, returning with a plate of shortbread. 'Someone gave them to me for Christmas. Don't tell her if you ever meet her, but I don't really like shortbread.'

She puts the plate on the coffee table, but neither of us touches it. I can't afford to: I've lost two pounds but I still have another eight to go.

I make a mental note to pay more attention to her eating patterns. I try to remember whether she was the same around food as a teenager. She's definitely thinner now than she was then, though there was never much of her back when we were young. I always assumed she was naturally slim, in the way her mother was, but in hindsight it's possible that she had an eating disorder. My mother made the odd comment here and there, but I was only a kid – I never paid too much attention. I was too busy idolising Siobhan to listen to anything my mother had to say.

She sits back down next to me. 'I've got a proposition for you.'

'Sounds ominous.'

'Nothing of the kind,' she says with a smile. 'Why don't you come and stay here for a while?'

My hands close tighter around the warm mug. 'You're serious?'

'I wouldn't offer if I wasn't. It makes sense – it'll give you a chance to find a new job without paying rent for a while. You can find somewhere new once you've sorted yourself out.'

'I... I don't know what to say. It means so much. Thank you.'

'So is that a yes?'

'It seems a lot to ask.'

'You didn't ask. I've offered. And look... this isn't a purely selfless move on my part. To be honest, I'd appreciate the company. This place can be too quiet at times.'

'I always wondered how you managed... living alone.' My words cast us into a sudden and somehow unexpectedly noisy silence. I can hear the ringing of my ears, tinny and high-pitched. 'I won't get under your feet,' I tell her. 'You won't know I'm here, I promise. And as soon as I find myself another job, I'll look for another place to rent.'

'There's no need to rush anything.'

A single tear falls from my left eye and trails slowly and dramatically down my cheek. I couldn't have executed it with better precision. I wipe my nose with my sleeve.

'Thank you, Siobhan. You've been so kind. Kinder than anyone's been in a long time.'

She puts a hand on my arm. 'There are some face wipes in the bathroom,' she offers, subtly letting me know that my mascara has run and my face is a mess. 'Take your time.'

I thank her again before going to the bathroom. After using the toilet and washing my hands, I stand at the sink, my palms pressed against the porcelain. The mirror reflects the state of me: reddened eyes, chapped lips; mascara streaking my cheeks in broken rivers of black. I look like a disaster. A train wreck of a human being. I smile. If nothing else, I can put on quite a performance when I need to.

FOURTEEN

SIOBHAN

Anna moves into the flat two days after I invite her to stay, despite having to pay rent on her flat for the next six weeks. I offer to pay for a removals van to collect her things, but she assures me that she doesn't own very much and it won't be necessary. She arrives just after lunchtime in an Uber, and the driver pulls two suitcases from the boot and a third from the back seat. It seems a pitiful accumulation of possessions for a life of thirty-one years, though maybe she prefers to travel light.

I wonder whether she's spent her adult life to this point running away, and the irony of the thought doesn't pass me by. We're all of us running from something, whether we stay in the same place or not.

She smiles awkwardly as the taxi pulls away, noticing my brief but inescapable assessment of her things.

'I've got the kettle on,' I tell her. 'Come on, let's get you inside.'

I take two of the bags and usher her into the building, wanting her to feel at home here. The last thing I need is for her to think I'm judging her.

'Let me take one of those,' she says, but I insist on managing both cases, lugging them up the stairs.

I pull them through to the spare bedroom. The door is open ready, the bed made; everything arranged just so, to make her feel as welcome and at home here as possible. There's a vase of tulips on the windowsill, and I bought some toiletries that I've laid out on top of the chest of drawers in case she's forgotten anything.

She drops her rucksack on the bed as she takes in the details of the room.

'Take whatever time you need. I'll leave you to unpack and get settled in.'

I pull the bedroom door closed behind me and go to the kitchen. I retrieve my phone from where I left it plugged into its charger by the microwave and continue scrolling the news report I was reading when Anna messaged me to say she was almost here.

SUSPECT ARRESTED IN CARRIE ADAMS MURDER CASE

Flynn. I think of him here in the early hours of Tuesday morning, desperately pleading for my help. I want to offer it, to do something, but I fear that things are now beyond my control. And the doubt that set in has taken hold. I don't really know him. I know nothing about him. For all I know, confiding in me about his relationship with Carrie might have been a ploy to try to get me onside before the police became involved.

The truth will rise to the surface, I tell myself. Somehow justice will be served. Yet I know this isn't always true.

A man has been arrested in connection with the murder of Carrie Adams, the radio presenter who was found murdered at her home on Friday 17th March. The man, who was known to

Ms Adams, was yesterday questioned by police but has been released pending further investigations. Ms Adams, 31, had been the presenter of the popular afternoon show at City Sounds Radio for a number of years. Her colleague, Dylan Sykes, said of her: 'Carrie was brilliant at what she did because she had a natural way with people – she was funny and warm, and she will be missed by everyone who knew her.'

There's a comments section beneath the article. I know I shouldn't look at it – it will inevitably be filled with the vitriol and unsolicited opinions of keyboard warriors and armchair experts – but I open it anyway, mentally preparing myself for what I know is about to come. It starts off without insult or offence, people passing on their thoughts and condolences to her friends and family, or commenting on what a terrible crime this is. Then comes the gossip.

Anyone else hear the call-in a week or so back? Reckon it might have been the person who did it?

I said the exact same thing to my boyf! Def too much to be a coincidence!

Wonder who this man is that's been arrested. Might be someone she works with.

I scan the rest of the comments, praying no one has mentioned Flynn's name, because despite my doubts, he remains innocent until proven otherwise. Thankfully no one has mentioned him. Though I assume it's only a matter of time before somebody does.

'Everything okay?'

Anna stands at the bedroom doorway, silently watching me. I hadn't heard her there.

'Fine,' I say, locking my phone.

'Is there any news?' she asks, as though she somehow knows what I was looking at. 'Have the police caught anyone yet?'

The words are spoken with a childish simplicity, evoking

images of officers in fancy dress chasing men in striped jumpers with oversized handcuffs.

'No,' I say, not wanting to mention Flynn. 'Not yet.'

She comes over to where I'm standing and places a hand on my arm. 'I don't know how you're coping. You know... keeping on going after what's happened.'

I meet her eye. She's looking at me in that way she used to, too intently, trying to probe my brain with her gaze. It has the same effect now that it did two decades ago. And I know what she's really trying to say. *You've done it before... it must be easier the second time around.*

'That's what we have to do, isn't it? Keep going.' I go over to the kettle.

'It's for the best.'

I turn at her comment, not knowing why it sends a shiver snaking through me, chilling me to the bone. 'Pardon?'

'It's the best idea,' she says. 'To keep going. Keep yourself busy.'

I eye her for a moment. She smiles sadly, pityingly. 'What is it?' she asks innocently.

'I forgot that tea I was going to make you,' I say, when the truth is that her words have unsettled me for reasons I can't put my finger on.

She takes a seat at the table as I make the tea, the silence stretching into too much time to think.

'Do you know when the funeral is?' she asks eventually.

'Not yet. I suppose it'll depend on when the investigation is over. They'll need to release her body.'

I feel sick at the thought of Carrie lying on a cold steel table, or stored in one of those chillers like you see on TV. I've no idea whether this is what really happens, but whatever the reality is, she is alone, somewhere none of the people who love her are able to join her.

'Are you okay?' Anna asks with concern.

'Fine.'

But the truth is, I can't stop thinking about her words. *It's for the best*. I've heard them before. I just can't remember where or when.

FIFTEEN

ANNA

It's lovely here. Better than lovely. From the window seat in the open-plan living room I can sit and watch the world go by, and there's a surprising amount of it considering the street on which the building stands. Siobhan is lucky that her living room windows are at the back of the house, where she gets a view of the wide expanse of park that pushes into the distance – a rare selling point for London properties. Amid the carpet of green fields that stretches beyond the wall at the back of the small yard, there's plenty of opportunity for people-watching. Over the past hour, I've observed two dog walkers arguing over one unleashed dog's attack on another, seen a mother cradle a crying toddler after he fell off a scooter, and watched a teenage couple making out beneath an enormous oak tree that stands just along the footpath.

Since I got here two days ago, Siobhan has looked after me like a child. I mean this in the best of ways. I'm not as annoyed by it as I'd expected to be; if anything, I'm grateful for her attention. It feels safe, being here. It feels like home. I wonder if she's doing it for me or for her. Being busy probably helps take her mind off Carrie's death, and I know despite her best intentions that her invitation wasn't extended for purely altruistic purposes. I am her distraction. Her project, in a sense. Despite everything she thinks and believes, she needs me far more than I need her.

I have a little money stashed away; enough to cover food and contribute towards bills for the next few weeks. I still have the numbers for some of the people whose houses I used to clean; tomorrow I will call a few to find out whether they'd like to have me back. I gave up on domestic cleaning when I got the job at the hospital, but in many ways it was better: most of the work was cash in hand, and if anyone gave me any bother, I could just stop working there and pick up another property easily enough, usually through recommendations.

But for now, I'm just going to bask in the feeling of being here, within Siobhan's life and among her things.

I go upstairs to her bedroom, something I've not yet done since moving in. I've wondered for a while now if she has carried a box of memories with her from home to home, small trinkets and photo albums; tickets and greetings cards. She's definitely the type. I start by looking under the bed, but it's one of those divan-type things and it's too low to the floor for much to be kept beneath it. There are fitted wardrobes with sliding doors that take up one wall. Inside, her life is organised with precision: clothing hanging in colour categories, shoes lined up in neat rows like stiletto soldiers; cosmetics and hair products shelved as though on display in a boutique salon.

Everything I touch is going to need to be replaced exactly as it was before I opened these doors. I reckon Siobhan is particular enough to notice if anything is out of place. She must have some sort of condition. It isn't normal for a home to look like the inside of a John Lewis store, and there's a part of me that wants to tear through the place – to pull dresses off hangers and smash perfume bottles against the smear-free mirrors. I hold in the temptation, swallowing it down with gulps of air that calm the simmering rage within me.

There's a small suitcase standing at the base of the left end of the wardrobe. I take it out and put it on the bed before unzipping it. Inside, there's a collection of summer sandals and a folded beach bag, as well as a sunhat that I recognise from one of the few social media photographs Siobhan has allowed to be made public. I'm about to return the suitcase to the wardrobe when I notice the half-zipped pocket at the front of it. There's something wedged inside. A photograph. I take it out and smooth it between my fingertips. At some point it's been crumpled, presumably by Siobhan. I picture her balling it in a tightened fist, trying to crush the memories, imagining that they might be erased if the faces can't be seen. Out of sight, out of mind. The attempt at destruction has left a map of fine cracks in the image, but at some point Siobhan obviously changed her mind and tried to flatten it back out, stashing it under a pile of books, perhaps, to try to undo some of the damage.

She looks exactly as I remember her as a teenager: willowy and thin-limbed, the long hair she always wore loose back then straightened so that it stretches down her back. I'd forgotten just how much lighter it used to be. Dirty blonde. She's wearing a cropped vest top and jeans that hang from her narrow hips; she looks like a member of a noughties girl group, and I feel for a moment exactly as I used to all those years ago: admiring of her, and jealous as hell. It looks as though the photo was taken at a house party, though it's hard to tell from the background. There's a hand on her shoulder. The owner has been cropped from the image, but I know who it probably is. Lewis Handley.

I don't remember much about him. Or rather, what I actually mean is that I don't remember much about him before his name and face were plastered across the front of every local paper. Ironic, really, that before his arrest he was a nobody. Or perhaps that isn't true. Maybe it was more the case that he was a nobody before he got with Siobhan, and that she was the one who made him noticeable. Without her, no one would have remembered his name. Without her, his life might have turned out so differently.

Why hasn't she thrown this photo away? I doubt she welcomes any reminder of the past, especially not the parts that involve Lewis. Yet she's kept this image of herself, too scared to let go of the girl she once was. I return it to the pocket in the suitcase. The fact that it's here is confirmation enough for me. Siobhan may have moved, but she never really moved on.

I put the suitcase back before finding myself distracted by a trouser suit hanging at the end of the wardrobe. It's rose gold and tailored, with high-waisted trousers and a short jacket – the type of outfit you'd see on a celebrity at a red-carpet event. She must look amazing in it. Successful. Powerful.

I take the hanger from the rail and lay the suit out on the bed before stripping out of the clothes I'm wearing. When I catch sight of myself in the floor-length mirror, I cringe at my underwear: greying white bra and oversized granny pants that have frayed at the seam of the left leg hole. Siobhan wouldn't be seen dead in anything resembling what I've got on, and the thought leads me to the drawers at the other side of the bed, where I find her collection of underwear.

As I rifle through the items in the top drawer, it occurs to me that she owns bras that probably cost more than what I'd earn in a day. My fingers move across cotton, silk and lace, and I take out a couple of things just to get a better look at them. Just to wonder what-if. And then I find myself removing the old items I'm wearing, kicking the knickers aside as though I'm shedding a layer of skin, and pulling on Siobhan's. They're slightly too tight, pinching at the top of my hips. But I'm still a work in progress, I remind myself. I put on the bra. It needs some chicken fillets, like we used to wear back in the day when we were little girls playing at being women.

I go over to the mirror and assess myself with a critical eye. There's no natural light on the mezzanine floor, but with the bedside lamps tilted at the right angle, I feel as though I'm under a spotlight, centre stage in her domain. My skin looks mottled, like it does when it's cold – purple and patchy. Does anyone really like the sight of their own reflection when they've only got their underwear covering their modesty? I might have lost a bit of weight, but the ripples of fat across my stomach still look like a trifle that's been tipped on its side during the car journey back from the shop.

When I put the suit on and turn back to the mirror, I'm happier with the person I see looking back at me. I smooth the front of the jacket, fiddling with the buttons to see whether it looks better undone or not. I've lost enough weight for it to almost look on me like it might on Siobhan, though I imagine I'm not quite there just yet. Not yet, but it won't be too long.

I find Siobhan's straighteners and plug them in, then pull them through my hair, trying to curl the ends under with some styling wax I found in the bathroom. I pull my fringe to one side, just as she wore hers to go out last night. I have a job interview in a couple of days, with a recruitment company. I've not done office work in years, but it's not rocket science and I'll soon pick things up again. If I decide to go for it, that is. I like it here at Siobhan's, and I know that once I get a job I'll be expected to look for a flat, as we agreed. It's just that now I'm here, I don't want to leave the place. I don't want to leave her.

'Hi,' I say into the mirror, practising my best smile. 'I'm Anna Fitzgerald. It's great to meet you. I'm so excited about this opportunity. I've always wanted to work with a dynamic and forward-thinking team like the one you've established here.'

In the glass, the expression falls from my face. I've almost made myself sick in my mouth. This is so forced, so faked, and all of it untrue. Except my name, obviously. The rest would be a lie. I have never been enthusiastic about any job I've ever embarked upon in my life. For me, work is a means to an end. An unfortunate necessity. We can't all live like Siobhan Docherty, with a career we feel passionate about and a drive that gets us out of bed with a smile in the morning. Until recently, anyway.

I push my hair behind my right ear, trying to shorten it in the style of Siobhan's. I tilt my face. 'Hi,' I try again. 'My name's Siobhan Docherty. It's a pleasure to meet you.'

My rehearsal is interrupted by the sound of the doorbell. I go downstairs and look through the spyhole of the main door, and it's fair to say that the face I see is not one I was expecting. She looks more like Siobhan than I'd realised or remembered, but my memories of a lot of things are sketchy at best.

I open the door. 'Hi, Aunt Sarah. How are you?'

Her expression morphs in seconds from confusion to shock to anger, her face a flip book of emotions.

'What are you doing here, Anna?'

'I live here now,' I tell her with a smile. 'Hasn't Siobhan mentioned it to you?'

'Is she here?'

I shake my head. 'Not sure when she's due home. Sorry.'

She hesitates for a moment, about to say something, but changes her mind. Instead, she turns and walks away, gripping her handbag at her shoulder as though it's the only thing keeping her upright. I go to the gate and wait to see her turn the corner. Gone. One thing's for sure: she won't come back. Not while I'm still here. Because Aunt Sarah was always wary of me. And she was always right to be.

SIXTEEN

SIOBHAN

Before I go to work, I stop at the library to return the book I borrowed on the day I was reunited with Anna. After using the self-service machine, I go up to the second floor, where there's a meeting room that rarely seems to be used. It's empty again today, so I go inside and take off my coat. I need to call my mother to wish her a happy birthday.

I ordered flowers and some fancy toiletries online that should be delivered at some point today, but whether they'll be welcomed I'm not sure. My mother has always been a difficult person to buy for: she doesn't really have many hobbies, and her views on most things seem to be that they're a waste of money. But I couldn't just get her nothing, so flowers and the obvious it was.

I'm not sure whether she'll have heard the news about Carrie. My mother doesn't use social media, so unless she's seen it on the television, she's unlikely to be aware of her death. Her murder. The thought sends a shiver through me, and I find myself glancing over my shoulder despite knowing I'm alone in the room.

She doesn't answer, so I leave a message wishing her

happy birthday and telling her I'll try to call her again later, once I've left the station. I wonder where she is. She never seems to go far or do much, or perhaps that's just what she tells me. It's always seemed that she's never wanted to admit that she might be enjoying any kind of life in case anyone regards this as a betrayal of my father's memory. No one sees it that way, but I suspect this is what my mother fears. She was always fiercely loyal to her family, but it's sad to think that for almost twenty years she has denied herself the happiness that my dad would have wanted her to have. She was a young woman when he died, only thirty-two. She still had a lifetime to live, but her heart stopped when she learned that his had, and though it was shocked back into a slow-thudding pulse by the unforgiving requirements of parenthood, it never beat the same again.

My thoughts stay with her from the library to the radio station building on the South Bank, and when I get there, it feels like I'm seeing a ghost: because here she is, my mother, standing on the pavement just to the side of the main doors. She looks across and sees me before I cross the road at the traffic lights, though she looks away abruptly, face turned down, mouth small and tight like she's trying to suck out an ulcer from the inside of her cheek.

'Mum,' I say, as I approach her. 'Is everything okay? I just tried calling you. Happy birthday.'

My mother never just appears in London like this. She's only ever been to visit me here a handful of times, and those occasions were always pre-planned, with us meeting at the train station so I could help her navigate the route to my flat. We tend to meet up at her house, where the air is clearer and the water tastes nicer, according to her. She can't understand why anyone would want to live in a city, presumably because she's never experienced it for herself. Our home town of Halbury was the closest she got to an urban landscape, and after everything that happened there, it's not surprising she's sought solitude ever since.

'Has something happened?' I ask.

She pushes her bag up onto her shoulder from where it's slid down her arm. 'I've been to your flat, Siobhan. I thought I'd surprise you. It was me who had the surprise, though.'

Anna. I wonder whether they came face to face, but they must have; Anna doesn't have access to the doorbell app, so the only way my mother could have seen her there was if Anna had answered the door to her. I wonder why I didn't hear the notification on my phone. I'm usually alerted when there's anyone at the house, but perhaps I've got it accidentally muted. I make a mental note to check it later.

'How long has she been living with you?'

'She's not living with me,' I tell her. 'I mean, she's staying with me, but it's not permanent.'

'Does Anna know that? She seemed pretty comfortable, from what I could make out.'

'Did you go into the flat?'

'No.'

She offers no reason or explanation as to why she didn't go in – whether it was her preference or Anna's doing – and I don't probe for any further response. As far as I know, the last time my mother saw Anna was the same time I did, all those years ago, before our meeting at the library. All I know is that she has no time for her. Yet she's never seemed to have the words to explain why.

I'm all too familiar with the face she's pulling: mouth twisted into a question mark, left eyebrow tilted skywards, jaw tensed with the pressure of holding back what she wants to say.

'I didn't know you two were back in touch,' she eventually manages.

'We weren't. I mean, we haven't been for long. We bumped into each other at the library.'

Mum makes a humph noise that makes her sound like a braying donkey.

'What?' I ask.

'Nothing. Seems convenient, that's all.'

'What do you mean?'

'Well, does she even live in London? And since when? Since when did Anna become a reader? When was the last time you even spoke to her?'

'Same time you last did,' I remind her.

She falls silent for a moment. I wonder whether Anna is really the issue here. More likely it's her mother, Auntie Claire. Something happened between the sisters years ago, but no one seems to know what. It became the family secret, the elephant in the room that everyone knew about but ignored, until eventually a strained relationship became a fraught one and a fraught one became a barely existent one. And then there was nothing.

'I've just heard the news about Carrie. I mean, that's partly the reason I'm here. My God, Siobhan... why haven't you called me?'

Bit preoccupied, Mother. The ghost of a friend's corpse following me everywhere I go. And then the guilt... the never-ending guilt.

'I didn't want to worry you.'

She sighs noisily and it manages to make me feel about fourteen again. 'Are you okay?' she asks, her tone softening.

'No. Not really. It was me who found her.'

'Oh God, love,' she says, putting a hand on my arm. I notice the varnish at her fingertips is chipped where she's been biting her nails again, an old habit that she just can't seem to shift. 'Why don't you come home for a bit? Surely they've given you some time off work?'

'Yeah, they have, but...' I trail into silence. The worst thing I could think of now would be to go home, but I don't want to offend or upset her by telling her that. And how would I even begin to explain?

'But you don't want to take it.'

The way she rolls her eyes is inescapable, even when she turns her head to try to hide it. We're less than a couple of minutes into the conversation and she's already managed to make it about her. Carrie has been murdered. I found her body. But it's Sarah's feelings that are most important in this moment, just as they've always been.

'I can't go anywhere while the police are investigating the case,' I lie.

'They've told you that? Why would they say that?' She takes a sharp breath. 'They don't think you're somehow involved in this, do they?'

'No, Mother,' I say, a little too forcefully. 'No. But because I'm considered a key witness, they want me to stay close by in case I can help at any further point down the line.'

She knows I'm lying, but I'm grateful when for once she just says nothing and accepts what I tell her.

'It makes sense you having a lodger, you know. A room-mate... whatever you want to call it. I imagine it helps financially, and to be honest, it was always a surprise to me that you chose to live alone. But why Anna?'

'She's family,' I remind her.

'She's trouble, Siobhan. She always has been. And you've always been better than that.'

This is the problem. My mother sees what she wants to see. She believes what's easier to believe. And thinking I'm the reliable one, that I've always been such a good girl, honest and hard-working, is part of the issue. We've never been able to talk properly, because I've never been able to tell her the truth.

'Is this why you fell out with Aunt Claire? Because you always had the attitude that you were better than she was?'

I shouldn't have said it, and as soon as the words have left my mouth, I regret them. They sound nothing like me, bitter and spiteful. Things I don't want to be and don't want to be known by.

'You know nothing about Claire and me,' my mother says quietly.

'No, I don't,' I agree. 'Because you've always refused to talk about it.'

Her lips thin. 'You're making a mistake,' she says. 'You can't see it because you always try to find the good in people, but there's something different about Anna – there always has been. I'm sure she's been charming since you've reunited, because she's very good at that, getting people to see what she wants them to see.'

'I need to get to work. I'm sorry you've had a wasted trip.'

'Siobhan—'

'It's my life.' I cut her off, more abruptly than I intended. 'You don't get to tell me how to live it any more.'

The look on her face says I may as well have just slapped her. She shoves her bag onto her shoulder and adjusts her hair, refusing to show any further sign of just how much my words have hurt her. Immediately, I wish I could take them back.

'It'll all end in tears,' she warns.

SEVENTEEN

ANNA

I don't come out of my bedroom until 11 a.m. on Friday. I've been living in the flat for almost a week now, though it feels in a lot of ways like I've been here for ever. I'm where I was always meant to be. I heard Siobhan earlier on, and by the time I head to the kitchen I assume she's already gone to work. She usually leaves by 8.30, so I'm surprised to find her sitting silently at the breakfast bar in the kitchen, scrolling absently through her phone.

'Sorry,' I say, putting a hand self-consciously to my chest. I'm only in the vest top and shorts I wear to bed. 'I didn't realise you were here. Are you not working today?'

She shakes her head without looking up at me. 'Not feeling great.'

'Are you okay? Do you need me to go and get you anything?'

'No thanks.' She still hasn't looked at me, and I wonder whether I've done something to upset her.

'I was just applying for jobs,' I tell her, not wanting her to think I'm idling around doing nothing, even though that's exactly what I've been doing. Siobhan's generosity means my savings should see me right for the next month or so.

'How did the interview with the recruitment company go?'

She looks at me for the first time, and only now do I see how exhausted she looks. She can't be sleeping. It must be all the worry about Carrie's death, and about whoever's responsible still being out there somewhere.

'No luck,' I lie. 'Not enough experience.' The truth is, by the time I reached the offices I couldn't be bothered so I went and ate some pizza instead, regretting the calories afterwards.

'Keep trying. Something will come up.'

'I've got another one on Monday,' I tell her, lying again.

'Where?'

I feel as though I'm being interrogated, but I try to keep my cool. 'Council offices,' I say smoothly. 'Contract cleaner. I can't imagine they'll be swamped with applicants for that one, so fingers crossed.'

Siobhan stands, her face breaking into a sudden smile. 'You'll need to look your best then. Come on... get dressed.'

'What's going on?' I ask, unnerved by the change in her behaviour.

'We're going out.'

'Where?'

'A surprise,' she tells me. 'Go on. Get yourself ready.'

I hear her on the phone while I'm in the bedroom, thanking someone on a loop before ending the call. When I leave the bedroom, she already has her coat on, with two umbrellas brandished like spears.

'You'll need this,' she says, passing one to me. 'It's supposed to rain this afternoon.'

We head for the station and get on a train. Siobhan continues to refuse to tell me where we're going, saying nothing more than that I'll see when I get there. When we exit the station at King's Cross St Pancras, she takes my arm and leads me towards the fountains at Granary Square. I feel myself tense as she runs a hand over my coat sleeve.

'Please don't argue with me about it when we get there, okay? It's my treat.'

We stop outside a hair salon. It only takes a brief glance through the window for me to know I could never afford this type of place. Also, I wonder what's so bad about my hair that she feels a need to change me.

'You deserve some you-time,' she says, though I've had plenty of that just sitting in that flat all day, thinking about what happens next.

'This is too much,' I protest.

'Honestly, Anna, it's not. Call it a thank-you.'

'For what? I'm the one staying at your place rent-free, remember?'

'It doesn't matter,' she says, brushing the comment away with a sweep of her hand. 'You've been there for me. You've done more than you know.'

She pushes the door open and steps aside to let me through, looking away, embarrassed now by the sincerity of her words. This isn't what Siobhan does. We don't attach a feeling to what the other means, not verbally, anyway. I know how much I've been there for her, both years ago and now. I don't need her to tell me what I've done. But hearing it still fills me with a swell of something unfamiliar. A feeling I could get used to.

A young woman with impossibly long eyelashes and huge silver hoops hanging from her ears greets Siobhan by name. I wonder how often she visits this place, and how much it must cost her each time. I've never seen a salon like this. Everything seems to be made of glass; not just the floor-to-ceiling mirrors that stand in front of every chair, but the reception desk, the surfaces that house straighteners and hairdryers; the shelves that store fancy bottles of products that probably cost more than my weekly wage. It's like being in a hall of mirrors where every surface reflects back a different angle of myself. They also reflect back the Instagram-perfect staff members, who all look as though they've been filtered in real life, faces unblemished and hair styled without a strand out of place.

Another member of staff shows me to a chair in front of a mirror, while Siobhan waits on a sofa near the reception area. The stylist introduces herself as Ellie. She takes my coat and replaces it with a black plastic cape before disappearing for a moment. I watch in the mirror as Siobhan reaches for a magazine from a glass-topped coffee table. Her dark hair falls over her right eye as she leans forward, obscuring half her face. I get out my phone and run a quick search on styles, knowing that when Ellie returns, she's likely to ask me what I'd like her to do.

When she comes back, she hands me a glass of champagne. 'Can I get you anything else before we start?' she asks, though she doesn't specify what else is on offer.

'No thanks.'

'Okay. What are we doing today then?'

'I've had a look at some cuts,' I tell her, as though I'd known I was coming here today. I gesture to the phone in my lap. 'You don't mind, do you?' They must get fed up of people flashing images of models at them in the hope that similar hair will change their faces. 'Something like this. A "lob" – is that what they call it?'

The haircut in the photograph I show her is very specific, with sharp edges and a sweeping side fringe that covers the model's left eye. I see the way Ellie looks up to the mirror and glances at Siobhan. 'Like your friend's?' she says.

'She's my cousin. But yeah… like hers would be good.'

She smiles thinly. I don't care what she thinks. Imitation is the sincerest form of flattery: isn't that what they say?

'And what about a colour?'

I tell her I'd like it darkened, preferably a chocolate shade of brown, and again I see her eyes roam to Siobhan. She disappears again and returns with a large book that she opens to reveal a colour chart. Her finger moves across a spectrum of shades before landing on a deep shade of brown. 'This one?'

'Perfect. Thank you.'

I try not to watch Siobhan in the mirror while Ellie sets about mixing the colour for my roots, but it's hard to tear my eyes from her. The way she pushes her hair behind her ear, always with a thumb and forefinger; the way her lips linger against her champagne flute for a couple of seconds before she takes a sip.

I remember watching her in this same way in the garden one summer evening, during one of Uncle Garrett's infamous barbecues. There were more children than usual there that day: Siobhan's parents had told her she could invite some friends from school, and though she'd only chosen a few, they all had siblings, so the garden was overrun, and not for the first time, I went forgotten. There was a wooden Wendy house in one corner, outgrown by Siobhan long before. I think her parents had intended to get rid of it, but they'd never got around to it, and it was still there on the night of that last barbecue, years after the one I recall now.

It was so hot in the Wendy house. I was only wearing shorts and a T-shirt, but the T-shirt was made of fabric that was too thick for the weather, and there were embarrassing patches of sweat beneath my armpits that had stained the peach a deep shade of orange. I watched the smoke rise from the barbecue, escaping from the gaps round the closed lid. I heard the voices of the other children at the end of the garden as they played tag on the lawn, and all the while I grew hotter and hotter, feeling my face flush and sweat trickle down my spine.

It's funny the things we remember, years after an event. I don't recall much else about that evening, but I remember the feel of the sweat and the stench of charred chicken, and I remember Uncle Garrett's voice when he called Siobhan over.

'Show 'em what you can do,' he instructed, moving an arm

theatrically in front of him before swiping it to the side like a ringmaster in a circus big top. Siobhan laughed that tinkly laugh, a sound that rang from her like the introduction of an acceptance speech even as a child. She moved back onto the lawn, knowing what her father was referring to without having to ask. She'd done this before. They'd been rehearsing it. And they'd been saving it until this moment, when there were plenty of friends and neighbours present who could watch and clap and congratulate her on just how brilliant she was.

I was the gymnast. Or at least, I was the one who wanted to be. Siobhan had started lessons after I had, after my mother had made the mistake of telling Sarah about the class she'd signed me up to. And of course, she had to be better than me. And she was. She was better without trying, and as I watched her perform a double backflip across her parents' lawn, her class-mates cheering her on as though she was taking part in an Olympic final, all I could focus on was the memory of my last failed lesson – how I'd fallen off the beam and the rest of the group had laughed at me.

God, I hated her in that moment. I hated the way she could do everything without trying – things that took me an age to even contemplate attempting, let alone achieving. I hated that she looked so agile and capable and that everyone loved her and everyone applauded her. But then I loved her so much I felt it tighten in my chest like heartburn. I loved that she was an older, better version of me, because who else would I live up to? My mother was a train wreck, careening into every available passing male at high speed before veering off track and landing at a junction of self-destruction and self-loathing, where she would invariably choose to stop and set up camp. Siobhan was the closest thing I had to a sibling, and like any sister would, I loved and hated her in equal measure.

'Are you okay?'

Ellie snaps me from my daydream. When I glance in the

mirror, I realise a tear has snuck from my eye, snaking its way down my left cheek.

'Fine,' I say, hastily wiping my face with my palm. 'Just yawned, that's all.'

'The colour's all on now, so we'll just leave you here for a while, okay? Would you like a magazine or anything?'

'No thanks.'

There's nothing more ugly than a person's reflection in a hairdresser's mirror while there's a work in progress still taking place. I look awful. Unwell. The dark colour against my pale skin manages to make me look like some sort of ghoul. I know it'll lighten when it dries, but it won't lighten that much, and when I check Siobhan in the mirror again, I wonder whether the stylist has even matched it accurately. Perhaps she's gone for a darker colour on purpose, sensing just how much I want it exactly like Siobhan's.

I wait for what feels like hours before she returns to lead me to a basin, where she rinses my hair and asks me if I'd like something I've never heard the name of before. With no clue what's she talking about, I simply nod and say yes please. It's not me paying for it, so I suppose it doesn't matter. A strong scent of vanilla and spearmint fills the air. This is what it's like to be rich, I think. To be pampered and preened and treated like royalty. How fucking boring, to live every day like this.

By the time she's drying and styling my hair, I can't wait to get out of this place. The afternoon has brightened, and with all the glass surrounding me I feel as though I'm in a greenhouse, like I might sprout a fucking tomato from an orifice if I'm left to cook any longer. The shite pop music they're playing on repeat is making me want to tear my ears from the sides of my head, and the inane gossip of the two members of staff at the next chairs is driving my headache to a crescendo in my skull.

I try to switch off from it all, focusing my energy on the transformation that's starting to shape in front of me. As Ellie pulls the straighteners through the front of my hair, I see myself in the mirror in a way I never have before. I love it. I love the way my hair shapes my face and manages to make my eyes more striking. I love the way the fringe gives me a European look. But more importantly than those things, I love the way it makes me feel. Better. More like Siobhan. Because I always believed our lives were meant to be intertwined, but perhaps the truth is that I deserve better than that. More. Maybe the truth is that I was always meant to be her.

EIGHTEEN

SIOBHAN

I leave Anna at home, telling her I'm going out with colleagues from the radio station. It's a lie, and she's presumably guessed that, because why would we all go out drinking when one of our friends has just been murdered? She says nothing, though I can tell she's angling for an invitation. It would be too much. Maybe one evening, but not tonight. I really need to be on my own, away from everything that's familiar.

I sit in a bar in Canary Wharf drinking my third cocktail, though I've been here less than an hour. I chose the place at random; I thought it best I didn't go somewhere I've been before, particularly with anyone from work. It occurred to me that I might hook up with someone casually, go home with them for the night to avoid having to go back to my own place, but even with the fuzz of alcohol in my brain, I realise this is a bad idea. Now, I realise I just look sad and desperate, alone in a bar on a Saturday night, the rest of the place filled with groups of friends. So I text my ex, Nick – possibly an even worse idea than coming here in the first place.

Are you out?

Nick is always out. We met out and we stayed out for most of our two-year relationship, until I discovered he was going to remain out for ever and had no intention of ever giving up the lifestyle he'd had since he was a student. I didn't even expect him to give it up. I wouldn't have wanted him there with me every evening, for us to fall into the trap of mindless television and stale conversation that seemed to afflict so many of our coupled friends. I just thought he might start to go out a little less, that he might adapt his patterns slightly to accommodate me.

I get a text back within minutes.

Yeah. You?

I tell him where I am. He says he's about fifteen minutes away, near London Bridge, and would I like him to come and meet me. Because why else would I be texting him at 9.15 on a Saturday night? I send a reply. I finish my third drink before ordering a fourth. In no time at all, I've finished that one as well. I start to think he isn't coming. April Fool.

When he arrives, he looks more sober than I expected him to be, or perhaps it's my own cocktail intake that's making him appear less inebriated. He's still wearing the suit he probably wore to work, though he's lost the jacket somewhere. His usually clean-shaven jawline is peppered with stubble, and the late nights and eating-on-the-go are starting to catch up with him.

'I'm so sorry, Siobhan,' he says, leaning in to give me a kiss on the cheek. 'I heard about Carrie. I know how close you were. It's... fuck. It's horrendous.'

Not apparently horrendous enough for him to have texted me to see how I am, though.

He drags a bar stool noisily across the tiled floor and sits close to me, so close that our knees are almost touching. 'Are you okay?'

Better late than never, I suppose.

'Yeah.'

A stranger would be able to work out this is a lie, so I'm unlikely to be able to fool Nick.

'You don't have to pretend, Siobhan.'

'I know. But I'd rather.'

He tilts his head to one side and gives me a look I'm unable to read.

'You look good,' he says.

'Thanks.' Though I'm not sure it's an appropriate comment to make, or to reply to. I raise a hand to catch the attention of the barman, who comes over and says, 'Same again?' before asking for Nick's order.

'I've got a stalker,' I tell Nick, once the man has brought our drinks and gone to the other end of the bar to serve someone else.

'What?' His hand lingers on his glass. 'Why would you think that?'

'Someone keeps calling me and hanging up.'

'Unknown number?'

'Withheld.'

'Probably one of those annoying insurance companies.'

'Probably,' I say. But then I tell him about the roses delivered to work and the feeling I've been getting of being watched, and now that I hear it all out loud I realise I sound like an idiot. I hear myself as he must: paranoid and suspicious. Telling him about the baseball cap might make him take me a bit more seriously, but I don't want to go there: it's too specific and I'm unsure whether I'm that skilled a liar. There are so many things I never told him. There are so many things I've never told anyone.

'Do you think this is because of Carrie?'

His words floor me. I open my mouth to speak, but nothing comes out; it's like my voice has been dragged down my throat and is stuck there. Then I realise that I'm misinterpreting his question. He isn't suggesting I'm involved, so why did I take it that way? I suppose guilt must be driving me to see accusations in everything.

'There's been so much to process,' he continues. 'When we're grieving, and sleep-deprived, things always look so different.'

Now I understand what he's implying. That I'm making more of things than I should. That I'm seeing and thinking things that aren't real. Stress. Pressure. The complicated tangle of emotions that comes with grief. All used as a smokescreen to ignore the real problem that lies behind them. It reminds me of the time he tried to convince me he was no longer using cocaine. It reminds me why I ended things with him.

'You're saying I'm imagining things?'

'I'm not saying that at all.'

I swallow half my drink in one long gulp, knowing I should probably stop now. He says nothing, instead keeping pace with me.

Within an hour and a half we're back at my flat, the pulsing creep of a headache at my temples warning me it's time to call it a day. I should listen, but I don't. The place is quiet, Anna presumably asleep. I don't tell Nick she's there; there's no point. By the time she wakes in the morning, he'll be long gone.

We go upstairs to my bedroom, both on wobbly legs. He catches me midway up the staircase when I almost stumble backwards. I stifle a drunken giggle and grab his hand, using him to steady myself on my way to the bed before taking off my clothes and getting under the duvet. He removes his too, then he finds me in the darkness and kisses me.

'Come on,' I say, hearing the slur in my voice. 'Fuck me. Please.'

I move the duvet, sliding down his body until my mouth finds his groin. For a moment, it feels as though he's going to relent. Then he holds me by the shoulders and pushes me gently away.

'Siobhan. I'm not having sex with you.'

I sigh with frustration and move back up onto the pillow. His hand finds mine as the other pulls the duvet up to cover me. Since when did he become so annoyingly nice? It occurs to me now that if he'd acted this chivalrously while we were together, we might never have split up.

'I don't—'

He cuts me short. 'Come here.'

He stretches his arm across the bed and I curve into the shape of it. His chest is warm.

'Why are you here if you're not going to have sex with me?' I ask.

'You called me. I said I'd always be here for you no matter what, didn't I? So here I am.'

'I'm scared.'

He pulls away to look at me. 'If you're really this worried, you need to tell the police what's been going on.'

I nod, because there's little other response I can give. I can hardly tell him that talking to the police about any of this is an impossibility.

'What does that mean? Are you going to?'

'Yes,' I lie. 'I'll tell them.'

'I'll come with you, if you like.'

I move back closer to him, appreciating his warmth against my face.

'What was that?' He sits up and puts a hand on my shoulder as though holding me down, keeping me from anything that might be downstairs. Anyone.

'It'll be Anna.'

'Who's Anna?'

'My flatmate.'

'You never mentioned you had a flatmate.'

'You never asked.'

I pull at his wrist, urging him to come back to the warmth of the bed. He's letting the cold air get in, and my arms have pimpled with goosebumps at the chill.

'Nick? What's the matter?'

'Put the light on,' he instructs me, his voice lowered.

'What?'

'Put the light on, Siobhan!'

I reach over and flick the switch for the lamp. The room is thrown into a brilliant white light, headache-inducing after the lull of the darkness. Nick shifts up onto his knees, looking through the balcony railing of the mezzanine floor into the living room below.

'What's the matter with you?'

'She was standing behind the sofa fucking watching us.'

'Don't be ridiculous.'

'Siobhan,' he says, turning to me, 'she was looking right at me. I could see the whites of her bloody eyes.'

I sigh and get out of bed. I reach for the dress I was wearing just a short time ago and throw it on. Downstairs, the living room is quiet. The bathroom door is ajar, but when I peer inside, she's not there. Her bedroom door is shut. I get a glass of water before going back to the bedroom.

'You imagined it,' I tell him.

'I didn't bloody imagine it. She was looking right at me!'

I drain half the glass before handing him the rest to finish. My brain feels as though my head has been clamped in a vice, and I regret every cocktail that came after the third.

'That bedroom door is really noisy. It wouldn't have opened or been closed again without us hearing it.'

'If you say so, Siobhan,' Nick says, his voice thick with frustration. 'You'd better get used to sleeping with one eye open, though.'

I say nothing. I can't explain it to him, and even if things were different between us, I wouldn't want to. There's no way he could begin to understand that even with her quirks, I'm safer with Anna here than not.

NINETEEN

ANNA

Carrie's funeral is held on a glorious mid-April morning, the kind of spring day that inspires a sense of hope even among the more cynical of us. I wake early, having set my alarm to make sure I was up before Siobhan. I have to do everything quietly; with the kitchen and living room areas both open to her exposed bedroom on the upper floor, every noise is amplified and it's hard to keep anything secret.

I make her breakfast. And when I say I make her breakfast, I mean I make everything from scratch: sour cream and sun-dried tomato tartlets, the pastry kneaded by hand; avocado salad with blueberries, and chilli-infused sweet potato frittata. She needs to keep her strength up. I want to give her something special on what I know will be a difficult day. I've always been the only one who can really make her feel better. The only one who knows how to take her pain away.

She comes downstairs at just gone 7.30 and I greet her with a coffee and one of those sympathetic smiles that says 'I know what you're going through' even when it's a lie. She looks unlike herself this morning: her skin is sallow, and there are deep lines stretching from her eyes that I've never noticed before. She's too thin. I can't keep up with the weight loss if she's going to carry on like this. She needs feeding up.

'Have a seat,' I say, gesturing to the table.

'What's all this for?' she asks, her eyes widening at the sight of the feast in front of her.

'Just a thank-you. And I know today's going to be hard. You need to keep your energy up.'

I'll just have to find a way to get some of my own now, I think. I'm bloody knackered after all this *MasterChef* shit.

She sits at the table, and I put a plate in front of her.

'Are you sure you wouldn't like me to come with you to the funeral?' I offer. 'For support.'

'No,' she says, too quickly, as I take the seat opposite her. She seems to realise how abrupt she's been, and adds, 'Everyone from work will be there, so there'll be plenty of support. Thank you, though.'

I watch her reach for a slice of frittata and take a bite, slowly and deliberately. Her complexion is a strange colour, tinted green under the kitchen's too-bright spotlights. She isn't going to get through today without breaking down. She needs me more than she realises.

'And everyone's wearing something red, you said?'

She nods. 'It's her sister's idea. It was Carrie's favourite colour. They want today to be a celebration of who she was.'

The coffee I've made is too bitter and too strong, but Siobhan says nothing as she takes a sip. We eat in silence, Siobhan going through the motions but barely seeming to consume a thing.

'I've made too much food. I can put it in the fridge for tomorrow.'

'I think I've had enough,' she says, though she's only had a couple of mouthfuls of the avocado salad and a quarter of her slice of frittata. 'It was delicious,' she adds, apologetically. 'Thank you.'

'It's the least I could do.' I push back my chair and start clearing the table. 'You'd better go and get yourself ready.'

Siobhan glances at the clock, but stays for a moment at the table. I get a burst of memory, like déjà vu, and for a moment I'm transported back to my aunt and uncle's house, Siobhan and me sitting in her bedroom, the duvet pulled up over our knees. It was a couple of weeks after Uncle Garrett had died. The house, usually alive with sound and life, had fallen into a silence that had at times felt suffocating. I see us together there so clearly I could almost reach out and touch the hair I brushed that day, stroke after stroke, trying to soothe the pain that had knotted in her brain like a tumour. I put down the plates I'm holding and move like a ghost to stand behind her at the table, my fingers finding her hair as they did that day.

'What are you doing?' She pulls away from me sharply, ducking from my touch.

'I'm sorry. I don't know, I... I was just reminded of something else.'

I go back to the task of clearing the table, sensing Siobhan watching me with suspicion as I work.

'Leave it,' she says. 'I'll do it later.'

'I'm not leaving you with this mess,' I tell her. 'I made the—'

'Leave it!' she snaps.

Slowly my hand returns the empty coffee cup to the table, moving without my brain's instruction. I can't remember her ever speaking to me like this before, not even all those years ago, after everything had happened. She doesn't deserve me. I deserve better.

She gets up from the table and goes to her bedroom to get ready. I leave the kitchen as it is; I'll clear up once she's gone and isn't here to reprimand me for doing so. In my own bedroom, I sit at the edge of the bed, mulling over what just happened. Siobhan is more damaged than she realises, and I'm the only person who knows this. That makes me the only person able to help her. I'm the only one who's ever known what's best for her.

I go back into the living room when I hear her come downstairs. She's wearing a fitted knee-length black skirt with a deep red blouse tucked in at the waist, her bobbed hair straightened so that it falls to her shoulders.

'You look lovely,' I tell her, but she says nothing. Perhaps that's not an appropriate thing to say to someone who's about to attend a funeral. Neither is 'I hope everything goes well,' but I say that too, anyway.

After she leaves, I change quickly. I don't own a single item of clothing or accessory that's red, so I go upstairs to look through Siobhan's things, finding a cream scarf with red flowers that will have to do. I change into my trusted interview/date/funeral dress and tie the scarf around my neck, unable to do anything with the thing that doesn't look as though I'm off to audition as a rep at a holiday camp. But it's good enough for today. Carrie for one won't have any objection, at least.

The funeral starts at 1 p.m. I take two buses to Shoreditch, then check the distance to the church on my phone. Only half a mile, but far enough away that if I walk the longer route, I'll get there just after the service starts. I don't want to be early, or Siobhan might find an excuse for me to leave. If I'm just a little late, there'll be nothing she can do other than accept that I'm there.

I quickly regret the heels I'm wearing, but I had no other shoes that were appropriate. Despite my choice of footwear, however, and walking the long way, I somehow arrive too early. The churchyard is filled with mourners, everyone wearing at least one red item. There are scarlet silk scarves and crimson ties, pillar-box ankle socks and ruby coats. One woman totters down the path in a pair of glittering red six-inch stilettos, looking how I imagine Dorothy from Kansas might have if she'd taken up pole dancing.

I spot Siobhan near the church doors, speaking with a man I don't recognise. He says something and she wipes her eyes; he puts a hand on her arm and says something more, presumably offering words of comfort. I feel heat rise beneath my dress as I cross the road to wait on the other side. The hearse must have already arrived, Carrie's coffin already inside, because a few minutes later, people begin to stream into the church. I go over to join them as the last few mourners make their way inside. There's piano music playing, and at the front of the church, propped on a huge easel, there's an enormous photograph of Carrie. She's wearing a bridesmaid's dress and is posing in the gardens of what I presume is a hotel, her face tilted to the sun, her pale throat catching its rays. I have a flashback, her body beneath mine on the bed, the veins at her temples bulging pale blue as I tightened my hands around her neck.

I look for Siobhan. She's sitting in the second row from the front, but there's nowhere to sit either beside or behind her. There are plain-clothes detectives standing near the doors, failing spectacularly in their attempts to appear anonymous. They're here looking for clues. I've seen something about that before: how killers will often go to their victims' funerals, sometimes for no other reason than to revel in the fact that they can. I scan the pews and see an empty space a few rows behind Siobhan. I whisper apologies to the people who have to stand to let me pass, and sit just in time for the vicar to start.

Funerals are odd things really. Everyone sits in silence and listens to a eulogy from a person who didn't even know the deceased. I wonder if the vicar does a copy-and-paste job, like schoolteachers writing reports about kids they've not really noticed for the past three terms. I bet it's awkward if the wrong name gets dropped into a speech by mistake. And in their weirdness, funerals are a bit like weddings in some respects. I bet half the people here, all sitting now with their hankies and their fake tears, hadn't seen Carrie in years. And half of that half probably didn't really like her – the kind of acquaintances people get lumbered with and then are too polite to shake off, like taking home a stray dog to feed because the bloody thing wouldn't leave you alone. Of those who *had* seen her – even in some passing sense, in a supermarket, or at a gathering arranged by a friend of a friend – there'll be the ones who say things like 'I only saw her a few weeks ago', as though that somehow makes the death more shocking or unexpected. I hate small talk. And small talk at funerals is the worst.

When the vicar's speech finishes, I realise I didn't hear a word of what he'd said. A blonde woman gets up from the front row, and when she turns, I see she's an older version of Carrie: the less fortunate sibling who wasn't quite blessed with the better elements of the gene pool. She clears her throat as she stands at the lectern, her head lowered to the paper she grips between her tightened fingers.

I should feel something. In every inch of each of my bones, I feel as though I should *feel* something. But I don't. And I can't. I know there's something different about me; I've known it for as long as I can remember, since I was just a little girl, old enough to understand that people cry when they're sad and laugh when they're happy. That time I watched a neighbour's dog get hit by a van outside our house, I knew I was supposed to react as everyone else did, with panic or sympathy or some sense of sorrow for the elderly owner who'd lost her main source of company in this cruel and lonely world. When that boy in my class whose name I can't now remember didn't come back to school after the summer holidays, and the teachers were holding back tears in assembly – Year 3's Mrs Gardner not quite as successful as the others in maintaining the flood defences – I realised I should have felt sadness too. And when Uncle Garrett was suddenly gone from our lives and Siobhan and Aunt Sarah were unable to speak with the pain of it all, I knew I should have felt something. Anything. But I didn't then, and I can't now.

I know I shouldn't be able to sit here, at the funeral of a woman whose life I ended. But though I remember being there, every detail of those moments as colourful as an oil-painted memory, it still doesn't feel as though it was me. *That girl's got more front than Brighton*; that's how I once heard Aunt Sarah describe me. She was right, I suppose. But she was jealous too. Jealous of the fact that no matter how hard she tried to change the fact, her daughter would always be closer to me than she'd ever been to her. I was the only one who could make her feel better, who could take her pain away.

As though sensing my thoughts, Siobhan turns and glances behind her. She looks right at me, sees me here among the mourners, and her expression falls to one of dismay, too instinctive for her to do anything to disguise the fact. I offer her a small, sad smile, but she turns to look back to Carrie's sister, who has only now been able to start speaking.

'When we were growing up,' she begins, 'I always wanted to be like Carrie.'

There's a reason I'm here, I remind myself. A good reason. The best of reasons. This – all of it – is for Siobhan. But perhaps no longer just for her. I remind myself that I deserve to be here. Anything that was mine always belonged to her too. Now, I'm equally entitled to what's hers.

'She was funny and kind and clever, and everyone loved her.' The sister's voice breaks. She's not going to make it to the end of this.

With her back turned to me, I can see the tension in Siobhan's shoulders. I know she can feel me watching her, aware that my focus will rest on her throughout the rest of the service.

'Being with Carrie was like looking in a mirror. She was me and we were the same in so many ways, but she was a better version of me – the me I always wanted to be. And it was a good thing, to have this better version around. Carrie made me aspire to be more. She made me a better person. My life was better just for having her in it.'

Siobhan turns back to look at me, just as I'd known she would. Our gazes meet fleetingly before she looks away. Like looking in a mirror. A better me... the me I always wanted to be.

TWENTY

SIOBHAN

On the Monday after Carrie's funeral, the atmosphere at the station is tense, rumours moving between studios as silently and stealthily as ghosts, bleeding invisibly through the walls. People try to keep them away from me, but I know what's being said about Flynn. His arrest is public knowledge now, and it doesn't seem to matter that he was released without charge. *Pending further investigation...* that's the bit that sticks. His relationship with Carrie, now known to everyone, has made him prime suspect, just as he'd anticipated. Yet he's returned to work, knowing that hiding away will likely only make him look more guilty.

There's still a part of me that wonders whether there's even the slightest chance he might be. I don't want to think that, but I can't help it. I've seen another side to him now, and all it takes is a moment. The wrong circumstances, and I suppose any of us could be a killer.

'You okay?' I mouth as I take off my coat and hang it on the back of my chair. Flynn is sitting at his desk, a pair of headphones covering his ears. Mila is at the other side of the studio, pretending to be absorbed in some paperwork, though my guess is that she's primed to take in anything that might be said around her. I don't trust her not to repeat what she overhears in this studio to people in the others. It's impossible to know who to trust any more.

Flynn just shrugs. He looks exhausted. Broken. I think of him outside my flat at 1 a.m. My phone ringing just moments after I'd stopped talking to him. Is it possible that might have been him? But why? I know it doesn't make any sense, but so much of what's happened lately is senseless.

Flynn had wanted to go to the funeral, but told me he'd decided it was best not to. He didn't want to upset Carrie's family, who'd known nothing about her relationship with him. I knew Carrie well enough to realise why she'd chosen to keep it a secret. My guess is that she enjoyed the sneaking around – that it felt exciting to have something between them that only they knew about; something she could gain a thrill from every day at work. Because although she was professional and brilliant at what she did, Carrie was also a thrill-seeker. I just wonder now whether she'd really considered Flynn in all of it, or whether he was simply collateral damage in her quest for excitement.

From across the studio, Mila asks me a question. I'm so lost in my thoughts that I have to ask her to repeat it, and I'm sure I hear her sigh impatiently at my mental absence.

'The notes from the meeting,' she says. 'I thought they were left on my desk.'

My desk. She must hear the words as I do, though if she does, she doesn't have the sensitivity to edit them. I feel myself grow hot beneath my dress, my chest flaring with a heat that intensifies faster than I'm able to control. It rushes to my neck and my cheeks in an upward flood, and I turn to the window so Mila doesn't see it. I watch the world move beyond the glass, a stream of pedestrians trailing the pavements. At the railings that stop people falling into the

Thames, a young man stands with his back pressed to the metal, his thumb scrolling his phone, his free hand shoved into the pocket of his jeans. His head is lowered, his dirty-blonde hair mussed and in need of cutting. My shoulders sag with an invisible weight, and when he glances up from his phone, it feels as though I'm frozen, my feet stuck to the floor. He's so much like Lewis that for a moment I feel I must be looking at a ghost. I press my hands to the windowsill and my chin to my chest, willing the blood to my brain. With my eyes shut tight, I try not to think about what happened that night – the last time I saw him face to face, when he told me he would call me.

When I open my eyes and look out of the window again, the man at the railings is gone.

I'm not sure how much longer I can do this. Dylan told me to take time off after Carrie's death, but I didn't want to: I feared the loneliness and the isolation of the flat, and I didn't want to be on my own. But I'd underestimated just how difficult being here every day would be. Her desk will always be her desk, no matter which presenter sits at it. Her things might have been cleared away, but I continue to see them as though they're haunting me. And regardless of whose voice is transmitted from this studio, I continue to hear hers, and I'm not sure that will ever change.

'Siobhan.'

I turn at the sound of Dylan's voice. It's as though he's somehow heard me thinking about him.

'Everything okay?' He nods me over, a prompt for me to leave the studio so that neither Mila nor Flynn overhears our conversation. 'You shouldn't be here.'

'Where should I be? At home, on my own, overthinking?' I follow him to his office.

'I just think you need to take a break. You're grieving.' He closes the office door before putting a hand in his pocket and taking out a piece of paper. 'I think you should see this,' he says, unfolding it.

When he offers it to me, I take it reluctantly. It's a printout of an email, sent from an anonymous account. It's titled *FAO Dylan Sykes*.

> *Dear Mr Sykes,* it begins. *You should know that one of your staff, Siobhan Docherty, was years ago involved in someone's death. The truth was covered up at the time to keep her protected, but in light of the recent murder of Carrie Adams, I feel it's only right you should be aware of who you have working at the station. I will leave you to draw your own conclusions.*

Beneath the message there's a link to a regional newspaper article. I see the word 'fire', but I don't need to see any more.

'Where did this take you?' I ask, gesturing to the link before handing the sheet of paper back to him.

'Fire at a derelict farmhouse. Man killed.' He eyes me questioningly. 'Do you already know about this?'

I could lie. I could tell him that I know nothing, that the email is a malicious hoax sent by the same person persecuting me with unwanted gifts and nuisance calls. But he will look into this further, if he hasn't already done so. I've run for long enough, and if I lie now, I will only make myself look more guilty.

'Yes.'

I tell him everything. Most of it, anyway. I tell him I was sixteen years old and that Lewis was my boyfriend. I explain the history of the farmhouse, the legal battle for ownership that meant it was left empty and isolated far past the time it should really have been demolished. I tell him that it was commonly used by the kids who lived in our town, as a place to meet up and hang out, usually without any intention to cause trouble.

And I make sure he knows that as far as either of us was aware, Lewis and I were alone that evening.

It was an accident. A terrible, tragic accident that ended two lives.

'It's not the kind of thing you'd want people to know, is it?'

Dylan sighs noisily and looks up at the ceiling. 'You need to take some time off.'

'Are you suspending me?'

'For what? A misdemeanour that occurred almost two decades ago?'

Misdemeanour. The word echoes through the room. No one saw it like that at the time, and I never believed anyone would see it in that way now. I don't even see it that way myself. We were guilty, both of us.

'I just need some time to think, Siobhan. We all do.'

'Who are you going to get to replace me?' I ask, feeling as protective over my position here as I am of Carrie's. The thought of someone else sitting at my desk and doing my job fills me with a sadness I hadn't anticipated. I love it here. I never want to leave the place, though I realise that nothing is for ever.

'That's something I'm going to have to work out. See the rest of this week through and then take a fortnight off, at least.'

I find myself shaking as I leave the office. He may not have fired or even suspended me, but it feels as though he might as well have. No matter how he chose to word it, this is the beginning of the end of my time here.

It's hard to concentrate amid the echoes of my conversation with Dylan, but I manage to keep going enough to function somewhere near normal. Just before the show starts, I get a call from Anna, telling me she's downstairs. She's never shown up at my workplace like this before, and I hope this isn't the start of a habit. I want my private and professional lives kept apart as much as possible.

When I go down, I'm grateful she isn't waiting by reception.

Instead, she's standing outside the main doors smoking a cigarette. The air is still on the chilly side for mid April, and she's wearing my black and white houndstooth three-quarter-length coat, the one I bought in a second-hand shop in Brighton a couple of years ago.

'You don't mind, do you?' she says, gesturing to it when she sees me looking. 'You said it suited me.'

'Since when did you smoke?'

She shrugs. 'I didn't think you'd disapprove. You're still a smoker, aren't you?'

'Only when I'm stressed out.'

She raises an eyebrow, puts a hand in her pocket and holds the packet out to me. I decline the offer, though it's tempting.

'What are you doing here, anyway?'

'I brought you lunch.' She passes me a paper bag. Inside, there's a salad, a pot of mixed berries, a couple of granola bars and a bottle of water. The salad is home-prepared rather than shop-bought; not just bagged lettuce leaves thrown into a Tupperware box, but shredded carrots and red cabbage, chick-peas, chunks of avocado and tiny slivers of radish. I almost feel bad now at feeling irritated by her showing up here unannounced. But not that bad. We've still not discussed the fact that she came to Carrie's funeral after I'd told her I'd go alone. At least she didn't turn up at the wake after the service.

'Thank you. That's so kind of you.'

'I'm worried you're not looking after yourself. You need to eat.'

'Okay, Mum.'

It's said with a smile and meant as a joke, but as soon as the words leave me, I realise they were the wrong ones. The history between our families means there's little space for friendly mention of either of them. Anna knows how my mother feels about her. How she's always felt about her.

'Got much on this afternoon?' I ask, filling the awkward silence that has settled between us.

'Another job interview,' she tells me, running a hand theatrically across her middle. 'I'll be out of your hair soon enough.'

'There's no rush.'

I wait for her to thank me or offer some kind of response, but she does neither.

'I'd better go back up,' I tell her. 'The show's starting soon.'

I hurry back up the stairs, willing myself not to turn to look at her again. A single thought has stuck with me and refuses to be shaken off: that she looks unnervingly like me; that I could have been looking in a mirror.

TWENTY-ONE

ANNA

I've not been back at the flat for long when the doorbell rings. I can't see outside – only Siobhan has the app – so I go downstairs and look through the spyhole. There's a young man on the doorstep, maybe mid-twenties. When he takes a step back, I see he's carrying a small package. I open the door and he does a noticeable double take. A smug vanity surges in my chest.

'Parcel for Siobhan Docherty,' he says. 'It needs a signature.'

I pause before saying, 'That's me.' I smile, the lie having left my lips as easily as an exhalation.

I shouldn't have said it. Correct him, my brain tells him. Tell him it was just a joke. You're not Siobhan. But I've never been a fan of listening to what my brain wants to tell me. I've always preferred to go with my gut.

He hands me the electronic signature reader and I realise I now have to sign Siobhan's name. I've no idea what her signature looks like.

'Thanks,' I say, scrawling an approximation. Our fingertips brush as he takes the reader back from me and hands me the parcel.

'Nice round here,' he comments. He gestures to the house. 'Been here long?'

'A few years.' Our eyes meet. He's got nice eyes, sort of grey-blue. He's good-looking, and probably knows it. He's studying me way too intently. Delivery drivers don't usually make eye contact, let alone look at me as though he wants to follow me upstairs. I can't remember the last time anyone looked at me this way. I don't know if anyone ever has. Dean certainly never did. But then I didn't look then like I do now. I wasn't this version of myself.

'I've got a friend who's just moved in not too far from here,' he tells me. 'He's new to London.'

'Where's he from?' I don't really care – it's not the friend I'm interested in.

'Uh... Reading.' He grins. The friend doesn't exist.

'Okay. So does this friend need some help finding his bearings?'

This is not me. I don't do this. Anna is not this confident; Anna doesn't flirt outright with men she doesn't know and has only just met. But I'm not Anna at the moment. And this is way more fun than I'd expected it to be.

'Depends who's offering the help, I suppose.'

God... he's *really* good-looking. I deliberate over what my brain is telling me to do and say, stalling on the possibilities of everything that could go wrong. Then I speak the words anyway. 'Well... you'd better take my number. To pass on to your friend.'

He puts the package on the wall to the side of us and takes his phone from his pocket. I give him my number. I see him pause as he taps it into his phone. '836,' he repeats, confirming the last three digits.

'That's the one.'

He returns the phone to his pocket.

'Sorry,' I say, with a confidence that was until recently alien to me. 'I didn't get your name.' I give him my best Siobhan smile, slightly lopsided; strong, not too cute.

'It's Jack.'

'Nice to meet you, Jack. And thanks,' I say, gesturing to the parcel.

'I wish it was bigger and heavier, to be honest. I'd have to carry it into the house for you then.'

'I'd take you up on the offer,' I quip back, 'but I don't invite strangers into my home.'

He grins again. One of his front teeth overlaps its neighbour just ever so slightly. He laughs as though he's told a joke inside his head but decided to keep it from me. 'Very sensible.' In the pause that follows, I feel the chemistry between us like static in the air; if I were to touch him now, I think he'd shock me with an electricity I'd feel through to my bones. 'I guess I might see you about then, Siobhan. You know... when you help out my friend.'

This. This is how it feels to be Siobhan Docherty. I spent so many years wondering what it must be like for her, and now I know. And every second feels better than I'd ever imagined it might.

'Maybe,' I say casually.

I watch him return to his van before making my way back into the house, my head and heart on a high I can't find anything to compare to. When I go back up to the flat, I'm tempted to open the box to see what's inside, but I don't. Whatever's in there, Siobhan is welcome to it. Nothing could come close to what I've already gained from today.

TWENTY-TWO

SIOBHAN

The Tuesday show hasn't yet started when the police arrive. They're not in uniform, but I recognise the female officer as the lead detective on Carrie's case; the one who took my statement at the station. The male officer was there the evening I found Carrie in her flat. I couldn't recall the woman's name at the station and I still can't remember it now – though when she sees me here, the look she gives me is far less sympathetic than it was that day.

Flynn looks up from his desk as the officers enter the studio. Mila's rambles about a delivery driver who left her parcel in a wheelie bin that was then emptied by bin men before she'd had a chance to retrieve it comes to an abrupt halt, and her face flushes as though she's contemplating the inaneness of her complaints in the shadow of Carrie's murder.

'Afternoon,' the male detective says, his greeting not offered to anyone in particular. Until my name falls from his lips, that is. 'Ms Docherty. We'd like you to come with us to the station, please.'

My mouth falls open. My jaw moves as though I'm about to say something, but I don't know what, and the moment is instead filled with an uncomfortable silence in which Flynn and Mila have time to eye me questioningly. I feel hot under their attention, though I know I've done nothing wrong.

'Of course,' I say, not wanting to cause a scene by making a fuss. 'What's this about? I've given my statement... I've told you everything I know. Have you found someone? Do you know who did this?'

'It's probably best we deal with this back at the station,' the female detective says. Why can't I remember either of their names? Perhaps I should have paid more attention, but it was impossible to hold on to details when all I could think about was the fact that Carrie was dead. All I could focus on were the details of her murder – snapshots in high definition that flicked through my memory like a macabre flipbook. My brain had no space for anything else apart from the fact that it may all have been my fault.

'Do you want me to come with you?' Flynn offers. He eyes the detectives defiantly, and I consider now whether I've been wrong to doubt him. This protectiveness doesn't seem the response of a guilty man. Surely if he saw me as a potential distraction from the police's interest in him, he'd be enthusiastically willing me to the car I imagine is waiting for me outside.

'I don't think that'll be necessary,' the male officer answers on my behalf.

'Mila needs you here,' I say, resenting the interruption. 'I'll be fine. Thanks, though.'

I get my coat and leave the studio with the officers. We pass Dylan in the corridor, the worst of timings, yet his face suggests he already knew the police were here. After yesterday's conversation about the fire, he must only think the worst of me now. I pass him without speaking. Perhaps it makes me look guilty, although anything I might say is only likely to have the same effect.

I stay silent in the car on the way to the station, and when we get there, I'm shown to an interview room. I ask if I'm under arrest and whether I need to contact a solicitor, the way people do in television police dramas when they know they're about to be accused of something they didn't do.

'This is just a conversation,' I'm told. 'For now, at least.'

But I don't believe what they're saying. In fact, it feels as though I've walked into a trap, so I ask to contact a lawyer friend and make them wait until he arrives.

I've known Harry for a number of years, having first met him through Nick. I've not really much clue as to how good he is at his job, but at the moment he's the best chance I've got. He sits by my side in an interview room, the detectives who came to the studio now sitting opposite us.

'Interview with Siobhan Docherty, Tuesday the eighteenth of April,' the man says, speaking for the benefit of the recording. 'Present are DCI Manning and DC Brett.'

At least now I know their names, I think.

'We've been reviewing the CCTV from Hanover House again,' DCI Manning tells me. 'We'd been concentrating on footage from the day of Ms Adams' death, but when we went back to look earlier, to the previous day, we found this.'

She clicks a button on a laptop and the sepia image stilled on the screen comes to life. The footage shows the pavement outside Carrie's building, capturing the steps and the intercom at the front door. For a few moments there is nothing. Then someone comes into sight: a person wearing a long coat with the hood pulled up. We watch them tap a code into the intercom before entering the building. They are then recorded again on an internal camera, heading towards Carrie's door.

I feel both officers' eyes on me as I watch the footage.

'This could be anyone,' Harry says flatly.

'It's quite a distinctive coat, isn't it, Ms Docherty,' the detective says, ignoring the comment. 'Do you recognise it?'

There's a lump in my throat. My voice is trapped behind it,

unable to push through the blockage. The officer's eyes are fixed on me, observing every second of my discomfort. I imagine she's looking for guilt; for the telltale signs that I'm keeping something hidden.

'This coat belongs to you, doesn't it, Ms Docherty?'

I wish they would just call me Siobhan. 'It did,' I manage. 'Or one like it used to, at least.'

'Can you explain what that means?' DC Brett says.

'I gave it to a charity shop, months ago. Back before Christmas. I was having a clear-out.'

'Convenient,' DCI Manning says quietly, looking at the notes in front of her.

'There must be plenty of coats like that out there,' Harry says, not particularly helpfully.

'True. But the chances of one being worn by a person of similar height and build to Ms Docherty at the home of a colleague and friend seem slight, wouldn't you agree?'

'I'm not sure how you can tell a person's height from this,' he says, flicking a hand dismissively at the laptop.

'Quite easily, actually. We've had one of our experts take a look.' DCI Manning sits back and puts her hands behind her head. If her demeanour is meant to unnerve me, it's working. 'The strange thing about this is that the woman is picked up on CCTV entering the building, but not leaving. What do you make of that, Ms Docherty?'

'I don't know.'

Harry casts me a glance that warns me not to give any further response.

'We've a couple of theories. The first is the most obvious: that this woman left via a different exit, the only other one being a fire escape at the back of the building where there are no CCTV cameras. You'd have to be pretty well acquainted with the building to know it's there. Why would someone leave via a fire escape? It suggests they don't want to be seen, don't you think? This woman entered the building on Thursday evening and Ms Adams was murdered on Friday morning...'

Manning leaves the rest of her unspoken sentence floating silently in the air, an invisible accusation. She's looking at me now as though I'll offer the answer; as though I'm likely to just raise my hands and say, *you're right... well done... I did it.* Instead, I do as Harry silently suggested and say nothing.

'What time was this footage recorded?' Harry asks.

'Four forty-seven p.m.'

'The show my client works on doesn't finish until four.'

'Enough time to get from the South Bank to Shoreditch. It's only half an hour or so by public transport.' DCI Manning finally lowers her arms. 'We can agree this is a woman, can we, Ms Docherty? I don't think anyone looking at this would try to argue it could be a man. Whoever she is, the question now is whether Ms Adams knew she was there.' Her focus on me is unsettling. I feel a line of sweat gather at the back of my neck. 'Have you ever been given a spare key for Ms Adams' home?'

I shake my head. 'Never.'

'Have you ever had access to her key?'

'No. I've been to her place a few times, but I've never had a key. That isn't me in the footage. This can all be disproved,' I say, turning to Harry. 'I gave the charity shop my details, for Gift Aid. They'll have a record of it in the shop.'

A chill runs the length of my spine as I look back at the officers sitting opposite me. No, I tell myself. It's ridiculous. But the thought has snagged on my skin, and it refuses to loosen its grip. There's only one other person this could be.

'Were you envious of Carrie's position as presenter on the show?'

'What? No! I'm a producer, she's a presenter... they're two completely different roles. We have different skill sets entirely. I've never had any interest in presenting a show.'

'You used to present a show, though, didn't you? At university.'

How the hell have they found this out? It was years ago and it was nothing, just a hobby I did for a stint of no longer than a couple of months when I was in my second year. It had taken three years for a shred of confidence to return after what had happened, and within no time at all I realised I'd made a mistake. It wasn't for me. I'm the wrong personality, for a start. And broadcasting my voice across a public space was unlikely to help me in my quest to stay hidden.

'Briefly, yes. What's that got to do with anything?' I hear the tone of my voice, abrasive and defensive, and the expressions of the detectives sitting opposite me let me know they've registered it. I've done nothing to help myself, only made myself look more guilty.

'It must have been an ambition, at one point.'

'If I'd wanted to present, I would have pursued it. I didn't. I stopped volunteering a couple of months after I started, and by the end of that year I was focusing on production. That's all I've done since. Carrie and I had a great working relationship. We were a good team. We supported each other. And we were friends, too.'

DC Brett's right eyebrow raises in a high arch. 'Are you sure about that?' He reaches for his notes and slides out a sheet that he passes across the table to me. 'I'm sure you're aware that one of your colleagues has been investigated in relation to Ms Adams' murder. We checked his phone history and the messages between them. Take a look.'

I don't touch the sheet of paper. I'm scared to. Instead, I lean closer so I can peer at it, reluctant to see this exchange the officers clearly can't wait for me to read. DCI Manning is practically salivating with the anticipation of my reaction.

Flynn: You going out with the others on Friday?

Carrie: Don't think so. Siobhan's going to be there, isn't she? Fancy giving it a miss?

Flynn: Something happened between you two?

Carrie: Five hours a day is enough for anyone... know what I mean haha

I nudge the sheet to Harry without looking at him. Heat has risen in my chest, making my neck flare red. I never had any idea that this was how Carrie really felt about me, and knowing it changes everything. I thought we were a team. A good team. I thought she liked and respected me, but it turns out I was an annoyance to her. Her words cut deeper than I ever could have imagined. I considered her one of my closest friends. It seems I can't trust anyone, not even the dead.

'I never knew she felt that way about me,' I say, the hurt of her words, inescapable on the printed sheet in front of me, leaving me reeling.

'What is this?' Harry says dismissively, shoving the paper back across the table. 'Nothing, that's what it is. A throwaway comment. You plan on using it to accuse someone of murder?'

The detectives exchange a glance. Harry's done his job here. But I realise it's only for so long.

'Are you charging my client with anything?'

'Not yet,' DCI Manning says.

'Right then.' He scrapes his chair back across the floor. A laugh escapes him, sharp and sudden like a gunshot, though he's clearly not amused by anything. 'It's taken you a month to look through some CCTV footage,' he says scathingly, his mouth twisted in a smirk. 'A month. Really?' He reaches for my arm. 'Come on,' he says. 'They've wasted enough of your time already.'

Outside the station, fresh air hits me like the morning after a heavy drinking session.

'You okay?' Harry asks, genuine concern etched on his features. 'Try not to worry. They know this is all circumstantial, for now.'

For now. The words seem to echo through the car park. I can't linger on them, on the probability of my imminent arrest. All I can think about is that still from the CCTV footage. My coat. Me. Anna.

My mother was right: Anna is dangerous. But until today, I hadn't realised just how much. She terrifies me. There. I've said it. I always knew her interest in me wasn't healthy, but I excused it, finding pity for her awkwardness and her self-deprecation; I learned to regard her imitation as a form of flattery. My mother must have somehow known a truth I remained keen to avoid acknowledging, and not because I haven't wanted to believe what Anna is, but because, like the child that's always been trapped inside me, petulant and afraid, I've never wanted to admit that I was wrong and my mother was right. I've never wanted to consider the fact that her being right about Anna might change other aspects of our past.

Poor, sad little Anna. Friendless. Charmless. Harmless.

Only maybe she isn't so harmless after all.

TWENTY-THREE

ANNA

Siobhan texts me just before lunchtime telling me to come home for six o'clock. She tells me not to eat too much, so I'm assuming she's planning to cook. I didn't see her yesterday after she got home from work; she was back late, and when she came in, I heard her slope straight upstairs to bed. She seemed to purposely avoid me for some reason, apparently regretting the fact today. Perhaps dinner is her way of making up for it, or maybe she feels she needs to return the favour after breakfast last week. Either way, it's starting to feel as though we're a married couple. The thought makes me claustrophobic. I want to *be* Siobhan, not be with her.

I do as instructed. I skip lunch altogether, though by the time I reach my interview, my stomach is rumbling. I sit in a small glass waiting room with the three other candidates, wondering whether any of them has lied in such detail as I have on their application. Name: Siobhan Docherty. DOB: 13 September 1988. Address, current post, qualifications, experience... I've lied about the lot. Well, not really lied, I suppose. They're all facts. They're all the truth. They're just not *my* truth.

There are three women and one man here. The job is in marketing. I'm not sure even Siobhan has the relevant experience, but I plan on using the 'transferable skills' route to impress them. That, and my new look. My new-found confidence. I smooth down the skirt I took from Siobhan's wardrobe: a beautiful expensive knee-length silk one, the kind that swishes in a pleated blur of bottle green when I move from side to side. I tried on several outfits before settling on it as the right choice for today: professional yet glamorous; smart, but just sexy enough to give me an edge.

Outside the window of the waiting room, we watch a catering company bustle about with boxes and chairs, preparing the larger room adjacent to us for some kind of event.

'Anyone know what's going on there?' I ask.

'They've got some corporate clients coming in later this afternoon,' a woman says, her voice authoritative and smug, and her answer reveals what a shitshow today really is. She's an internal candidate. She must be, because how else would she know this?

A moment later, the penny seems to drop with the male candidate. He rolls his eyes and takes his phone from his pocket. Maybe he's considering his next interview already, because this one is likely to be a waste of time for everyone other than the self-satisfied cow who's now watching a champagne tower being erected by two kids who don't look old enough to have left school. So the rest of us are here to make up the numbers, I think – the box-ticking legal requirement of advertising the post and carrying out an interview process for the sake of appearing unbiased and inclusive. What a load of bollocks.

My phone pings in my pocket, and I remember I've not yet turned it to silent. I take it out and open the message.

Hey you. When are you free to meet up? I'm asking for a friend, obviously. Jack x

I feel a wave of something unnameable warm my stomach and settle there. I hadn't really expected to hear from him. But this is Siobhan... no one lets her down.

I don't message back. I'll do it later. Siobhan would play it cool, wait a few hours before responding. Just a casual reply, nothing too keen.

When my name is called, I make my way to the room where the interviews are being held with the attitude of someone already defeated, because that's essentially what I am.

'Ms Docherty,' the man at the opposite side of the table says. 'Please take a seat.'

'Take it where?'

The woman seated next to him looks up sharply from the notes in front of her, her thin-rimmed glasses falling to the tip of her nose and only managing to stay on her face thanks to the ski-slope curve above her nostrils.

'I beg your pardon?' she says, her voice as thick and cloying as clotted cream.

'Don't beg, please,' I tell her. 'It's so degrading.'

They're looking at me open-mouthed now, neither of them sure what to say next. They probably don't want to say anything at all, more than likely hoping I'll turn and leave, but I'm enjoying their discomfort a little too much, so instead of relieving them, I sit down and give them my best smile. My Siobhan smile.

'I... uh...' The man sifts through some paperwork, feigning looking for something necessary for this moment.

'You have an impressive CV,' the woman says flatly, resentful of the facts in front of her.

'Thank you.'

'And your current employment is at...'

'City Sounds. It says it right there in my CV. I thought you might have read it before today?'

The woman's face flushes. 'I don't find your attitude to be particularly agreeable.'

'I don't find the fact that you've invited me here today particularly agreeable, not when you've already got someone else lined up for the job.'

'I... uh...' the man says again.

'I... uh...' I imitate him, wobbling my head from side to side. 'Is everything okay? Do you need some form of assistance?'

The woman's cheeks are sucked into her face, her lips puckering into a circle of wrinkles even the Botox can't keep at bay. 'I think it might be a good idea for us to terminate this interview here.'

'Excellent idea,' I say, over-enthusiastically. 'Probably the only good one you'll have today, I suspect.' I put a hand to my mouth and blow her a kiss as I stand. 'Ciao for now,' I say breezily, then I saunter from the room in the way I imagine Siobhan might, although I know that really this would never happen. Siobhan would never behave the way I just have. She'd never have the guts.

When I go back out into the main reception area, the catering company have finished constructing their champagne tower. Light reflects from the glass construction, sparkling beneath the spotlights overhead. It's an impressive sight, in terms of both scale and effort.

I let the door ease closed behind me and pause a moment as I watch a couple of staff argue over which trays the canapés should be placed on. The clock on the far wall tells me it's already gone 4.30, and it looks from the growing sense of panic that the guests are due any time soon.

As I head for the exit, I have to walk past the champagne tower. It's not yet been filled with alcohol, which is disappointing. Still, I swipe a glass from the lowest layer, relishing the cry that leaves one of the catering staff and absorbing with glee the look of horror that spreads across the face of her colleague.

The tower comes crashing to the ground in a fractured glitter ball of light and reflection, sending showers of glass spraying across the room as it hits the tiled floor. I continue walking, sensing the expressions of shock on the faces of the other candidates still sitting in the waiting area. As I reach the door, the bitch who interviewed me rushes out in a whirlwind of panic.

I turn to give her a wave before I leave, and it's the best feeling ever.

TWENTY-FOUR

SIOBHAN

Anna killed Carrie. I hold the thought with me, heavy in my heart, unable to put it down and leave it for a moment. It's like carrying a screaming, fractious baby that doesn't belong to me. I can't escape the noise of it, and I can't just leave it. I need to act in response, but I feel so numbed and exhausted by everything that my brain can't begin to consider a reaction. Anna killed Carrie. Anna killed Carrie while wearing my clothes. While already looking like me. She managed it before her physical transformation had even truly begun.

Anna wants to ruin me.

My mother's warnings seem to make so much more sense now, though I doubt even she realised her niece's true potential. Dangerous, wasn't that how she described her? I never considered it in this sense, that Anna might be violent. Murderous.

I can't go back to the flat until I've cleared my mind. I managed to avoid Anna yesterday, but I'm not going to be able to prevent our paths from crossing at some point. By the time she gets home tonight, I need to be able to look her in the eye and pretend that everything's fine. I need to leave London with the certainty that as far as she is concerned, I trust her.

I walk until my legs ache, miles and miles of London trod underfoot as I try to make sense of everything that has happened. I stop near Camden Passage, a pedestrianised street in Islington filled with antique and vintage shops, realising that I must be at least eight miles from home. There's a café at the end of the street, and I go in and order a coffee and some lunch, having eaten nothing since yesterday.

It occurs to me that I'm only a mile or so from the Rhythm and Brews bar; at some level, my subconscious must have brought me here today. After I finish eating, I continue to walk. I tap the postcode into my phone and follow the directions, not really sure what going there will achieve. When I arrive, the street is busy. The weather is good, and people are out window-shopping and picking up food on their lunch breaks. There's a bench across the other side of the street from the bar. A packed bus stops nearby and a crowd of people spill out onto the pavement. The last people to get off are an elderly couple in coats that look too heavy for the recently mild weather. She holds his arm, her handbag slung over the other, helping him as he wobbles down the steps on frail legs. They stand at the kerb as the bus pulls away, waiting for the lights to change so they can cross the street safely.

Something about them reminds me of my grandparents. His thin grey hair, tufting at the ears. Her hunched shoulders beneath her tartan coat. When I was a child, my grandparents seemed ancient to me when they were still in their fifties, in the way everyone over the age of thirty seems old when you're so young. Then, after my dad died, their own deaths swept them up in a whirlwind, taking them within three months of one another less than a year after they'd lost their youngest son. This is what grief does. It hollows you out and then it destroys the shell that remains.

The lights change to red and the couple start to cross the street. The man is moving faster than his legs are comfortable with, knowing the green man will soon begin to flash and the traffic will start moving again. It occurs to me now how little time these lights allow for someone who is elderly or less mobile. It seems a sad reflection of modern life, that we are all in too much of a rush to consider other people's difficulties with the things we might take for granted.

I watch as he falls. It seems to happen in slow motion, one foot tripping over the other, his wife losing her balance as she tries to hold him upright. He lands with a thud on the tarmac, his wife stumbling, just managing to break her own fall. I rush to help them. Someone else has got out of a car, and he assists the old lady while I crouch beside her husband.

'Are you hurt?' I ask him. But his answer is interrupted by the blasting of a car horn. Someone revs their engine and swerves around us, barely missing the old lady. My heart pounds with the callousness of it, but when I look at the rest of the traffic, his response seems to be the reaction of the majority.

'What's your name?' I ask the man on the floor.

'Malcolm.' He winces in pain. 'I think I've done my hip in.'

More car horns are blasted. The man who got out of his car to help is calling for an ambulance. Malcolm's wife looks white. It's then I get that familiar feeling, one I know all too well by now. Someone is looking at me, but not just someone watching the drama in the middle of the road unfold. I know who it is, and I have a sudden urge to run.

'They're on their way,' the man tells me, putting his phone in his pocket. 'Come on,' he says to Malcolm's wife. 'It isn't safe for you to wait here.'

He takes her by the arm and leads her to the pavement, and I panic at the thought of being left alone in the middle of the road with this man who could be more badly injured than we realise. More than this, I panic at the thought that I can't be here. I can't do this.

I turn. He's there, on the pavement outside the bar where he works, his muscular arms on display beneath the T-shirt he wears emblazoned with the bar's name and logo. Malcolm's wife is sitting on a chair outside a nearby fish and chip shop, being tended to by a woman I assume must work there. I turn back quickly. He can't see my face.

I'm grateful when the driver of the car that's been left in the middle of the road returns.

'I have to go,' I tell him, regretting the words but knowing I don't have a choice. 'There's somewhere I've got to be.'

'But—' he begins, but I don't give him a chance to finish. I grab my bag and dart back to the far side of the road, a van driver blasting his horn and shouting abuse at me through his window when he narrowly misses me. I run to the end of the street and turn left, and I don't stop running until I reach St John's Gate. By the time I find a bench, my thighs are burning and my heart pounds with such intensity I feel as though I'm going to throw up.

I've got to get to a supermarket and buy food for dinner this evening. I have to get showered and changed; I need to remove any evidence of the day from me before I see Anna back at the flat.

I've known for some time that someone has been watching me. It started with phone calls, then unwanted gifts. I started to watch back, familiarising myself with patterns of behaviour, in much the same way my own routines must have been scrutinised. I felt him getting closer, and then that day, just after I'd been reunited with Anna at the library, he was right beside me, handing my bag back to me on the pedestrian crossing.

I take the flattened cardboard takeaway coffee cup from my bag and work it back into some sort of shape. I'd retrieved it from the bin in the park after he'd followed me to the coffee shop. His name is printed in black permanent marker, the rushed scrawl of a barista who had probably penned a hundred names already that morning.

JACK.

Jack Lovell.

My stalker.

TWENTY-FIVE

ANNA

I'm late getting back. I purposely lengthen my journey home to the flat, not wanting to be roped into the task of helping out with dinner. Besides that, it's a nice evening, comparatively mild against recent weather efforts, and every extra step is an additional push towards the weight goal that is now just a couple of pounds within my grasp. I thought I would feel better for it, but I'm not sure I do. I might look better, but the renewed energy I was promised when I read all that crap online about weight loss and a new me is yet to show its glowing post-workout face. Perhaps *I'm* the problem. There's a nagging doubt clinging to me like a mollusc gripped to a rock. Something's going to go wrong; it always does.

There's music playing when I get into the flat. This isn't unusual: Siobhan's lifestyle is soundtracked, her playlist as prolific as her use of eyeliner. But tonight isn't her go-to choice of sounds, and the lighting is muted, candles arranged in clusters on the sideboard and dining table, like a fancy restaurant without, hopefully, a bill at the end. She has her back to me; what with the music and the noise of the blender, she didn't hear me come in. An intrusive thought worms itself into my brain as I watch her stir some colourful concoction that looks like neon vomit: me closing the gap between us, my hands moving around her throat. Carrie's face appears in front of me in the softly lit room, her features with the blurred edges of a ghost.

'Anna,' Siobhan says, a hand thrown to her chest. 'I didn't hear you come in.'

'Sorry. I didn't mean to make you jump.'

She looks me up and down. The outfit I wore to the studio was one thing, but this appears to be quite another. Her top lip is sucked in, betraying her disapproval. I wonder just how much the skirt cost, and whether even it's the cost of the thing that's bothering her when it might just be me and the fact that I'm wearing it.

'I've been to an interview,' I explain quickly. 'I should have asked if I could borrow something, but it came up last minute and I didn't have anything suitable. I'm so sorry. I'll get it dry-cleaned for you.'

'Don't worry about it,' she says, her words flat. 'It's fine.'

She looks away, returning her focus to her task, but I know it's not fine. And it's not just the clothes. There's something else. She doesn't want to look at me.

'Can I do anything to help?' I offer, hoping I've arrived too late to be needed. 'I mean, not now, obviously. Not wearing this. Let me go and get changed first.'

I go into the spare bedroom and close the door behind me. I've never referred to it as 'my' room – it isn't, and I'm on borrowed time. Just how long I have left, I don't know. It'll be decided by Siobhan, just as she likes to think every decision is hers to make. Until recently, that is.

I pull the clothes off hastily, but take greater time and care in laying them out on the bed. God knows how much it's going to cost me to get a silk skirt dry-cleaned, but I've said it now so I'm locked in. I pull open a drawer, my first instinct drawing me towards a pair of leggings and a T-shirt. But Siobhan has gone to so much effort and looks so lovely that I can't just roll out of the bedroom dressed as though I'm about to eat a pizza on the sofa. Not really wanting to have to return to it, I put on the dress I wore when I met her for dinner. When I check my reflection, disappointment greets me in the glass. I expected to look like Siobhan dressed as me, but I don't. I look like me again – just me, but with Siobhan's hair, or a lame attempt at it, at least.

Something catches my eye in the mirror: the parcel I never gave her on Monday. It's still sitting beside the bed where I left it after I'd brought it upstairs, not having had a chance to mention it to her since.

She's at the dining table, arranging plates, when I leave the bedroom. She must hear me this time, yet she doesn't turn to look at me, and I wonder now just what I've done. Something has happened. I worry what she knows.

'This came for you,' I tell her. She turns to take the parcel from me, putting it on top of the microwave.

'What can I do?' I ask.

'Nothing. It's all done.'

When she moves back, I see that the table is adorned with various plates of tapas: little cubed potatoes in a tomato sauce, king prawns curved around a pot of chilli dip, glistening mushrooms, and something unidentifiable that could be green peppers or those gross little fish things that come in tins. The air is thick with the smell of garlic and something else I don't recognise. No expense has been spared, and no effort either. Yet as I sit at the table and take in the details of the feast, I can't shake the feeling that there's a purpose to all of this. I'm here tonight for a reason, and I'm not sure I want to know what it is.

'This looks incredible,' I tell her. 'I feel bad. You've done so much to help me... I should be the one putting on a fancy dinner. This makes my breakfast look like a Tesco meal deal.'

Her silence manages to be noisy. She crosses the room and

takes a bottle of white wine from the fridge. Collecting two glasses from the cupboard, she hands one to me, still managing to avoid making eye contact. She knows something, I think. But what? There's nothing for her to have found out. It can't possibly be anything to do with Carrie. If she knew anything, she'd have found an excuse to get me straight out of her home. The last thing she'd be doing is making an effort with dinner and wine.

'How did the interview go?' she asks, sitting opposite me. 'Did they say when you'll find out?'

'Next couple of days. I think it went okay, but I'm not holding out much hope, to be honest. Internal candidate.'

'Always annoying.'

'Very.' I wonder how she'd react if I told her what I did at the interview, and that I used her name and CV. I imagine her face if she bumped into someone one day and they said, 'Siobhan... I heard all about the incident with the champagne tower.'

'Tuck in,' she says.

I watch her spoon some potatoes onto her plate. Everything she does is delicate and precise. She tends to her dinner with the same focus a painter would offer a lifelong project, every movement an intended piece of art. Somewhere in my head, I know it isn't right to feel the desire to destroy it all with the intensity I do, but I've rarely listened to my head, and my gut wants to watch chaos take the place of her particularity.

'Any other news?' she asks.

I think about the text I received from Jack. The response I sent him when I was on my way back from the interview. Turns out, I couldn't wait. The flirtation that burned from the screen with a few simple exchanged sentences was palpable. 'I'm going on a date on Friday.'

Siobhan smiles. 'Great. I'm glad you've met someone. Who is he?'

'His name's Jack.'

She drops her fork. It clatters to the floor and she reaches down to get it.

'Everything okay?'

'Fine. Sorry... I'm so clumsy.' She reaches across the table to help herself to some mushrooms. She's still avoiding eye contact. 'So... how did you meet this Jack?'

'He delivered your parcel.'

She splutters and puts a hand to her chest. 'I'm fine,' she says, with a wave of a hand. 'Just spicy, that's all.'

Her face has gone pale. I wonder whether she's coming down with something. She doesn't seem herself at all tonight.

'Going somewhere nice?' she asks. 'On Friday?'

I don't know why I'm reluctant to answer the question. Why do I feel that if I tell her where we're going, she might turn up there unexpectedly – that I might spot her among the other diners, watching us from behind a menu like the kind of really bad private investigator you see in spoof spy films? She's bound to be jealous when she sees how good-looking Jack is. Much nicer than that ex she brought home with her the night she didn't bother to invite me out.

'I'm not sure yet.'

'Well,' she says, stabbing her fork into a cube of potato. 'That is exciting. I hope it goes well.'

We eat in silence for a while. I wonder if she's simply jealous that I've met someone. It seemed a sad move for her to invite Nick here – a step backwards. I know his name because I heard her say it, and I knew he's her ex because... well, I've made it my business to know everything about Siobhan's life that might be useful to me in the future.

'There's something I wanted to talk to you about,' she says, before finishing the mushroom on the end of her fork.

Here we go, I think. She's going to ask me to leave.

'I'm taking some time off work.'

'Okay.'

I wait for her to tell me that because she's going to be home more often, she needs me to move out. We can't be in each other's space all day. Then I wonder if maybe she wants our roles to be reversed. I promised her I'd find a job soon. Perhaps she's hoping I'll be out while she stays here, that maybe I can keep her financially for a while in the way she's kept me.

'I shouldn't really have gone back, you know, after...' She trails into silence, unable to speak the truth of Carrie's death aloud. Seeking a distraction, she reaches for an olive and pops it into her mouth.

'I'll find somewhere else to live by the end of the week.'

'No,' she says quickly. 'That's not what I'm...'

But she doesn't finish the sentence. She can't, because the olive has slid down her throat, and when she tries to speak, all that escapes her is a strangled gargle. She reaches for her drink and takes a swig of wine, but it comes back up in an unsightly spray. She looks at me wide-eyed, her face contorted in panic. I should get up. I should go to the other side of the table and help her. But I don't. I watch as her face turns from pink to puce, wondering now what will happen when she dies. I won't gain anything from her death. I may live here, but that won't mean a thing if she's left a will. And if she's going to die, I need her to do it somewhere else – somewhere no one will know it's even happened. Anna Fitzgerald can disappear without anyone noticing. Siobhan Docherty can't.

I get up and go to her, pulling her up from her seat. I'm not really sure what I'm doing when I wrap my arms around her from behind and tighten them beneath her ribs. I pull hard, in and up, like I've seen demonstrated on television, but nothing happens; she's still choking, the noise of it becoming more ugly by the second. I do it again. Nothing. Then I try a third time, and this time a single olive, still whole, shoots through the air, landing on the wooden floor near the dishwasher.

Siobhan gasps and gulps down air like someone chugging

on water after finding an oasis in a desert. Her chest wheezes and she slumps into her seat like a deflated balloon. The thought occurs to me that I've just saved her life, and for a moment I curse myself. Maybe I should have let her die. Perhaps it would have been easier if she had. Either way, I'm now stuck with the choice I've made.

For a while, neither of us says anything. I stand awkwardly at the side of the table, looking on as she recovers her composure, realising just what a close call that was. After a minute, I go to the kitchen to get her a glass of water.

'Are you okay?' I ask, handing it to her.

She takes the drink without thanking me. 'I'm fine.'

I return to the chair opposite her.

'I don't want you to leave here,' she tells me eventually, once her breathing has returned to normal. 'What I was going to say is that I'm going away for a while. Just for a break from everything. I was going to ask if you'd mind looking after the flat while I'm gone.'

'Of course not. I mean, if you're sure that's what you want.'

This is perfect, I think. It buys me some extra time.

'Thank you,' she says, eventually. 'You saved my life.'

But her eyes say something different, and I know what she's thinking: that I may have saved her life, but it took me a few seconds too long to decide to do it.

TWENTY-SIX

SIOBHAN

As soon as Anna has gone to bed, I lock myself in the bathroom with my phone. Everything is ruined. I brought Anna here as a decoy, knowing that if I encouraged her lifelong obsession with me I could manipulate a physical transformation that might be enough to fool Jack into mistaking her for me, if only for long enough to buy me some time to get away. I knew the day he passed me on the pedestrian crossing that he was starting to move closer, and I knew his intentions could only mean me harm. I'd done the right thing in making myself available to Anna. Part of me felt guilty for using her to save my own skin, but I couldn't see another way out. Now, knowing what I do about Carrie, that guilt has evaporated. Anna deserves everything I had planned for her. But now that she's met Jack, all the preparation I've put in place will count for nothing.

Just a couple of hours ago, I watched Anna watch me choke, waiting for me to die. I knew what she was before she came here, but only to a degree: I knew that she was obsessive, weird, infatuated with me in the same way she'd always been since we were kids, but I hadn't known until I watched that CCTV footage at the police station that she was also a psychopath. A murderer. Tonight, I saw it with my own eyes. She would have let me choke. She would have left me to die, had something not stopped her at the last moment.

But if the past few months have taught me anything, it's that it's always better to keep your enemies close.

I access the app for the doorbell and go back to Monday. I skip through footage of Dominic and Freya coming and going, as well as Anna arriving home after she'd been to the radio station to bring me lunch. Not long after this, Jack appears. He's wearing a cap pulled low to hide his face from the camera, but there's no mistaking it's him. I turn the volume low in case Anna might be lurking outside the bathroom door, listening in. I hold the phone to my ear and hear Jack tell her he has a parcel for Siobhan Docherty. My heart plummets with the realisation that everything is over.

I listen as he asks for a signature. And then I hear Anna's voice, so sugary sweet it's sickly, say, 'That's me.'

My breath escapes me. I move the phone from my ear and skip the footage back a few seconds, replaying it to make sure I haven't made a mistake. I listen to them flirt with each other. Then I hear Jack call Anna by my name.

He thinks she's me. They're going on a date on Friday, and he thinks Anna is Siobhan.

I could cry with relief. I knew the plan was risky. I knew there was a good chance it would fail. I could never have imagined it would turn out better than I might have hoped for. I started a process, but Anna has walked straight into a trap. She has inadvertently made everything so much easier for me.

I close the app and go out into the living room, half expecting to find her here. She's not. What is here, though, still waiting for my attention, is the package she passed on to me: the one Jack brought here on Monday. I go to the kitchen for a pair of scissors before heading up to my bedroom. The parcel is sealed tightly, thick strips of Sellotape making it impossible to open with my fingers. I slice through it and peer inside before I allow myself to touch the contents. It's a book. I pull it out, and for a moment the title makes my heart stop in my chest. *Matilda, Who Told Lies and was Burned to Death.* I drop it on the duvet beside me, as though it's alight and has just singed my skin. The cover is creepy, illustrated with a pencil drawing of a Victorian child who looks dead behind the eyes. I'm familiar with the name of the poem, though I can't remember ever having read it. But I know what it means. I know all its implications.

I take the book from the bed and push it to the back of the shelf inside the wardrobe. As I do so, I catch sight of the hat I hid there, staring at me accusingly: the baseball cap I was sent anonymously in the post. I know now that Jack sent it. There's only one person who might have owned it – or one like it – because nobody else is relevant to me in any way that makes sense for it to be sent all these years later. When I google his name, my heart drops like a stone into my stomach. It couldn't have been his: it isn't possible. Yet it's the exact same type he was wearing in the photograph all the newspapers used of him, and Jack's only intention in sending it must have been to torture me with the memory.

A rush of cold air brushes past me, and I turn instinctively, drawn towards its source. But there is nothing and no one in the room with me, other than perhaps his ghost. I know his face as well as I know my own. He has never left me. Pale complexion, gaunt cheeks; the sunken eyes of a man riddled with addiction. A face too small for its skull, skin following bone along the contours of his jaw. I know all the details still, so clearly I'm able to visualise him in front of me, my memory bringing him back to life like a mirage, hazy and intangible. I feel an icy knot travel down my spine.

'I'm sorry,' I say softly, as though he might be able to hear me, and forgiveness may be sought so easily that all I need do is ask it of the air.

I manage to avoid Anna for a couple of days. On Thursday, I stay in bed until mid-morning, something I never do, but the excuse I text Anna is a genuine one: I feel terrible from my ordeal the day before. My throat is raw, burning almost, and my near-death experience has left me with a headache that stays with me until the evening. She calls up from downstairs a couple of times: the first to ask me if I want a cup of tea or some breakfast; the second to let me know she's going out. I don't ask where she's going. I don't care. I get up and roam around the flat for a while, wandering aimlessly from room to room while planning in my head what I'm going to do next. Jack thinks Anna is me. Jack wants to hurt me. Anna is crazy enough to assume my identity. They are both unhinged, both deserving of the other. I need to get away from here as soon as possible.

On Friday afternoon, Anna comes out from her bedroom apparently ready for her date with Jack.

'You're not going out wearing that, are you?'

Her face falls. She looks crushed.

'I'm so sorry,' I say quickly. 'I didn't mean that as it sounded. I just meant...'

But I don't know where to start. She's wearing a woollen dress that's so shapeless she may as well have a burlap sack hanging from her shoulders. And don't get me started on the boots: knee-high, flat-heeled, shiny black monstrosities that from a distance resemble a pair of wellies. No one's ever going to believe she's me if she goes out wearing that.

'You meant I look terrible,' she says quietly.

'I didn't say that. Look, I know it's a bit cold out, so you want to be warm and comfortable. That's sensible. But sense doesn't need to get in the way of style. Come with me.'

She follows me up to my bedroom, and I gesture to the bed. She sits and waits as I pull a range of dresses from the wardrobe. She's playing a game, as she always is, craving the attention she always claimed never to need. She knew exactly what she was doing when she put on those clothes.

'They won't fit me.'

'You haven't tried them yet. And they will... there's nothing of you.'

I catch her mouth tweaking into a slight smile, though my words weren't intended as a compliment. She's lost a lot of weight since she moved into the flat. What was she hoping I would think: that the stress of it all must be responsible for it? Poor Anna, I think, unable to keep the snideness from my thoughts – it can't be easy for her, having lost her marriage, her job and now her home, all in the space of just a couple of years. She must be in need of a friend. Someone to boost her confidence.

Someone to make sure she pays the price for what she's done.

I bite my tongue as my thoughts grow angry. She mustn't see any sign that I know about Carrie. And I can't show her that I know she's going out tonight pretending to be me.

'Try this one,' I suggest, passing her a deep blue off-the-shoulder dress that I haven't worn for a few years now, not since a friend's wedding reception.

'Bit much for a dinner date, isn't it?'

'Depends what sort of first impression you want to make.'

She frowns. 'I don't want to look slutty. Or desperate.'

I raise an eyebrow and she begins to apologise. 'I'm sorry... I wasn't saying the dress is slutty. It's a beautiful dress. I'm sure it looks gorgeous on you. Sophisticated. I just... I'm not sure it's very me.'

'Is this more you?' I say, reaching for the skirt of her woollen sack dress. 'Come on, Anna,' I coax her. 'Try something new. If you always do what you always did, you'll always get what you always got.'

'Nice one,' she says, standing. 'Shall I get you a print of that for the living room wall?'

I unzip the blue dress while she takes off the one she's wearing, turning aside to give her some privacy. 'Let me know when you're ready,' I say, and I leave the dress on the bed and go to the window.

I stand to the side, where I can see her reflection in the floor-length mirror. I will never stand with my back to Anna again, not now I know who she really is. She thinks she knows me, that she knows who I am, but she knows nothing. She may be dangerous, but in the right circumstances – the wrong ones – there's the potential for danger in all of us. And I have always been one step ahead of her.

'What do you think?'

I turn. She's posing awkwardly with one hand on her hip and the other clutching the side of the dress.

'Relax,' I say. It doesn't look right, even when she loosens her grip on it. It's too baggy around the bust, and the colour isn't strong enough on her.

'You don't like it on me.' She begins to pull the dress off, and I catch a glimpse of her greying bra. It looks as though it's been through a thousand washes with her interview dress, and I can't believe she's chosen it for a date. This is a first date, though, I remind myself. Perhaps she has no intention of letting him see her underwear this evening.

'Anna,' I say, putting a hand on her bare arm. 'It looks lovely. You're just not finished yet. Would you like me to do your hair for you?'

'Would you mind?' she asks, her face brightening.

I plug in my straighteners, and she pulls the dress back on before sitting at the edge of the bed. I get a brush and run it through her hair, slowly and deliberately, the way she used to do mine when we were children. I remember it all, if only she knew. The way she looked at me. The way she tried to copy everything I did. Once, after a sleepover at my house, I found a lock of my hair tucked into a sandwich bag and stuffed into the toe of one of her trainers. She'd cut it off in a neat snip while I'd been sleeping.

I wonder whether her mind has taken her to the same place mine has returned to. Her shoulders are raised and tightened. I put my free hand on her left shoulder, applying pressure to push it down.

'Relax,' I tell her. 'You're always so on edge.'

She says nothing. From the corner of my eye, I catch a glimpse of the lamp on my chest of drawers. It has a domed glass base. I picture myself going to it, yanking the lead from the socket, using it to smash in her skull. I see the blood pumping in jets from her head, so vivid that it shocks me with its violence. This isn't me. This isn't who I am. But I can't stop thinking about Carrie. Anna will get what she deserves, but I'm not going to be the person to deliver it.

'So what's this Jack like then?' I say, taking hold of the hot straighteners. 'You haven't really said much about him.'

'I don't really know much yet.'

'What does he look like?'

She describes him in detail that's frighteningly accurate for someone who only met the man for a couple of minutes. I feign interest in her gushing verbal portrait of the man, already all too aware of what he looks like.

Anna looks at me in the floor-length mirror. 'He's out of my league.'

'Don't say that.' It's all I can manage. My voice is clogged in my throat, thickened like a cloud of candyfloss. I return my attention to her hair, but my concentration is somewhere else, dragged to a past I wish I could claim was someone else's.

'Ow!'

She jolts forward, her hand flying to her neck.

'Shit,' I say. 'I'm so sorry. Are you okay?'

When she moves her hand away, there are two distinct red lines where I pressed the straighteners against her skin. I wasn't aware I was doing it.

'I'll get you some ice,' I say, putting the straighteners on the heat pad and hurrying to the stairs. I feel her eyes on me as I go, sensing that she realises something is wrong.

I get a bag of peas from the freezer and wrap them in a tea towel, trying to compose myself. She mustn't see that anything is wrong. Everything is normal, I tell myself, chanting it over and over in my head as though repetition alone will be enough for me to believe it.

When I go back to the bedroom, she is still nursing the side of her neck. She takes the wrapped bag from me and presses it to her skin.

'I'm sorry,' I say again. 'I'm so clumsy.'

'It's okay,' she says, and if she thinks otherwise, there's nothing in her expression or her tone to suggest it. 'Are you all right?'

I shrug. 'Just tired. I'm going to have an early night. I'll be fine.'

'I can cancel. We'll rearrange for another night.'

'No, honestly, please don't do that.' I put a hand on her arm. 'You deserve this.'

'Thank you,' she says. 'For everything.'

She lowers the bag of peas and assesses the red marks in the mirror. 'Nothing a bit of concealer won't cover.'

'I'll do your make-up, if you like,' I offer.

'Are you sure? You've already done enough.'

'I promise not to poke you in the eye with the mascara.'

I begin to apply foundation before I contour her face in the same way I do my own. Bronzer, winged eyeliner, mascara. A slick of nude lip gloss.

'You look beautiful,' I tell her when I'm finished, and I know she believes it.

'You're a magician with that eyeliner.'

I force a laugh as I return the make-up items to their bag. 'I hope everything goes well tonight,' I tell her, and I have never meant anything with such sincerity in my life.

TWENTY-SEVEN

ANNA

When I arrive at the restaurant in Covent Garden, fashionably late by ten minutes, I expect to find Jack already at our table, waiting for me. By the time the waiter reaches me, I've had enough time to do a quick scan of the room and see he's not yet here. A mild panic kicks in. What if he's changed his mind? I'm going to look an idiot if he stands me up – or, even worse, if he's discovered I'm not really Siobhan.

I give Jack's name when the waiter asks who booked the table, realising now I don't know his surname.

'Lovell?' he asks, scanning the bookings list.

'That's the one,' I say breezily, as though I'd known this already.

As I follow the waiter into the restaurant, I start to think of the worse possible scenarios. What if he doesn't turn up? What if Jack Lovell isn't really his name? If I've lied about mine, why shouldn't he have lied about his? I figure the chances of two compulsive liars finding their spirit animal across the top of a DHL parcel are slim, so I hope for the best and try to reassure myself that he really is who he says he is and that rather than having stood me up, he just has terrible timekeeping.

The waiter leads me through the restaurant to a table for two in the corner of the room. Only half the tables are occupied, and thankfully the ones next to ours are empty, but I'm still conscious of being alone, so I browse the menu to avoid potential looks of pity.

The prices are comparable to the ones at the restaurant where I met up with Siobhan that first time after we saw each other at the library. I couldn't afford them then, and I sure as hell can't afford them now, though Siobhan reassured me that I shouldn't need to pay tonight; as far as she's concerned, Jack should foot the bill on the first date. It seems a bit of an outdated attitude for someone so independent, but I'll take her advice on it. It'll be nice to be wined and dined. The closest I ever came to that with Dean was a pancake roll from the Chinese takeaway at the end of the street and a six-pack of lagers from the off-licence next door.

I glance up when I hear the waiter welcoming someone near the front door. Jack looks even better than he did on the day we met, smartly dressed in a dark shirt and light trousers. He's like a model from a Next catalogue, one of those ones who seem not to have made much effort with their hair but it's probably taken them three hours to style. He looks too good to be seen with me. Too young for me, as well. He shouldn't want to date me. But then I remind myself that I'm no longer me, and that's the point.

His eyes meet mine across the restaurant before he says something to the waiter that makes the other man smile. He seems so confident. I wonder what was said. For a moment, I feel an unpleasant heat rise in my chest, worried that some joke about me has just been passed between them – some snide observation about the way I'm dressed, or a comment designed not to be overheard by female ears. Stop it, Anna, I tell myself. Not every man is like Dean.

'Siobhan,' he says as he approaches, the name rolling from his tongue like melting chocolate. 'Sorry I'm late.'

He leans down and kisses me on the cheek with a confidence I wasn't expecting, despite his exchange with the waiter. He pulls out the chair opposite me and sits down, leaving a trail of aftershave lingering in the air behind him, something musky and not too overpowering. I hate the response my body gives to his smile. It's nothing like me. I don't do this.

'Have you ordered a drink yet?' he asks me.

'No. I was waiting for you.'

It's too soon after Dean. I don't know how to do this – how to function or behave as a single woman, someone capable of holding the interest of this man who is so different to me. So out of my league. But perhaps I don't need to function as me. He thinks I'm Siobhan, so at least for tonight, that's exactly who I'm going to be.

He smiles as though I've just told a joke without realising he already knows the punchline. 'What do you usually go for?' He picks up the wine menu. I'm not sure I should drink, not when it makes me so unpredictable. I've always preferred to remain in some sort of control, even when I've merely been making a pretence at it. 'White?' he says. 'Red?'

He's assuming I drink wine, so I guess I'll go with it. I just won't have much. What would Siobhan choose? 'White,' I suggest. My tone sounds apologetic when I've no idea why. This man is making me behave in ways I would never usually act.

He catches the attention of a passing waiter and orders a bottle of Pinot Grigio, which even to someone who barely knows red from white seems a safe and unimaginative option.

'You look lovely,' he says, once the man has left the table.

'Thank you. So where's your friend?'

He grins. 'Sorry,' he says, raising his hands. 'You got me.'

'Well,' I say, sitting forward. 'I'm kind of glad he's fictional, to be honest.' I hold his gaze, my lips curving into a suggestive smile. This is what Siobhan would do. This is how she gets what she wants.

'So tell me about you,' he says, leaning his forearms on the table. 'I know your name is Siobhan Docherty, but that's pretty much all I know.'

'That's more than I know about you.'

'Clever answer,' he says with a smile. 'Okay. Well, my surname is Lovell. I live in Hackney, I work in a bar. I do some delivery work on the side because the pay's so bad. I came to London to be an actor. Embarrassing, isn't it?'

'Not at all. Everyone should chase their dream.'

'Even when that's all it is?'

The waiter returns with a bottle of wine in a metal bucket filled with ice. He pours us both a measure and asks if we're ready to order food, but we've not even had a look at the menu yet.

'I'll come back in a few minutes.'

I'm tempted to tell Jack I'm not hungry, which is the truth: the diet has finally started to work its magic and my appetite is finally suppressed. I'm sure my stomach has shrunk. I want to suggest we skip dinner and head straight to his, but I bet Siobhan doesn't do sex on a first date.

'There's too much to choose from,' I say, browsing the menu with little real interest.

'Close your eyes and point at something,' Jack suggests. 'I'll do it too. If you don't like it when it comes, I promise to swap with you.'

I feel him watching me as I close my eyes. I scan my finger across the menu before stopping. 'What have I got?' I ask him, my eyes still closed. I sense him leaning across the table. His fingers graze mine as he takes the menu from me.

'Lamb tagine,' he says. 'Could have been worse.'

'I'm a vegetarian,' I say quickly, remembering now that

Siobhan doesn't eat meat. Damn. I'd been hoping my finger would land on the ribeye steak, but I can't eat that, not if I'm taking this as seriously as I need to be.

He closes his eyes as I open mine. Now that I'm able to properly look at his face, I see that his skin is young, unblemished. This close, I reckon he can't be older than twenty-seven. I wonder if it's appropriate for me to be on a date with someone that age, although no one would bat an eye at a thirty-one-year-man dating a twenty-seven-year-woman. It's barely an age gap at all. Unless, of course, it turns out he's younger.

You're thirty-four, I remind myself. Siobhan is thirty-four. It makes the gap suddenly seem a lot wider.

'What am I getting?' he asks, and I realise I'm supposed to be checking out his menu choice.

'Vegetable moussaka. How convenient... we'll have to swap.'

The waiter returns and Jack orders our meals.

'You never answered my question,' he says, once we're alone again.

'Which one?'

'I asked you to tell me more about yourself.'

'Not really a question,' I say pedantically.

'Okay. In that case, you never responded to my request.'

I take a first sip of wine. It is dry and lovely and I let it sit on the tip of my tongue for a moment before I swallow it. 'My life's not particularly exciting either. I live in Greenwich, as you already know. I work in radio, I like music and eating out, and that's about it. The summary of my life.'

'You work in radio,' he says. 'That's cool.'

'I'm a producer. I do all the behind-the-scenes stuff, so not really.'

'Where did you grow up?'

'Halbury. It's a few miles from Rochester. What about you?'

'Reading. You know... like my imaginary friend. Do your parents still live there, where you grew up?'

I look down at my bitten fingernails. I should have got fake ones or something, or at the very least put on some varnish to disguise the state of them. Siobhan never wears false nails, but her own are nice enough that she doesn't need to. 'My mother does.'

Jack is looking at me a bit too intently. I don't want to do this on a first date: I don't want to share my secrets and my history, not when they're not mine to reveal. There are too many details I need to remember, and I'm not used to this: I need to pause for a few seconds before I can answer anything. I didn't think he'd be this type of bloke, to be honest. I thought we'd just have a few drinks and a laugh and end up back at his place.

'I'm sorry,' he says. 'I feel as though I've upset you, but I'm not sure how.'

'You haven't upset me. I don't upset that easily.'

First fail: this probably isn't true. I know Siobhan, so I know just how easily hurt she can be – by words, by secrets, by lies.

'Tell me something interesting about you,' I say, purely to take the attention off myself. 'Not all that age, job, where you're from stuff. Something few people know.'

He raises an eyebrow. 'I once appeared in an advert for toothpaste.'

I laugh so hard I snort, and my wine goes up my nose. Next thing I know, it's made its way round the U-bend and down the back of my throat, and I'm choking on the heat of it as it burns me from the inside. I picture Siobhan at dinner, choking on an olive. *Do you believe in karma?* I'd once asked her, weeks ago now, not long after we'd been reunited. Now, perhaps maybe I should.

I manage to compose myself quickly, but my eyes are watering, and when I run my fingertips beneath my eyes, they reveal the mascara that's bled onto my cheeks. 'I'm so sorry,' I tell him. 'I wasn't expecting that.'

He doesn't look embarrassed, as most men might if their

date had just snorted a length of Pinot Grigio before nearly choking on it. I've attracted the attention of half the restaurant, yet Jack either hasn't noticed or just doesn't care.

'Sorry. So tell me... can this advert still be found on the internet?'

'Unfortunately, yes. The internet's not our friend in that sense, is it? Letting people see too much of our pasts.'

I feel too hot under the weight of his gaze. He's looking at me strangely as he waits for a response I'm uncertain of, not really knowing what he expects me to say to that.

'Well,' I say. 'If a toothpaste commercial is the worst of your skeletons, I don't think you've got too much to worry about.'

There's an awkward silence, which is broken by the arrival of our meals. We switch plates after the waiter has left us, but Jack still reaches over to try a mouthful from mine. It all feels a bit too intimate for people who are on a first date, but I'd rather the weirdness of this than the discomfort of the conversation that preceded it.

After we've eaten and the wine has been finished, Jack asks if he can see me home. He doesn't suggest extending the night by visiting a bar, and he doesn't ask me back to his, and I wonder whether I've done enough. It feels as though I won't be asked out on a second date. It's my fault. I may look like Siobhan now, but I'm still not enough *her*. I thought I could do this, but I obviously need to work harder.

We get the Tube to London Bridge and chat about music as we head back to the flat.

'So,' he says, when we get there. 'This is goodnight, I suppose.'

'Thank you for seeing me home.'

'No problem. Wouldn't want you walking alone in the dark. London's a dangerous place.' He takes my hand in his and squeezes my fingers gently. I wonder for a moment whether he's going to kiss me, but he doesn't. 'Goodnight, Siobhan.'

'Goodnight.'

He waits to see me go inside. I feel giddy and confused as I head up the stairs, my head dizzy with the wine and the enigma of him. It felt for most of the night as though there was something he wanted to say to me or ask me, something he was holding back for reasons he didn't want to share.

The flat is drowned in darkness. It seems unusually silent; too quiet for Siobhan to be at home. I flick on the living room light. The place is spotless and smells of lemon-scented kitchen cleaning spray. I kick off the heels that have been slowly murdering my feet all evening and dump my coat and bag on the sofa.

It's then that I notice the note on the dining table:

Decided to leave tonight to beat the morning traffic. Hope you've had a lovely evening. See you in a week or so. S x

TWENTY-EIGHT

SIOBHAN

I am back in the house where I spent my teenage years, the suitcase I brought with me upstairs in the bedroom still painted the sickly shade of pale lilac I chose when I was thirteen, when we first moved here. At some point, a couple of years later, I planned to change it, but the thought that I'd be leaving the place soon enough always kept me from bothering to do anything about it. This house was never going to be home. Mum did what she could to try to give me a happy childhood after Dad's death, but she was never going to be able to succeed, no matter what she did. There was always a sadness that would creep in even on the days that were better ones. I'd never realised how good our life had been until it was ripped from beneath us.

Mum and I eat dinner together at the wooden table etched with the ghosts of my childhood doodles: her signature dish of five-bean chilli that was my favourite as a teenager. I told her I was going vegetarian not long after Dad died. Whenever I thought of that last barbecue, my stomach would churn with involuntary images that invaded my brain like the details of a horror film I regretted watching: unidentifiable raw flesh charred and burned, the smell of death and decay ingraining itself in my nostrils as though it was real.

'This is a surprise,' she says again, the same words she'd offered when I called her on the way here last night to tell her I was coming. Not a pleasant surprise. Not a nice one. Just a surprise.

'I really hope I haven't interrupted any of your plans this weekend.'

She spoons a second slop of chilli into my dish. 'You've not interrupted anything.'

I take a forkful, feeling my cheeks water instantly at the mush between my teeth. It tastes like dog food. It isn't the chilli; it's me. Nothing tastes as it should. Even water leaves a disgusting aftertaste on my tongue, everything tainted with the flavours of guilt and fear. I never knew until recently that you could taste adrenaline, but you can, like an acidity at the back of your throat that burns long after the fear has been swallowed.

'What's happened, then?' my mother asks.

'Nothing. Nothing's happened.'

She stabs her fork into a lump of beans that have clogged together.

'Still got Anna living with you?' she asks, her mouth pursed as though she's just sucked on a lemon.

'No,' I lie, because it's less complicated than telling the truth. 'She's gone. I said it wouldn't be for long.'

She looks at me questioningly, and I feel myself squirm beneath her attention. Coming back here has made me feel like a teenager again.

'What did she do?'

'She didn't do anything. It was a temporary arrangement, that's all.'

Mum pushes the food around her plate with a fork.

'I'm sorry,' I say. 'For what happened on your birthday. I

shouldn't have said what I did. I shouldn't have reacted like that. I know you were just worried about me.'

She says nothing. She continues to prod her food, not making eye contact with me.

'Why have you always hated her?' I ask.

She presses the fork prongs so hard against the plate I think they might snap. Her knuckles have turned white.

'Mum?'

'I don't hate her,' she says sharply.

'Okay. Maybe hate is too strong a word. You don't like her, though. You never have. I just wondered why. She was just a kid.'

My mother's fork clatters to the floor as she shoves her chair back. 'Why are you here, Siobhan?' She takes her plate of food, barely touched, and leaves it by the sink before busying herself with the dry dishes stacked on the draining rack.

'I wanted to see you.'

And that's the truth. I did want to see her. There may be more to it than that, but I need to spend this time with her. I need time to somehow say my goodbyes without her realising that's what they are.

Her sigh is audible. She knows there's something I'm not telling her. We haven't seen much of each other these past few years: she doesn't want to go to London, and I don't want to come back here. Returning to this town drags the scab off a wound I've been nursing – or more to the point, not nursing – for over two decades now, so whether or not I want to see her is irrelevant. We both know I would never choose to do so here.

'Mum,' I say eventually, after the last dish has been returned to its rightful place. 'When did you last speak to Claire?'

With her back still turned to me, her shoulders sag like deflating balloons.

'I don't remember,' she eventually replies.

She isn't telling me the truth. 'You must speak to her every now and then. Just to see how she is.'

My mother turns sharply to me. 'What's all this about, Siobhan?'

I want the truth, I think. All of it. I'm here to say goodbye. I'm here to spend a last few days with you, because Jack is going to kill Anna, believing that it's my life he's ending. I need to disappear. I need to be out of the country and as far away from this place as I can get before he realises his mistake, before an identification or post-mortem reveals it isn't me at all.

Anna has always wanted my life. Now, I'm giving her my death.

'I just needed a break from everything for a while, Mum. After what happened to Carrie, and then meeting Anna again... I'm exhausted. I just wanted to come home.'

I watch as the words soften her, as her expression morphs from frustration to pity. 'Oh, love,' she says, coming over to the table. She pulls a chair next to mine and sits beside me, then puts her arms around me and holds me to her, something she hasn't done in a long time; something so unfamiliar that I tense at the feel of her body against mine. 'I'm so sorry, Siobhan.'

'What are you apologising for?'

'I should have done things differently. We should have left this town. I should have been braver.'

'You did what you could, Mum. It wasn't your fault.'

I don't know how to react when she starts to cry. I can't remember the last time I saw her cry. My mother's emotions have always tended to simmer beneath a carefully composed exterior, bursting into flames of heat and rage when left unattended for too long. It wasn't always that way. In the months after my father's death, she used to cry all the time, though she always tried to hide the fact by disappearing upstairs or into another room where she thought I couldn't hear her. She was trying to protect me, but it had the opposite effect. I used to wonder why she was ashamed of her tears, and her refusal to show them meant I came to think of my own as something I should feel guilty about; that they too should be kept hidden away. For a long time, I didn't cry. I suppressed the sadness until it became a tight ball in my stomach, and it stayed that way until I discovered the old cottage, where I learned that drinking would mask the pain for a while.

'But things might have turned out differently for you if we'd moved away.'

She could never imagine how accurate this statement is. Of course she knows how much Lewis's arrest affected me, and she knows a little of the guilt I've carried since. She never asked me if I was there that night; she didn't need to. Even knowing the truth, she never spoke a word of it, not to me or to anyone else. When she was asked whether I was home that evening, she said I was. She told police the name of the film we'd watched together, recorded from the television a couple of weeks earlier. If they'd asked me about it, I would have been able to tell them the details, because we *had* watched it together, just a few evenings before the night of the fire.

If we'd left this town after Dad had died, that night at the old cottage would never have happened. Two lives would have been saved. My mother has no idea how far-reaching the consequences of that night have been. She has no concept of the fact that almost two decades on, I still can't escape the repercussions.

'I'm doing fine, aren't I?' I tell her. 'I've had a good life.'

She moves away from me, her hands holding my arms at my sides. Her eyes narrow as she studies me, and I realise my error in using the past tense. 'I'm *having* a good life,' I add, with a forced smile.

'Are you, though?'

'Yes, Mum. I'm happy. Or at least, I was. I mean, Carrie's

death has changed everything. But I've survived once. I can do it again.'

My mother wipes her eyes. 'I know I've not said it enough, but I'm proud of you, Siobhan. I'm proud of the woman you've become, despite all the odds stacked against you.'

Don't say it, I think. I can't hear these words. I don't deserve any of them.

'What's the matter?' she asks, sensing my reaction.

'Nothing. I'm fine. Honestly.'

She leaves her chair and goes to fill the kettle. 'I don't know about you, but I've gone off the idea of food. Do you fancy a cuppa instead?'

'That would be lovely.'

I watch as she sets about making tea, her back turned to me. She is only fifty-four, with so much life still ahead of her, if only she knew it and knew how to use it. I want to tell her what I did, my part in all of it. I want to confess as though I'm in church, speaking with a priest; I want to ask for forgiveness for the lies I wrapped myself in and the truths I never told. I want to tell my mother everything and tell her I'm sorry, that I should have been different. That I wish I'd done something that night: something that might have altered the course of all our lives.

But I can do none of these things without arousing suspicion. When I disappear, I need to do it silently. These next few days will be the last I see of her, yet I still can't bring myself to ask her the one question to which I need an answer more than any other: what really happened to Dad that night?

TWENTY-NINE

ANNA

I didn't need to worry about the possibility that Jack might not want to see me again. We meet up another three times in the week that followed, each of those meetings instigated by him. He sends me texts before 8 a.m. to say good morning, and on the evenings I don't see him, he messages me to wish me goodnight. It all feels nice. Normal. But I know already that normal isn't meant for me. I tried it once, with Dean, and look where that got me. But it still feels quite nice to pretend.

On Thursday, we arrange to meet at Caledonian Park in Islington. He starts his shift at the bar at 4 p.m. and won't finish until the early hours of the morning, so he suggested meeting now to make the most of the weather. It's a beautiful sunny spring day, so we go for a walk after I manage to dissuade him from the idea of eating out. I can't afford it. My savings are coming to an end; I'm going to have to call around some of my old clients and see if they'll have me back to do their cleaning, just a temporary fix while I look for something more permanent. I'm still hoping I can find something as Siobhan, but there's only one way it'll ever work.

Jack is waiting for me outside Caledonian Road station

when I arrive. He takes my hand in his almost without looking at me and leads me to the pedestrian traffic lights further down the street.

'All okay?' I ask. He seems distant, not himself. Not that I really know him well enough to know what 'himself' is.

'Fine. Just tired.'

We cross the road and make our way to the park. The sound of children screaming and laughing can be heard as we approach the playground area, with its tired-looking wooden climbing frames and swings that have had their chains wound too short by bored older kids who stay after dark. Children need little to entertain themselves. It's a shame we can't stay that way really.

'When are you going back to work?' Jack asks.

I stop. Pause. Think. I need to make sure my brain is fully engaged whenever questions relating to my job or my personal life arise. I can deal with subjects such as favourite films or musical preferences – and I've swayed into a vegetarian diet with ease – but anything more specific needs to be met with care. I've been close to slipping up too many times.

'Siobhan,' he says, stretching the name over three syllables while waving a hand in front of me as though I've gone to sleep. I still haven't grown used to hearing it as my own.

'Sorry. Yes. I mean, I'm not sure yet. It's all still... raw. You know?'

'I can imagine. I lost someone too. My brother.'

I stop walking. He's never mentioned this before. In fact, he never mentioned having a brother at all, though we've spoken about family on a few occasions, with me always turning the conversation back to him, keen to avoid the details of my lies.

'Oh God. I'm so sorry. You never said.'

'It's not an easy thing to bring up with people.'

We start walking again, Jack taking the lead. He squeezes my hand gently, and it feels strange, this public show of affection. Dean and I never held hands. I can't remember ever holding hands with anyone other than Siobhan, back when we were too young to be self-conscious.

'How old was he?' I ask. 'I'm sorry... we don't have to talk about him if you don't want to.'

'I'd like to talk about him. No one ever talks about him – that's the problem. After the funeral, people just carried on with their lives as though he'd never existed.'

'Perhaps they were worried about upsetting you,' I suggest.

His cheeks puff out before he blows air through the small circle his mouth forms. 'Maybe. But I'd rather feel temporarily upset than keep carrying it all on my own.'

'What happened to him?'

'He hanged himself.'

It wasn't the answer I was expecting. I thought he was going to tell me that he'd been killed in a car accident, or that they'd discovered a tumour that was already beyond treatment. I didn't suspect for a moment that he had taken his own life.

'I'm so sorry. That's awful.'

Jack stops walking and turns to me. He puts his hands on my shoulders and holds my gaze for slightly longer than is comfortable, doing that thing he did on our first date, as though he wants to say something but can't quite bring himself to just come out with it.

'Do you know what the most awful thing was, though? No one else took any responsibility for it. No one paid a price for it except my brother.'

I feel the temperature fall around us, as though the sky has just dropped a few feet, trapping us beneath a blanket of cold air. What does he mean, paid a price? Paid a price for what?

And then his face changes. He takes my hand in his again and smiles, the air around us shifting as though those last few moments didn't really happen. 'Sorry,' he says, too breezily. 'I didn't mean to dampen the mood. Do you fancy a coffee?' And with that, he leads the way through the park to the high street at the far end, where we find a café with outdoor seating and sit together talking about this and that and nothing, neither of us mentioning the subject of his dead brother again.

When our drinks are finished and it's nearly 2 p.m., Jack insists on seeing me home, despite the fact that it's the middle of the afternoon and it's almost an hour-long round trip for him to get back to the bar.

'You'll be late for work,' I tell him.

'Not if we leave now.'

We go back to the Tube station in silence, both of us contemplating our separate problems. I imagine Jack is consumed with thoughts of his brother. For me, it's Siobhan who fills my mind. Or, more specifically, how to get rid of Siobhan. Because that's what this has come down to. I wanted to get close to her again, to revel in the energy I'd always gained from being around her. But I'm enjoying her life more than I expected to. What started as a little challenge to myself has grown in gravity: this is the life I want to lead, not just now, but always. It's unfortunate, but there's only one way to make that work. Siobhan has to disappear without anyone realising she's gone. To all intents and purposes, it's Anna who must die. It's Anna who'll be missing, lost without a trace.

I've read about people who faked their own deaths, and in most of these cases it's easy to see where they went wrong with it. If you're going to disappear, you have to do it entirely. No one can miss you. There needs to be no one to notice you're gone. Fortunately for me, the only person who'd care about me is my mother, and as we fell out a number of years ago, she won't be surprised when she doesn't hear from me. By the time she wonders whether everything is okay, I'll be long gone. I'm sorry it's come to this, I really am, but I've considered everything and this is the only way. Siobhan has to die.

She'll have to call the radio station and tell them she's not coming back to work. I'm not sure how I'm going to orchestrate that just yet. They'll need to believe she's decided upon a career change, but after everything that's happened with Carrie, it shouldn't be too difficult to convince them. She'll be having an early mid-life crisis. Reassessing her future in light of everything. If I can't get her to do it somehow, I'll have to make the call myself, pretending to be her. It's all good practice. I'll cut ties with the people she works with. I'll make sure I never go to the places any of them are likely to hang out, because I'd like to stay in the flat. I'd like to stay in London. Siobhan's life is here, where she came to disappear the first time around.

'Everything okay?'

Jack rouses me from my thoughts. I step aside to let someone walk past me on the escalator. 'Fine. Just thinking about work, that's all.'

He makes no response, and I'm grateful for the silence.

We sit side by side on the Tube, neither of us speaking as we're rattled back towards Greenwich. Like the last time he saw me home, he waits for me to go inside. I wave goodbye before closing the front door and am about to unlock the door to the flat when I hear someone say my name. Siobhan's name.

'I'm going to have to start charging for this, you know. At least it's got your name on it this time.'

I turn to see a man at the door opposite. He's dressed in Lycra shorts that are borderline indecent and he still has a cycle helmet on his head, either recently arrived home or just about to leave the building. He does a double-take, stalled by my appearance. 'Sorry,' he says. 'I thought you were Siobhan.' His eyebrows knit as he studies my face. Takes in the similarities between us.

'I'm her sister,' I say – the first thing that comes into my head.

'Oh. Right. Of course.'

But he looks sceptical, and I realise I'm not going to be able to stay here, not if I want to make this work.

'Everything okay?' I ask casually.

He smiles, giving his head a shake as though trying to wobble some sense into himself. 'Yes. Sorry. Fine. Here you go. Could you give this to her for me, please.' He passes me the box he's holding. 'Is she all right?' he asks, tilting his head to the side with that faux sympathy people put on when they don't really want to be bothered by your problems. 'You know... after everything.'

'Fine. Why wouldn't she be?'

'Oh. I just thought... you know... with her colleague and what's happened...'

Shit. Carrie. My thoughts have been so focused on Jack and how to get Siobhan out of the picture once and for all that I'd forgotten all about her.

'She's just trying to keep busy,' I tell him. 'Keep her mind off things.'

'Of course,' he says quickly. 'Best idea.' He steps away, heading back to his door so he can make a quick escape. 'If either of you needs anything, though...'

'Thank you.'

I wait for him to leave before letting myself into the flat. I put the box on the coffee table while I take off my coat and shoes.

I notice the smell first. It's unpleasant, but not unfamiliar. It's a bit like damp, like the smell of wet washing that's been left in a machine drum for too long, stagnant and fetid. I get a knife to cut open the tape that's holding the top of the box in place. When I pull the lid back, a flurry of movement startles me. I jolt back, managing to catch the palm of my free hand with the blade, slicing through the soft flesh between my thumb and forefinger. But I don't feel any pain. I'm too distracted by the sight of a swarm of cockroaches scurrying from the open box and making their way across the coffee table.

I scream. I'm surprised at the sound of it: it doesn't sound like me at all, too high-pitched and girlie. But I fucking hate beetles and spiders and any kind of creepy-crawlies, and I don't think I've ever been this close to a cockroach in my life, and now the little bastards are everywhere, still pouring from the box in their hundreds. I've no idea what to do to stop them. I reach over to flip the lid shut, but all I manage to do is ping a load of cockroaches further across the room. I find my phone and call Jack.

'What's up?' he asks, answering after just two rings.

'Where are you? Are you at the station yet? How quickly do you reckon you could get back here?'

'Whoa,' he says. 'You missing me that much already?'

'Please,' I say, my voice panicked. 'Can you come back here? I need help.'

'I'm on my way,' he says, and he stays on the line until he arrives at the door of the flat, attempting simultaneously to calm me down while trying not to laugh at my predicament.

'Oh Jesus,' he says, when he sees the cockroaches everywhere, climbing the walls and the furniture. I wipe my face, ashamed of the tears I've allowed to escape. I can deal with funerals and strangulation, but cockroaches are a step too far.

'What the hell happened?' he asks.

'They were in that,' I say, pointing at the box.

'Who'd send something like this?'

The question has already crossed my mind. I keep reminding myself that this wasn't intended for me, that this unexpected gift was sent to Siobhan, but I can't tell Jack that. And now I realise that he's never been inside the flat before. This is his first experience of the place.

'I've no idea. Some sort of practical joke, I'm guessing.'

He glances at me with a raised eyebrow. 'Not very funny,' he mutters.

I scream as something crawls up my leg inside my jeans. I start to jump and writhe like someone fighting a seizure; I must look ridiculous, but rather than laugh, Jack drops to his knees and starts patting at my calves, trying to catch the cockroach before it makes its way any further north. I feel something hard against my skin, then Jack's hand moves up my leg, grappling for the rogue pest. It might be funny if it was happening to anyone else but me.

'I'm so sorry,' he says chivalrously, flicking the squashed roach from his palm as he stands.

'What am I going to do?' I ask forlornly, surveying the pit that Siobhan's living room has become. She'd throw a fit for real if she could see the place. I wonder again who could have sent the box. Surely it couldn't be some sort of practical joke initiated by her neighbour, although he did look pretty odd, to be fair.

'What are *we* going to do,' Jack corrects. 'Just sit up there a minute,' he instructs me, pointing at the kitchen worktop. 'Let's find out how to get rid of them.'

I do as he suggests, and watch as he taps a search into his phone. Moments later, he asks if I've got any baking soda. Of course, I've no idea whether there's baking soda in the flat. I very much doubt it: Siobhan doesn't do baking, or any eating that involves much more than a salad.

'I'm not sure,' I say. 'I'll check the cupboards, but I don't think so.'

I stay on the worktop while I open the cupboards in turn. As I suspected, there is no baking soda.

'I'll have to pop to the shop a few streets away – they should have some. What am I supposed to do, just throw the stuff everywhere?'

Jack smiles. 'I don't know. Look, let's go and get some, and I'll come back with you and help.'

'You'll be late for work.'

'It's fine. I'll call them.'

It only occurs to me as we're leaving the building that I never buzzed Jack in when he arrived here after I'd called him.

'How did you get inside the front door?' I ask, letting it fall shut behind us.

'What do you mean?'

'When you came back. You didn't press the doorbell. How did you get in?'

'The woman from downstairs was on her way out.'

'Oh. Okay.'

I sense him eyeing me as we carry on walking down the street. 'Everything all right?'

'Yeah. I mean, this whole thing has shaken me. It's gross. I'm not going to be able to sleep tonight, I'll be too worried about a cockroach finding its way up my nose or something.'

'I'll stay with you, if you like,' he offers, before quickly adding, 'I'll sleep on the sofa.'

'Thanks, but I won't be sleeping anywhere until I know every one of my little guests is gone.'

The flat! I think suddenly. I did my best to make sure every trace of Anna was hidden, in case I decided to bring Jack back here – nothing with my name on it, no cards or letters left lying around that might inadvertently give me away. But if he wants to help me get rid of the roaches, he's going to be everywhere in the place and there's nothing I can do now to deter him. I need to get him distracted somehow, long enough to give me a few minutes alone in the bedroom. The last thing I need is for him to find the box of needles and morphine I took from the hospital, still stashed at the back of the wardrobe.

THIRTY

SIOBHAN

I wake early after a terrible night's sleep. I kept hearing noises, so vivid and seemingly real that I went downstairs in the dark expecting to find a stranger there. I stood in the hallway outside the living room with a kitchen knife clutched in my fist, as though I'd know what to do with it if I was to find someone on the other side of the door. If I was to find Jack there. The rational part of my brain knew there was no chance that would happen, though. He's distracted – for the time being, at least.

When I went upstairs again, I couldn't get back to sleep. As a child, I was always a deep sleeper; my mother used to tell me that she'd never had any of the issues other parents of young children complained about: the sleepless nights, the nap refusals, the regressions that would throw the pattern of the whole house off kilter. I slept soundly, unlike Anna, who left poor Aunt Claire a walking zombie for the first few years of motherhood. I think it must have been contentment. I was safe and happy and life was good. Then everything changed, and I don't think I've slept an uninterrupted night once between that night and this.

Now it's almost 8 a.m. and I'm still lying in bed, still trying to chase away thoughts of the ghosts that haunt me. After Dad died, I was fixated on the memory of his voice saying my name. Sometimes, in the darkness as I lay in bed, I would hear it quietly on repeat as though he was still downstairs in the living room. *Siobhan... Siobhan.* And I convinced myself that it was real, that he had called for me and I hadn't responded. I hadn't gone to him. I'd let him die alone.

I reach for my phone and tap out a message to Anna, desperate to distract myself from my thoughts.

> *Hope everything's okay back home. How are things going with Jack? X*

I don't expect a reply any time soon, but I get one within a few minutes.

> *Brilliant. I'm seeing him again tonight. Hope you're getting some much-deserved rest. Take all the time you need – everything fine here x*

I return the phone to the bedside table. It's all going exactly as expected. Jack isn't going to do anything impulsive: he doesn't seem that type. He's waited all these years to take his revenge, so I doubt a few more months will make any difference to him. He'll want a clean kill. An invisible murder, with no trail left behind him. I will simply disappear. Anna will disappear. It will all be premeditated, planned with precision, nothing left to chance. And it's this that worries me. I believe from what I've seen of him and from the time he's spent executing his revenge that he is thorough and particular in every aspect of his preparation. Someone that precise doesn't make mistakes. And for that reason, at some point he will realise the mistake he's made in believing Anna is me, and he will do everything he can to put it right. The more he sees of her, the less time I have.

I shouldn't have stayed at my mother's house for so long, but it's been harder than I expected to leave. This last goodbye feels the longest, and I'm not ready to let go.

I wonder now, for the first time, whether Jack might have done this before. The idea has never occurred to me: that he might seek out revenge in the way other people strive for life goals – holidays, exams, careers. But who else could he possibly have this much contempt for?

I think of that day, over six weeks ago now, when he picked up my bag on the pedestrian crossing while I was on my way to work. He was watching me that Saturday morning when I went to the coffee shop; he'd followed me there before and I knew he was there again that day. I picked up the disposable coffee cup he'd abandoned in the bin at the park and checked the name that had been scrawled on the side by the young barista who'd served him. Then, unbeknown to him, I had started to follow him back.

I found out the name of the bar where he worked, as well as the area where he lived. Hours of trawling through his colleagues' social media profiles eventually found me his surname, but what was more difficult was finding out who Jack Lovell really was. I didn't know anyone of that surname. There was a reason for that: it wasn't his surname. Or it hadn't been originally, at least. My guess is that Lovell was his mother's maiden name, a name he must have chosen when he wanted to become anonymous – anonymous to me, anyway.

I knew that Anna still took an interest in my life. I'd been aware of her at places where she thought she'd gone unseen: the library, restaurants, the street where I worked. Nothing had changed. We might not have seen each other for years, but she was still as obsessed with me as she'd been when we were children. She'd gone quiet for a few years while she was married to

Dean, but after they'd separated, her fixation with me had been resurrected. She fell into patterns, and it was easy enough for me to discover on which days she went to the library to fill in job applications online. I felt bad when the idea came to me. I would be sacrificing her life to save my own. It made me a terrible person. It was the product of a sick mind. But then I found out about Carrie. My gut had been right. This was everything she deserved.

Why don't I remember Jack? He must have been there all those years ago, at one moment or another. I had been to their house; I had sat in their living room and eaten at their table. At some point, I would have seen him. I would have spoken to him, never able to imagine in my wildest dreams that years from then he would still be in my life, hounding and persecuting me in a way that's surely exclusive to the vengeful. The bereaved.

We don't know how deeply loss will affect us until the day it happens. Until those months and years that follow, when the pain embeds itself within us as a permanent foreign body. No one can know how they'll react. I wonder if this was how it was for Jack. His brother's suicide was the catalyst that sent his life into a spiral. Before that, from what I've found out, he was high achiever, set to study medicine at university. He was going to tread a different path; give his parents a son they could be proud of. Then a single day changed everything.

I pull up the photograph of him stored on my phone: the one I'd found on one of his colleagues' social media profiles. Young, ambitious, full of potential. And, like so many of us, living a lie. Because before he was Jack Lovell, his name was Jack Handley. He is Lewis's younger brother.

THIRTY-ONE

ANNA

The day after the box of cockroaches is sent to me – sent to Siobhan – I invite Jack over for dinner. His first experience of the flat wasn't the best one, and after we'd gone to the shop to buy baking soda, it took us over four hours to make sure we'd rid the place of as many cockroaches as we were able to find. As far as I know, they've now all gone. I've had to deep-clean the flat three times since I found the last one, though, not wanting to take any chances. Luckily, I'm good at what I do. If Siobhan was to arrive home unexpectedly, she'd find the place spotless, even cleaner than when she left.

Jack missed his shift at work. He told me he'd got a warning from his boss, but he doesn't seem too bothered by it. I suppose bar jobs are easy enough to come by, and it isn't what he wants to do with his life in the long term anyway. I'm not really sure what he wants. We've still not had sex. I'm starting to wonder whether he even wants to. There's being chivalrous and then there's just being weird, and his behaviour has occasionally veered to the latter. But I'm in no position to judge weird.

Our last two meetings have been strange ones. There was his odd behaviour in the park, when he told me about his brother's suicide, and then the cockroach thing must have made him think God knows what. It's a wonder he's here at all. Tonight will be different. I'm going to be different: the perfect host, the perfect cook, the perfect lay. Siobhan, in every sense of the woman.

I hear the intercom ring at just gone six. I go downstairs to let him in. He's carrying a bunch of flowers and a bottle of champagne.

'Thank you,' I say, taking them from him. 'Come on up.'

I notice him scan the place as he follows me into the kitchen, still assessing the potential for possible rogue roaches. It takes me three cupboards to find a vase, but I'm hoping he's too distracted by his scrutiny to notice that I don't know where things are kept in my own home. I've no idea what I'm going to do when Siobhan comes back. He won't be able to visit then, not unless I can guarantee that she won't be home while he's here. I've not thought everything through well enough, but when I look at Jack, I don't care about that, not tonight.

I fill the vase with water and stand the bouquet in them, then put the champagne in the fridge.

'Can I get you a drink?' I offer, watching as he removes his jacket. I place the vase of flowers in the middle of the coffee table. 'Beer? Wine?'

'I'll just have a glass of water for now.'

The lasagne I made earlier is already in its dish, so all I have to do is put it in the oven and take the salad I prepared this afternoon out of the fridge. I bought mince, only remembering once I'd already got it home that I don't eat meat. I had to go back out and shove it in one of the neighbour's bins, in case Jack happened to go in the fridge later and see it hidden at the back.

'How long have you lived here?' he asks.

'A few years,' I say vaguely.

'Nothing in the post today? No nasty little surprises from anyone else?'

I pass him a glass of water. 'Thankfully, no. Honestly, don't overthink it. I'm not. It was probably a mistake, meant for someone else.'

His eyes are fixed on mine as he gulps down half the water. 'Didn't the box have your name on it, though?'

Shit. 'Forget it,' I say casually. 'I have.'

But of course, this isn't true. I've racked my brains with thoughts of who might have sent that box to Siobhan, and why, but I've got no closer to any kind of explanation. I can't come out and ask her either. If she knows about it, she might decide to come home, and that would end in disaster. I'm not ready for her yet.

Jack sits and we talk as I set the table and then eat dinner: mundane and generic subjects such as the weather; anything to keep from a topic that might inadvertently throw me into further awkwardness. It might sound strange, but sometimes the lies can be quite exciting. Knowing I need to stay on my toes and keep ahead of myself, in full character as Siobhan, is a continual adrenaline rush, that kind of feeling you get at the first dip of a roller coaster, just as the carriage tilts forward and the air hits your face, leaving you breathless. I might be addicted to the feeling of it.

He helps me clear the table before we take our drinks to the sofa. He sits close, our legs touching, and when he leans in to kiss me, I notice the same weirdness I've been aware of during a few of our dates. He's here, but he's somehow somewhere else.

'Everything okay?'

When he looks at me, it's almost as though he's angry. There's something behind his eyes, some kind of unresolved tension that he won't give a voice to. He's holding back for some reason, but I don't know why. I've thought maybe he doesn't fancy me, that he's changed his mind, though I doubt it: every man fancies Siobhan. It was always like that back when we were at school. There are two types of girls: the popular ones and the invisible ones. And it's hard being in the shadow of a person everyone loves.

After Uncle Garrett's death, people seemed to admire her even more. It was sympathy, I get that now, but as a child, all I saw was the lengths they'd go to in order to appease her. My own mother would fawn over her as though Siobhan was her daughter, momentarily forgetting about me. I'd lost someone as well. But that seemed to go by the wayside. It was all *Siobhan needs this* and *Siobhan needs that. Siobhan needs us. We need to be there for her.* So I did what every good girl would, and did as I was told. And I've been there for her ever since, whether she's been aware of it or not.

I kiss him again, but when I move my hands beneath his shirt, he holds my wrists to stop me. I wonder what he's hiding under there that he's too embarrassed to let me see. Maybe he hasn't been blessed in the way most men think matters. I mean, a person with a face that perfect has got to have some kind of shortcoming. No one can have it all. No one other than Siobhan.

'If you're having second thoughts—' I start.

'No,' he replies quickly. 'It's not that.' He puts a hand to my face and gently pushes my hair behind my ear. 'I just don't want to rush things.'

Rush things? I've been on scooters that have moved faster than this relationship. If that is what this even is. I'm not sure. I'm not sure it *can* be a relationship, not with everything that's going to need to come next. I haven't thought far enough ahead to know where I want things to go with Jack. Realistically, I know they can't go anywhere. At some point he's likely to find out the lie I've told, and when he does, there'll be no going back. In a way, he'll be my guinea pig. I need to mess things up, just once, so I can learn from the mistake and never make it again. That way, I'll be able to make the full transition into Siobhan's life, error-free. I just need to ensure that when she disappears, she's gone for ever. It seems a shame really that Jack needs to serve a purpose as collateral damage, because if he finds out about my lie, he's going to have to die too. It's unfortunate. I was starting to like him.

'You don't mind, do you?' he asks.

Yes, I think. It's a bit annoying. 'No, of course not.'

'I've got a whole weekend off work for once. Let me take you out tomorrow night. I'll buy you dinner as a thank-you for this evening.'

'You don't have to do that,' I tell him casually.

We chat a bit longer and drink some more wine, but I'm careful not to have too much. A slip of the tongue is far more likely to happen after a few glasses, and I can't afford that, not now.

'Can I stay with you tonight?' he asks. 'I won't... you know. I just want to be with you.'

I don't really see the point, to be honest, but I can hardly tell him that. I'm supposed to be friendly and hospitable, like Siobhan. I want to say no, to make up some excuse for why it isn't a good idea. Then I remember the cockroaches. How there might be more of the little bastards lingering in the corners and behind the furniture, just waiting to make a reappearance once I'm asleep.

'That'd be nice,' I tell him.

So he stays the night, and once he's undressed to just his boxers, I can see for myself that there's nothing for him to be ashamed of. He falls asleep with his arm across me, but once he's settled into a deeper sleep, I escape from beneath it. It feels like being pinned down, suffocating and restrictive. Dean and I never used to sleep like this, with our bodies touching. When you think about it, it's odd, like being smothered while being unconscious. I wonder whether Siobhan feels the same about it. I wonder whether she's still awake, and if she isn't, whether she's dreaming about me.

THIRTY-TWO

SIOBHAN

Before my mother gets home from her Saturday morning food shop, I leave the house and make the three-mile walk to the place we used to live. After that night, people questioned how we could stay in the town where our life as we'd known it had been so tragically brought to an end. A fresh start was suggested, as though by relocating, my mother could reinvent herself in her new role as a widow and I could move on through my teenage years as though I wasn't the girl whose father had fallen down the stairs and died while she'd been asleep in her bed. Life goes on. But ours didn't, not really. It passed through the motions of time, our faces changing as age altered us both, but it never moved beyond that night.

My mother responded to each of these well-intended comments with the same reply: it wouldn't be fair to move Siobhan from her school and the familiarity of her friends and teachers. *Hasn't she been through enough upheaval already?* I once heard her say to my aunt Claire. Sometimes though, I wondered whether that was just an excuse. I don't think my mother ever wanted to leave this place. It was the only town she'd ever known: she and her sister had grown up here, their lives shaped by the people and the landscape. My grandmother still lived nearby, and she was elderly and frail, too unwell for my mother to leave her. I couldn't wait to escape the place. Everywhere I went, the ghost of that night followed me. In keeping me close to my friends and my school, doing what she'd thought at the time was best, my mother kept me tethered to the nightmare of that night and the guilt that clung to me like scarred skin that refused to be shed. I was always sure it must have felt the same for my mother, and I wondered why the hold this town seemed to have over her was so strong.

It starts to rain before I arrive. I pull my hood up and head towards the T-junction that leads to the lane to the next village in one direction and the dead-end path of my former home in the other. Just being on this section of road throws up memories that have for so long now been buried. I remember the feeling of getting off the school bus near the corner shop on the main road and running along this stretch of tarmac, the open fields near my parents' house just a couple of hundred metres away. On warm summer days, I would lie in the grass, still in my school uniform, and pick handfuls of daisies to work into chains, wearing the first around my neck while I made another for Anna, then another for my mother, and finally a fourth for Aunt Claire. We'd done something in Year 1 that I'd never forgotten – a thing called the Invisible String. We talked about who we loved and who we felt connected to, and it was this, my teacher told us, that made a person feel safe. Anna was only a toddler at that time, barely turned two. She was just beginning to find her words, and she would call me 'Born', because 'Siobhan' was a challenge even for some of the children in my own year group.

My mother, my father, Aunt Claire and Anna. There were my grandparents too – a grandmother on both sides of the family, and my dad's dad, who used to tell me stories about his life that I was never sure were real or made up. These people formed the centre of my world, the crux of everything that came afterwards. I was connected to them in a way no one could see, but I felt it always, like a magnetic force field. The Invisible String. I've wondered about Mum and Claire, and the knots of the string that binds them. There are things no one knows about, though it seemed to me as I moved into adult life that sometimes these things were kept smothered for a reason, and it was better that way. Now, I'm no longer so sure.

The property comes into sight. The front garden looks much as I remember it, with its wide stretch of grass and the border that was once alive with colour. But that's where all recollection ends. The building that stands where our old house once was is nothing like its predecessor. The large Victorian detached home of my childhood has been replaced by a modern property with floor-to-ceiling windows and a double front door three times the size of the ones on most houses. It is flanked by a pair of tall bay trees, the extent to which it seems the current owners' gardening ambitions extend.

It takes me a moment to realise that something else looks unusual and off balance, and when I step back to assess the land, I realise that the new house hasn't been built on the same piece of ground where the old one stood. I wonder if that was due to the new owners' superstitions; whether whoever bought the place in order to have it knocked down sensed the tragedy and all its ghosts as though they had seeped into the earth beneath the building.

I walk to the gate at the end of the long gravel driveway and stop there to take in the memory of the place, one broken piece at a time. There are no cars parked outside, so I'm guessing that whoever now owns it must be out. For three years after Dad died, the house stood empty. We moved in with Aunt Claire and Anna for a while, but their place wasn't really big enough for the four of us. After a couple of months, we moved into a rented house, and then six months later, my mother bought another place using the money from my father's life insurance. No one wanted to buy Hollybush House – named by the previous owners due to its front garden's central feature. It became infamous for its history, the story added to and altered over time.

My mother told me years ago that it was being demolished and a new property was being built in its place. I imagine the buyers must have believed that by knocking the existing building down, they might in some way be able to rid the place of its history. Yet just being here, on the land where it happened, is enough to make my skin prickle with a chill. I hear the sounds of laughter; I smell the smoke from the barbecue as though it is still burning out in the back garden, over two decades on. I see us all as we were that evening: happy, carefree; alive.

After food had been eaten and drinks had been finished, Anna and I had stayed out in the garden, playing together. She liked to think that being around me made her seem like one of the older girls, but sometimes since, with hindsight and maturity guiding my memories, I've wondered whether it wasn't more the case that being around her kept me younger. I was happy to be so. My parents' garden was a safe place, filled with all my best and happiest times. I didn't want to grow any older, to be sitting exams and taking on responsibilities like the kids just a few school years ahead of me seemed to have. I wanted to stay there for ever, where it was safe.

My father called us in when it was nearly dark. He let us watch some television together, and then Anna and I went up to my bedroom. I always let her sleep in my bed when she came over to stay for the night, even though there was a spare bedroom that had been decorated especially for her. We were more like sisters than cousins and I liked having her there, though she never knew when to call time on the ghost stories she would tell me, trying to scare me so that I wouldn't be able to fall asleep: keeping me awake so that she'd have longer to spend with me.

That night, though, it didn't work. I dropped off quickly, exhausted by all the fresh air and the excitement of the day. I don't remember whether Anna tried to keep me awake. If she did, I was too tired to be aware of it or recall it afterwards. What I do remember is being woken by her hours later, when it was still so dark I knew it must be the middle of the night.

'Siobhan,' she was saying, pulling at the sleeve of my nightdress. 'Please, Siobhan. Please wake up.'

She was crying. I couldn't see her tears, it was too dark, but I could hear her sobs between her words as she tried to catch her breath.

'What's the matter?' I remember asking her. 'What's happened?'

I thought she must have had a nightmare. Either that, or she'd woken up disorientated and scared, forgetting where she was. But then a sound cut through the darkness, splitting the room in two and slicing through the thoughts I was barely awake enough to process. It terrified me into wakefulness, jolting me from the mattress, my spine rigid, my jaw locked tight. My mother's scream. A scream so earth-shattering that I was never able to erase the memory of it from my mind.

Later, when the place was teeming with police and a forensics team, and a family liaison officer who'd introduced herself but whose name had passed over me in a blur of muffled sound was consoling my mother while her body shook with soundless sobs, I would feel as though I was on a film set, or stuck in a nightmare from which I'd not yet woken. People. There were people everywhere. But someone was missing. My dad wasn't there. His body had been hidden from view by the time I came downstairs, covered by a sheet so that Anna and I wouldn't be exposed to the horror of seeing him there. Yet they couldn't move him – the forensics team wouldn't allow it – and so we were lifted over him as though he was litter and they were trying to keep our feet clean.

I remember seeing Aunt Claire first, before I saw my mother: she was standing by the flowerbed at the front of the house, her mascara blurred black around her eyes, her face blank as she stared at the concrete between her feet. She and my mother had gone to the pub after the barbecue – their monthly girls-only night out. She was swaying slightly, giddy from the wine they'd consumed and the paradoxical sobering shock of what they'd come home to.

Anna held my hand as the two of us were escorted into the back of a police car. I must have been crying, but I don't remember; I just recall a wall of silence around me, like I'd been sucked into a bubble and all my senses were compromised. I remember a policeman telling us to put our seat belts on, then for a moment we were left alone, just me and Anna in the back of the car. I could still see my mother in the front garden, unsteady in her heeled shoes, her mouth open but no sound reaching me. Anna's hand was still in mine.

And I remember what she said as we sat there and waited, her fingers working their way between mine so that our hands were clasped together.

'It's okay, Siobhan. Everything will be okay. I will always look after you.'

THIRTY-THREE

ANNA

I wake up remembering that Jack stayed the night. I expect him to be already gone, and my brain instantly preps me for a cop-out note left on the dining table. *Thanks for a great night, but...* Instead, when I turn over, he's still here in the bed beside me. He's wide awake, looking at me, and the murky grey-blue of his stare freaks me out for a moment.

'Good morning.'

'Good morning,' I say back.

He puts his fingers to my hair, pushing it back from where it's fallen across my face. I realise I still have on yesterday's make-up. Siobhan's signature winged eyeliner must be smeared across my face like spindly flattened spider's legs.

'You look pretty when you sleep,' he says.

'You're very kind, but I know this isn't true.'

'You've seen yourself asleep?'

'I've seen myself awake,' I tell him. 'That's enough to know.'

I'd quite like him to leave now. This is starting to all feel a bit too cosy and domesticated, but without the benefit of sex. A bit like being married again.

'Shall I make us coffee?'

'If you can work out how to use the machine, please be my guest.'

'You can't work it?' he says, sliding out from the bed and reaching for where he left his T-shirt on the chair.

Fuck. I have to stop doing this. This is supposed to be my flat. 'It's temperamental.'

When he goes down to the kitchen, I check my phone. Nothing from Siobhan, which I'm assuming means all is okay. She's gone to Aunt Sarah's. I know this because I called the house phone yesterday and Siobhan answered. I put on an accent and held my hand halfway over the mouthpiece, muffling the sound so she wouldn't work out it was me. Then I told her I was from an energy company and asked if she wanted a competitive price for her gas and electricity. She politely declined before hanging up.

Jack brings two cups of coffee up to bed. In a different life, this might be something I could get used to: gorgeous man, fancy London flat; lazy mornings with nowhere to be. This is what my life could be. Could have been, if things weren't as they are.

'Shall we go out for some breakfast,' he suggests.

'Okay. Where are you thinking?'

'Nowhere in particular. Let's just walk and find somewhere.'

I want to have a shower, but I don't want to leave Jack alone in the flat, where he'd have time to snoop about among my things if he was feeling that way inclined. Among Siobhan's things. I make an excuse about going for a run later, saying I'll have one after that, so we get dressed and head towards the high street, neither of us sure where we're going or where we might end up.

In the end, we opt for a little café I've never been to before, about a mile and a half from the flat. We find a table near the window and browse the menu, which is pretentious in the way most modern places are, boasting food no one really wants to eat but that people order to make themselves feel better about their shit diets.

When it arrives, it looks a lot nicer than I was expecting it to. I'm starving, but I can't tuck in because this isn't what Siobhan does. Plus I've still got a couple of pounds to shift before I'm able to match her. When I catch Jack looking at me questioningly, though, I realise I have to eat. I can't do anything that will make him suspicious.

'What would you like to do tonight?' he asks between mouthfuls. 'We don't have to go out for food again.'

'I'm happy with whatever.'

I wait for him to invite me over to his, because it's never happened before. There's never even been a mention of me going. It's starting to make me wonder what he might be hiding, other than the two housemates he's mentioned a couple of times.

'Anything on at the cinema?' he asks.

I inwardly roll my eyes. We're grown adults, not fifteen-year-olds.

'Don't know,' I say, unable to hide my lack of interest. 'Seems a bit boring, though.'

I look up, past Jack's shoulder. And it's then that I see Sheena. She's doing the same as I am, looking past the shoulder of the man she's with, staring in my direction. Her expression says she knows me, but she's trying to rack her brain for where she recognises me from. She returns her focus to her drink, says something to her friend and laughs in response when he makes a reply. Then she looks back at me, her thoughts still preoccupied with trying to work out who I might be.

'Siobhan. Siobhan?'

Jack was saying something to me, but I've no idea what it was.

'Are you okay?' he asks.

'Fine.'

'You look a bit pale.'

'I said I'm fine.'

I see her looking over again, unsure whether she's made a mistake. She gives a shake of her head and turns back to the man she's with, and my stomach drops with the relief of her not confronting me.

'Actually,' I say, 'I think I could do with some fresh air.' I push my chair back.

'Let me just finish this,' Jack says, gesturing to his half-eaten breakfast.

I'm too late. I turn to see the man Sheena's with reach for his coat from the back of his chair. They're getting ready to leave. And to get to the door, they have to walk right past our table. Jack's eyebrows are knitted as he watches me, wondering why I'm acting so strangely. I sit down. I'm going to have to ride this one out somehow.

I sense them approach our table. This time, once she's right beside us, she gets a better, closer look, and her confused expression falls aside to make way for a look of surprise.

'Anna. I thought it was you, but I couldn't be sure.' She looks at Jack and smiles before returning her attention to me. 'How are things?'

Shit, shit, shit. I feel Jack's eyes on the side of my face, watching me as I try to work out what the hell I'm supposed to say to Sheena.

'I'm sorry,' I reply sweetly, laughing lightly as the words leave my mouth. 'Do I know you?'

If Jack wants to kick-start his acting career, he could learn quite a bit from me. I just don't want him to know this, though.

Sheena's eyes narrow. She may have been unsure from half a room away, but up this close, she knows who I am. She knows she's made no mistake.

She opens her mouth to say something, to press the point

that she knows me, but then she looks at Jack and holds it back, keeping whatever words were on the tip of her tongue to herself.

'I hope everything's working out for you,' she says, then she holds my eye for too long, warming my awkwardness with her stare.

'What was that all about?' Jack asks after they've left the café.

'I've no idea. There are some crazy people about.'

'Who's Anna?'

'I said I don't know, didn't I?' I snap. 'Come on... let's go. I've got a couple of errands I've got to run today.'

He finishes his food slowly and deliberately, making me wait while we sit in silence.

'Everything okay?' I ask once we've finally left the café. 'You seem... tense.'

'I'm fine. You don't really seem yourself either.' He raises an eyebrow questioningly.

I feel my face getting hotter and hotter, my disguise melting right in front of him.

'Look,' I say, trying to keep myself from sounding flustered. 'About tonight. I forgot, I, uh... I already arranged to meet a friend.'

He can see through the lie, I think. He's read into what just happened with Sheena. He knows. He knows.

But I reassure myself with the thought that he can't possibly know. I just need to buy myself a little more time.

'I'll see you whenever then,' he says, and he turns and walks away from me like a petulant teenager who's just had an argument with his mother.

I watch him go. I should be angry, and I am, but there's also a small part of me that feels the sting of disappointment. Fuck Sheena. The meddling cow might have just lost me everything.

THIRTY-FOUR

SIOBHAN

In the week I've been back at my mother's house, I've moved through the phases of my childhood, revisiting the haunting grounds of my past like a ghost hovering over each of its loved ones in turn, there but absent; seeing but not feeling. Somehow, in what must be some kind of natural defence mechanism my body has secretly carried with it throughout my return, I've been able to detach myself from the reality of every scene I have come back to, each memory connected with every building and landscape. I am myself, but I am not. While standing here now, outside the last point in the map of my return, I have removed myself temporarily from the horrors of that night. My mind is trained now not on what happened then, but on what must happen next.

I never thought I'd see this place again. It was dilapidated before the fire; after it, the roof was collapsed and the walls crumbling. I can't believe it's still standing, but the building is listed, and despite various planning applications and petitions by locals, no one has ever been able to win the case to get it demolished. It was once part of a farm, passed down through generations for nearly two centuries. Then, after the fire, no one wanted to go near it. The old cottage, as it was known by locals – despite the sprawling size of the place – went from ruined romantic rendezvous spot to macabre location of a death caused by arson.

There used to be something romantic about the place, in a Gothic kind of way, and though the building had been used as a hang-out spot by local teenagers for years, that night there was no one else there to interrupt its eerie but beautiful silence. We had the place to ourselves. It was unsettling and creepy and exciting all at the same time, and I trusted that Lewis would keep me safe, that there was nothing and no one there that could cause us any harm. But we weren't in danger. We *were* the danger.

There's an old stone wall around the property, outlining an expanse of overgrown brambles and shrubbery that I imagine must hide what was once a front lawn. The last time I was here, some of the windows still had glass; it's all gone now, the last of them blasted out by the force of the fire. I feel a tightening in my chest. Guilt. A sickness. We never meant to hurt anyone. We had no idea that anyone else was there that night.

I pull the newspaper page, brown and faded, from my pocket, unfolding it with shaking fingers.

HALBURY TEEN PLEADS GUILTY TO MANSLAUGHTER

Lewis Handley, 16, of Halbury, three miles north of Rochester, yesterday pleaded guilty to a charge of arson and manslaughter following the death of Alan Grove, 43, at a fire in a local derelict building. Handley claims to have been alone on the night the fire was started, denying he had any knowledge that Mr Grove was also in the building. Grove, who was known to local authorities, had been using the building to sleep rough.

He died of smoke inhalation; however, a post-mortem revealed he had suffered an assault shortly prior to this. Handley maintains that he defended himself when Mr Grove attacked him. However, the toxicology report that was carried out after death suggests Mr Grove had a substantial amount of alcohol as well as heroin in his system, which the prosecution argued would have meant he wasn't in a fit state to attack anyone. Handley will be sentenced next month.

I was there. I was guilty. Lewis and I started that fire together. We were sixteen, but we were naïve; kids playing at being grown-ups. It was cold, and we thought ourselves adventurers, renegades. We had romantic notions of sitting beside a campfire together, talking and drinking into the night while we watched the flames dance in the darkness. It didn't happen like that. The fire spread quickly, sucking up anything and everything that came within its reach: the old wooden furniture that remained there decades after the last owners had passed away; the litter and debris left by the teenagers who used the place as a meeting ground for illegal raves.

I remember running from the building that night, Lewis's hand holding mine when I tripped on the way down the path that led to the broken wooden gate that somehow after all these years is still standing. We were panicking. The fire had taken hold far quicker and stronger than either of us had believed it capable of. We were idiots. We had thought it would stay contained, that we'd be able to put it out. Instead, we were guilty of arson. Not just Lewis, but me too. I was there. I may not have struck the match, but I did nothing to deter him from doing so either. We were stupid. But neither of us were killers.

Once we were out through the gate, Lewis pulled me back. He was frantically patting down his pockets, searching for something.

'My phone,' he said. 'I've left my phone in there.'

'Forget it,' I told him. 'You can't go back in, it's not worth it.'

'But if it's found, the police will know. They'll know I started the fire.'

He looked at me, his face fraught with panic and fear. I told him for a second time that he couldn't go back in, but he didn't listen.

'Go home,' he said. 'I'll ring you in a bit.'

I called after him, terrified, as he shot back up the path and disappeared into the house. I wanted to follow him, but fear kept me rooted to the spot. The fire couldn't yet be seen from the lane, but I knew it was in there, growing in heat and intensity. I stood there not knowing what to do, whether to wait for him to make sure he was okay or just do as he'd told me and leave. I didn't want to go while he was still inside. What if he didn't come back out?

It was then that I heard my name. I turned, startled, to see Anna on the other side of the path, half hidden among the trees.

'Is everything okay?' she asked.

'Fine,' I said, hearing the shakiness of my voice and hoping that somehow she might not notice it.

'What are you doing?'

I looked back at the house. I had to get her away from there before the fire became visible. She couldn't know what we'd just done. But Lewis, I thought. Lewis was in there. He was alone. 'Nothing,' I told her. 'I was meeting someone, but they're not here. Come on.'

I took her by the hand and hurried her home, not asking what she'd been doing there until we neared her house. She told me she'd wanted to see me, though she never said why. I never thought to ask, not until much later, when all she said, once again, was that she'd just wanted to see me. I left her with Aunt Claire, neither of us mentioning where we'd been, and as soon as I got home, I called Lewis. My heart lifted when I heard his voice, and he told me he was okay, that he'd got out of the old cottage unharmed, his phone recovered.

The next day, the village was flooded with news of the fire. According to reports, it had ripped through the building. Windows had been blown out. The roof had collapsed. And a forty-three-year-old man who'd been sleeping rough in the months since his marriage had collapsed had been found dead in what had once been the dining room, killed by smoke inhalation.

Lewis and I kept a distance from one another and didn't call, as we'd decided was best. He didn't have to tell me he was racked with guilt, as I was; I knew him well enough to know it without the words. He was a good person. He was kind and gentle and considerate. He was honest. And it was this honesty that led him to the police station, where he confessed to starting the fire. He hadn't told me he was going. The first I heard of it was from Aunt Claire, who told me she'd spoken with one of his cousins.

Two months later, he pleaded guilty to manslaughter. I wasn't in court: my mother wouldn't let me go. I didn't need to go to hear what he was accused of. By that point, the whole town knew he'd been there when the fire had started. I couldn't escape the guilt that had hung heavy in my chest since that night. I was as guilty as he was, but no one was looking at me.

Lewis could have done what most people would have and told the police that I'd been with him, but he didn't. He took the blame for everything, and when he pleaded guilty to assaulting Alan Grove, everything I thought I'd known changed. The post-mortem revealed that Mr Grove had been hit with something heavy before he'd died from smoke inhalation. Police later found a piece of old scaffolding dumped not far from the cottage, just beyond the hedgerow. If he hadn't been assaulted, he would likely have been able to flee before the fire consumed the building.

I had no idea what had gone on after I'd left and Lewis had run back inside. He claimed in his statement to the police that he hadn't been expecting to see Mr Grove, still believing himself to be alone. The man had tried to attack him, and he'd retaliated with the closest thing to hand. Perhaps those things were true, and yet I could never erase from my thoughts the fact that he had hit him so hard it had knocked him unconscious. Would someone apparently taken by surprise in the way Lewis claimed to have been be capable of attacking another person with such strength and precision? Such violence. And this was Lewis they were talking about. I had never known him to be anything but gentle. He was kind and calm. Lovely. But then, perhaps I had never really known him at all. Perhaps we are all capable of anything in the wrong circumstances.

I understand why Jack hates me. Lewis's life ended long before his suicide, and I was responsible for that in part. Perhaps I should have gone to the police and told them that I'd been there that night too. But what difference would it have made? Lewis would still have faced the same charges. He would still have been sentenced. And no matter how much I wished I'd been able to, there was nothing I could do to change that.

Maybe Jack is right to make me want to pay for my part in what happened. There are consequences to every action. But I know, despite everything, that I am not a bad person. Bad people intend to inflict harm upon others. I never meant to hurt anyone. And I've lived with the guilt of Alan Grove's death my entire life. Wherever I end up going after this, I will continue to live with the guilt until the day of my own death. But that won't happen because Jack Handley has decided it's due.

My thoughts are interrupted when my phone starts ringing in my pocket. I take it out and look at the screen. Dominic, my neighbour in London.

'Hi,' I say, answering quickly. 'What's happened?'

Because Dominic never calls me. He only has my number

in case one day there is an emergency, so unless Freya has finally got around to making that cheese and leek pie he mentioned, I'm guessing that now is that day.

'The police have been here,' he tells me. 'They're looking for you.'

THIRTY-FIVE

ANNA

A few days ago, I contacted some of my old clients whose homes I used to clean. Quite a few were keen to have me back, so this afternoon I return to a house in Streatham. The place is gorgeous, in a little cul-de-sac that feels as though you're out in the countryside somewhere rather than in the middle of London. I thought being back at work might make me feel better in a way; that clinging onto a little bit of Anna's old life before I leave her entirely would be cathartic. Turns out, not so much the case. As I return the vacuum cleaner to the perfectly stocked and organised utility room – shelves adorned with a selection of expensive cleaning products lined up like little soldiers ready for a war on hygiene – all I'm left with is a reminder of how pathetic my existence until this point has been. Thirty-one years wasted, always giving to other people. But at least now I know all that's about to change.

The owner of the house, a woman I first met years ago when I started working for one of her colleagues, is out in the garden, so once I'm finished, I pop outside to tell her I'm done. She comes into the kitchen, where she takes a handful of crisp ten-pound notes from a jar on the windowsill.

'You've done an amazing job, as always,' she beams, taking in the spotless surfaces and gleaming cooker top that prior to my visit I'm sure hadn't looked that different. I doubt she cooks. The oven looks as though it's never been used. What's the point in having fancy expensive appliances if you're never going to switch them on?

'Gosh, Anna,' she says, putting a hand on her hip and tilting her head to the side like one of those old-fashioned musical dolls you wind up with a key. 'I just can't get over how different you look. I wouldn't have known it was you. I love the hair.'

'Thank you. Just fancied a change.'

'So how are you keeping?'

'Fine,' I tell her. I'm now divorced, jobless and living with my previously estranged cousin whose mother has always hated me. I've killed a woman since we last met, and I'm planning the demise of another. 'How are things with you?'

'Great. Busy, busy, busy, but you know, I wouldn't have it any other way.'

I smile widely, forcing it to reach my eyes. When I went out into the garden, she'd been sitting on a patio chair reading a copy of *Grazia* magazine and drinking a smoothie that looked like a glass of blended grasshoppers, but who am I to judge? I guess rich people's idea of busyness is different to the kind the peasants have to endure.

'Thanks so much for today,' she says, putting a perfectly manicured hand on my arm. 'It's great to have you back.'

'It's amazing to *be* back,' I gush, because this playing at being Siobhan is doing wonders for my performance of bullshit, if nothing else, and I need to keep in character if I'm going to make this work long-term.

'See you soon,' she says, following me to the door.

Not if I can help it, I think. With any luck, I won't need the extra cash much longer. I'll have access to Siobhan's bank accounts, her savings; her life.

She's barely closed the door behind me when my phone starts ringing. I take it out and look at the screen. Jack.

'Hi,' I say coldly, because this is the first I've heard from him since he walked away from me outside the café on Saturday morning.

'Siobhan... everything okay?' He sounds sheepish. Good.

'Fine,' I say, echoing the nonchalance he'd shown me.

'Look... I'm sorry. About the other day. I was a moody shit. There were things on my mind. I shouldn't have taken it out on you.'

His brother, I think. Is this what he's referring to?

'Don't worry about it.' And yet *I'm* worried about it. He must have wondered after we'd parted ways what that exchange with Sheena was all about.

'But I am. I want to make it up to you.'

I say nothing.

'Actually,' he says, 'I've got a surprise for you.'

Oh God. I hate surprises.

'What sort of surprise?' I ask vaguely.

I turn the corner at the top of the cul-de-sac, making my way to the bus stop a couple of streets away.

'That'll spoil it, won't it? I need to see you first.'

A car horn blares from across the road as a driver reversing out of a driveway nearly collides with another.

'Where are you?' Jack asks.

'Streatham,' I tell him, but as soon as I do, I regret it. If he asks what I'm doing here, I'm going to have to lie, and I'm not prepared for that.

'Really? That's great. Not too far from where I am, actually. I've been doing deliveries.'

Oh no. He's going to ask to come and pick me up in his van. I'm not sure I can do this today. I'm too tired and I can't be bothered. Also, I need a shower.

'I'll come and get you,' he suggests, seeming to read my thoughts and ignore them.

'No!' I say, a little too keenly. The lights at the pedestrian crossing turn green and I make my way across the road. 'What I mean is, I'm not ready yet. I'm a bit hot and bothered, to be honest – I need to go home and have a shower, get changed before—'

'I'm sure you're perfect as you are. Drop me a pin on your phone.'

I'm really not, I think, glancing down at my stained leggings and the oversized sweatshirt I threw on over my T-shirt. Siobhan would tell me off if she could see what I'm wearing.

I turn the corner at the top of the street, the bus stop in sight ahead of me. And then I hear another horn. Not so insistent and prolonged this time, more the snappy sound of someone trying to catch the attention of a person they know. I turn. There's a white van a few vehicles up. Jack is sitting at the steering wheel, waving.

My heart trips over itself. What is he doing here? But he's just told me what he's doing here: he's been making a delivery. It seems a bit of a coincidence, though, that he should be here on the same afternoon I happen to come to this part of London; a part to which I've not been in ages.

He slows the van alongside me, the passenger window wound down. 'Jump in,' he says.

I say nothing for a moment, unsure what to do or how to respond. I don't like spontaneity. Nor do I like the feeling of not being in control. And something feels off about all this, like he'd already somehow known I'd be here before he even called me.

'What's the matter?' he asks, smiling. 'Come on, I'm not about to abduct you.'

I realise I'm being paranoid. Paranoid and suspicious, because this is what I've trained myself for over the years: to expect everyone to be as unpredictable as I am. But this is Jack. So I get into the van.

'I've just got one last delivery to make,' he tells me as he pulls away from the kerb. 'You don't mind, do you?'

'No, that's fine. What's this surprise, though?'

'If I tell you, it won't be a surprise, will it?' He rolls his eyes and smiles, and when the song that's playing on the radio comes to an end and the next one begins, he turns it up, singing along gently to himself as he heads towards the high street.

'You must be missing work,' he says, giving the radio a nod. 'When are you thinking about going back?'

'I'm not sure. It's still early days after everything that happened.'

'Of course.'

We drive without speaking for a while, the radio the only thing to break the silence. I realise we're heading towards Bromley. There's been no mention of where he needs to go for the delivery, and when I look around the front of the van, there are no parcels or packages to be seen. It could be in the back, I tell myself, behind the panel, hidden from view.

'Where are we going?' I ask him.

'I told you. One delivery left.'

'But what is it?'

'Nothing you need to worry about.'

'Jack—'

'Okay,' he says, raising a hand from the steering wheel. 'Okay. We'll stop. I'll show you. I wanted to wait until we got to the surprise, but seeing as you're so impatient...' He reaches over to give my thigh a gentle squeeze.

Pulling into a quiet residential street, he turns the van so that it's facing back the way we came before undoing his seat belt and jumping out, leaving the engine running.

'Come on then,' he says. 'Let's get this done.'

I follow him to the back of the van. He's grinning like an overly excited kid on Christmas morning.

'You're worrying me,' I say, only half joking.

'Don't be daft. Come here.'

He stands behind me and pushes my hair from the back of my neck before kissing the patch of bare skin he's exposed to the sun. Then he puts something over my eyes and ties it in a knot at the back of my head. 'I'll tell you when to look, okay?'

I hear him open the doors at the back of the van.

'Ta-dah!' he says, with all the enthusiasm of a stage magician. 'You can look now.'

I raise my hands to whatever it is he's tied across my face, lowering it from my eyes. But I've barely had time to see the empty space inside the van before a blow to the back of my head renders me senseless.

THIRTY-SIX

SIOBHAN

When I get back to the house, my mother is sitting in the living room watching television. I say watching, but the sound is turned down so that whatever the presenter with the blinding teeth and two-tone hair is saying is barely audible. My mother's focus is elsewhere, on the garden beyond the window, where her perfectly tended planters boast colourful bedding plants arranged in neat lines like a dance troupe about to start a performance. Sometimes I've wondered whether her garden reflects her mind, though it's more likely that the opposite is true and that the garden is the antithesis of the chaos she carries.

Sunday evenings used to greet me with a familiar sense of dread back when I was a kid. I remember them vividly, their scents and sounds: the lingering smell of gravy and roast potatoes from lunch; the theme tunes from the television programmes that would air just before my bedtime. I would have that rolling feeling in my stomach, despite the fact that I didn't mind school. I suppose it became a habit, the same way most kids feel when the weekend draws to an end. Those Sundays stopped after Dad's death. There were no more

Sunday lunches; no more TV before bed, Dad watching from the chair he always sat in.

When you're young, you think your parents are unbreakable. They're the only real constant in your life: teachers come and go, friends follow a similar pattern; you become aware, gradually, that things change without your control, but at least your parents remain consistent, the one thing that can be relied upon. My father's death left a question mark hanging over any kind of permanence. I read once that grief is the only emotion that really makes a person grow up – that the first experience of loss is when we leave our childhood behind and find ourselves thrust into the uncertain realms of what it really means to be an adult. For me, that happened when I was still not yet a teenager, and everything that might have come after it was altered, stained with the knowledge that life was fleeting and could be taken away in an instant.

'Mum,' I say, waking her from her reverie.

'Everything okay?' she asks, not looking at me.

'I've got to go back to London.'

She turns now. She looks so tired; the kind of years-old tired that sits with a person and can't be shed with a few good nights' sleep. She isn't old enough to look this weary. 'Tonight?'

'The police want to speak to me again.'

The corners of her mouth twitch. 'What's going on, Siobhan? I mean, what's *really* going on? There's something you've not been telling me since that day I came to see you. Why can't you tell me what's happened?'

An answer pops into my head, intrusive and beyond my control. *Because I can't trust you.* I'd like to erase it from my mind, wish it back to wherever it came from, but I understand that at some base level it must have come from my subconscious. It must be what I truly believe, deep down. I've always felt it, somewhere, but I've never understood why.

'It's to do with Anna, isn't it?'

'I haven't got time now, Mum. I'm sorry. I don't want to miss the last train.'

'You can't go now, Siobhan,' she says, getting up from her chair. 'It's too late. Surely whatever they want to see you about can wait until tomorrow?'

'It can't. They think I killed Carrie.'

I watch her face crease with confusion. 'I thought you said you weren't involved? That you were just helping with inquiries because you were considered a witness?'

'It's complicated,' I say, hoping this will be sufficient to deter her. Of course, it's not. She follows me up the stairs as I make my way to my room to pack my things.

'Something's going on that you're not telling me about,' she says, standing in the doorway and watching as I pull my suitcase up onto the bed.

'Touché, Mother.' She meets my eye briefly before looking away. 'Do you want to tell me what you've been hiding from me all these years?' Silence fills the space between us. She looks guilty. Guilty of something she has carried all this time and even now isn't ready to part with. 'I didn't think so.'

I start shoving clothes and toiletries into the bag.

'I've no idea what's going on, or where Anna fits into any of this, but make sure you don't go opening a can of worms for yourself, Siobhan. The past's the past for a reason.'

'This is about Carrie,' I tell her, offering just a half-truth. 'It's nothing to do with the past.'

I watch as her expression morphs from bitterness to something I can't find a word for. 'Is Anna involved? Did she have something to do with Carrie's death?'

She can't find out. If my mother knows that Anna murdered Carrie, it'll ruin my chance of disappearing quickly. She'll be all over the police, hounding them to find her.

'Why would you say that?' I ask.

She opens her mouth to speak, but instead she sighs before

falling silent again. What aren't you telling me? I think. Just what is it you've *never* told me?

'Whoever killed her,' I say, 'it wasn't me. If the police don't know that yet, they will soon. I'm not going to run away from my problems.'

'And if they charge you with her murder?'

'Then they'll realise at some point that they've made a mistake.'

'It's not always that straightforward. Innocent people get sent to prison for crimes they didn't commit all the time.'

'It's not going to happen. I promise you.'

For the first time since we came upstairs, I remember what's hiding in one of the inside pockets of my suitcase. I feel for it now, groping the outline of its shape.

'Mum,' I say, going over to her and putting my hands on her shoulders. 'There's something you could do for me, if you don't mind.'

'What is it?'

'Could you make me a sandwich for the journey?'

She smiles sadly. 'I still think you should stay here. But I'll make you the sandwich.'

When she leaves, I move quickly. There isn't much time before she comes back upstairs. I take out the liquid-filled vial and find the syringe. Morphine. The stash I found in Anna's bedroom weeks ago was enough to sedate a small army. She must have been taking it from the hospital while she was working there as a cleaner, though I'd no idea when I found it why she had so much. I assumed she must have been selling it on the side to make some extra cash. Now, I wonder whether some of it was meant for me, when the time was right for her to carry out whatever she'd been plotting.

I fill the syringe. I've no idea what the dosage is, or even how much would be needed to knock a person unconscious. I imagine Anna is more familiar with the details. Perhaps she's used it on someone before. Perhaps she's already noticed that some has gone missing, or maybe she had so much that she hasn't even realised her stock has been depleted. Either way, I've always intended to carry it with me. Just in case. I don't want to spend every moment having to look over my shoulder, but until my disappearance has become a reality, this is my life for now.

I leave the cap off the filled syringe and tuck it away in my jacket pocket. By the time my mother returns with a foil-wrapped sandwich, I'm zipping my suitcase closed.

'Have these as well,' she says, passing me an apple and a cereal bar.

'Thanks, Mum.'

I put the food in my handbag, checking that my phone, my passport and my keys to the flat are also in there.

'I know you're not telling me everything. But I just want you to know that whenever you need to come home, you can. You could leave London, Siobhan. Perhaps that life wasn't meant for you after all.'

It wasn't, I think. But the life I once had here isn't either. There's a new life waiting for me, someone far away from here. Far from all of this.

I'm relying on Jack disposing of the body and Anna never being found. If this doesn't happen, dental records or DNA will reveal that she isn't me, and once they know that, people will start looking for me. If Jack is still a free man, he will continue to hunt me in his pursuit for revenge. That's if he actually kills Anna, and if he doesn't, that changes everything too.

I feel guilty about my mother, about lying to her about my plans. She will think her daughter dead. If Jack does kill Anna, she will grieve for me, oblivious to the fact that the dead woman – the missing person – is her niece and not her child. She doesn't deserve to suffer any more than she already has, but what choice do I have?

'Come here,' she says, and for the second time over these past few days, we hug one another in a way that has previously been alien to us.

'Goodbye, Mum,' I say, and when she looks at me, I wonder whether she's somehow aware of just how much the words are meant.

THIRTY-SEVEN

ANNA

When I start to come around, my vision is blurry. I've no idea where I am, but the cold that has settled over me is so dense it has seeped into my bones, chilling my blood with its intensity. It's dark when it shouldn't be. It shouldn't be cold, either. The sweater I put on when I'd finished my cleaning job feels wet, the dampness of wherever I am having soaked into the cotton. I'm not sure exactly what the time is, but I know it isn't late. Not that late, anyway. Not late enough that it should be this dark.

Shit, my head hurts. It's like the worst hangover I've ever had, added to eight rounds in a ring with Mike Tyson. The pain is so bad I think I might be sick. When I try to raise a hand to rub my eyes, I find my wrists are tied together. There's blood on my sleeve; I can smell it, sharp like rusting metal. Still fresh. I've not been here that long. I push myself upright, but it's like trying to drag a sack of soil over a speed bump. Where the fuck am I?

Jack. I was with Jack, in the van. The surprise. There was no surprise. The bang to the head: that was the surprise.

I try to think back over the sequence of events from this

afternoon. The past few weeks rush back in a flood of colour and noise: the cockroaches, Sheena in the café, Jack confiding in me about his dead brother. I've made such a mess of everything. He knows I've lied to him. He knows I'm not Siobhan. Wow. It's pissed him off way more than I'd anticipated. He could have just finished things with me and had done with it. There wasn't really a need for the knock-out-and-abduct routine.

Think. I'd just been to work. What was in my pockets? I've got no pockets; I didn't have a jacket on. Keys... phone... they're both in my bag. But I've no idea where that bag is now.

And then I hear his voice from somewhere across the room, a disembodied sound that reverberates in the empty space.

'How's the head feeling?'

Fuck you, I think. But I say nothing.

I hate myself for allowing my guard to drop. There was a feeling in the pit of my stomach, a little voice at the back of my mind telling me not to get into the van with him, but I went ahead and did it anyway, like a naïve idiot. But he may not be as smart as he thinks he is. I had a moment of weakness, and he's no idea just what I'm capable of. Although admittedly, now that my hands are tied and my brain can barely function to think, it might be fair enough to admit that he's in control.

There's a movement from the corner, but he remains out of sight.

'We need to talk about what you did.'

You'd think that one unhinged person might be able to recognise the signs in another, but apparently not. I know what I am. But I didn't have a clue that Jack was anything other than a gentleman. A bit weird this past week, but not dangerous. I've been so preoccupied with my own deception that I missed what was right in front of me. It occurs to me that he must be one of the truly dangerous type: the ones who have no recognition of just how loose a cannon they really are.

He moves towards me, and for the first time since we were

in the van I'm able to see his face. He looks nothing like the person I've spent so much time with over these past couple of months. I need him to get closer; near enough so that I'm able to scratch his face. If anything happens to me and my body is recovered, at least there'll be his DNA beneath my fingernails.

'How long did you think you'd get away with it?' he asks. 'For ever?'

'I'm sorry,' I say, trying to keep my voice light-hearted, as though he might realise what a total overreaction all of this is. 'It started as a bit of a joke, I suppose. I never meant things to go this far.'

His face manages to burn bright even in the darkness. 'A joke? You think it's funny? Don't you have any regret at all for what you did?'

Jesus, he's acting as though I've killed someone. Okay, so I did, but Carrie was nothing to him, and I doubt this is anything to do with her. He can't have any idea that I was the one who killed her and even if he did know, why would he care? He didn't even know her, as far as I'm aware.

But what if he did? Is Carrie what all this is really about?

'I didn't really expect to get away with it, I don't think.'

My words are like a flare. He lunges towards me, his body over mine, and grabs me by the neck. With my hands tied, I can't defend myself.

'You haven't got away with it. You might have thought you did, but he told me, Siobhan. He told me you were there with him that night.'

Siobhan. With my brain fighting for oxygen, his words swim in a confused haze in front of me. He doesn't realise the lie I've told. He still thinks I'm her. I've made a mistake in assuming my secret is out. But if he still thinks I'm Siobhan, why is he holding me here like this? And who the hell is this 'he' he's talking about?

He pushes me back so that I fall onto my side, my hip banging against the cold concrete floor.

'I'm not Siobhan,' I tell him, wincing in pain.

His mouth twists into a smirk. 'Nice one,' he says.

I raise myself onto one elbow, cursing beneath my breath at the pain that flares through my hip – a distraction, at least, from the headache. 'I swear to you, it's true. My name is Anna Fitzgerald. I'm Siobhan's cousin.'

Jack is shaking his head now, though I saw the flicker of recognition on his face when I said the name Anna. He's thinking back to Saturday, to my encounter with Sheena in that café.

'Bullshit,' he snaps. 'You've been calling yourself Siobhan this whole time. You told me you were her the first time we met.'

'I know I did. That's what I meant when I said it started out as a joke. I thought you'd realised I wasn't Siobhan. I thought that was why you'd brought me here, with all this fancy rope shit, because you were pissed off.'

He's looking at me with an uncomfortable mix of confusion and rage.

'Is there really any need for all this?' I ask. I sigh when he doesn't respond. 'I'm not Siobhan,' I tell him again. I know the words sound ridiculous. If I was him, I wouldn't believe it either.

'Then why do you look exactly like her?' he asks. He still doesn't believe what I'm telling him, though there's something in his voice now that betrays a shadow of doubt. He will believe me, if he just hears me out.

'I've been staying with her since I lost my job. We lost touch for years, then we met up by chance and she invited me to stay. The whole dressing as her thing, and getting my hair done like this, it was all just a bit of fun. I never meant anything by it. That's what I meant when I said it had started as a joke. It was nice being her, living a different life for a while. You were never meant to get dragged into it.'

It's as I speak the words that the thought hits me with the force of a wrecking ball. *You were never meant to get dragged into it.* But what if that's not true? What if that was the intention all along? My mind begins to race through the events of the past couple of months. The invitation to stay at Siobhan's flat. Being loaned her clothes and actively encouraged to wear them. Being taken to get my hair done at her hairdresser's, Siobhan knowing that I've always wanted to be just like her. She knew that I would willingly go along with it all. That I would do it gratefully, like a smiling idiot being led to her own grave. Siobhan, who I've loved unconditionally. Siobhan, who I have killed for.

The strange things she was sent in the post. Jack bringing that parcel to the door. Her face when I told her I had a date with a man called Jack. Was that why she'd acted so weird? Did she know who he was?

The past few months rush at me like a tsunami.

'What did you mean,' I say, 'when you said "he told me you were there with him that night"? Who were you talking about?'

'Don't pretend you don't know. You were there. You saw what happened. And you let him take the blame for everything, even when he protected you. You let him sacrifice himself for you so you could carry on living your perfect little life, so you could have your career and your fancy flat while he rotted in prison and came out to nothing.'

The pieces don't fall into place one by one. Rather, they rain down on top of me, deafening my already pounding skull with their noise.

'Shit,' I say. 'Your brother. The brother you told me about.' God, it makes sense now. It makes so much sense. 'It's Lewis, isn't it?'

Because I'd heard rumours, as everyone in the village had.

How the boy who was serving a sentence for killing that homeless man out in the old cottage all those years ago had killed himself just days after he'd been released from prison. But I'd never made the connection between him and Jack until now. Now everything and nothing makes sense. Jack has hunted Siobhan out. Spent time with her, got to know her... or at least that's what he thought. All building up to this. His final revenge. Only he's got the wrong woman. I just need to make him realise that.

'So you are Siobhan,' he says, moving closer. He grabs my face in his hand, his fingertips digging into my cheeks. 'Did you think I'd be so fucking stupid as to be fooled by that? If you're her cousin, like you claimed, how would you know about that night?'

'She told me,' I lie, the words falling from my mouth. 'When we were kids, she told me she'd been there when the fire was started.'

I scan the room. The boards nailed to the windows. The charred walls. We're in the old cottage. The place where everything happened. He's brought me back to where it all started, so he can finish it here, full circle.

'And you did nothing? Didn't think to tell anyone else? Thought you'd just let my brother take the blame?'

Shit. He's angrier now than he was before. I'm just managing somehow to make things worse. Think, Anna. Think.

'That day we met,' I say. 'The day you came to the flat with the delivery. When I gave you my number and you put it into your phone, I saw a flicker of confusion on your face. It bothered me because I didn't know what it meant, but I get it now. You already had Siobhan's number stored, didn't you? You didn't think you needed to take it from me, because you already had it. But when you tapped it into your phone... what happened? It didn't match with the one you had stored?'

His eyebrow twitches. Doubt. He's starting to believe me.

'If you kill me,' I tell him, his hand still squeezing my face, 'Siobhan will walk away from all of this. For a second time. I should have said something, but I was just a kid. I'd just turned thirteen when the fire happened. I was scared. I loved her. Just like you loved Lewis. She was always like a sister to me. I'm not Siobhan. You might think it's fucked up that I've been pretending to be her, but let's face it, you've been doing an impressive job at your own acting routine too. Remember that woman who came over and called me Anna at the weekend? I used to work with her at the hospital. I'm not a radio producer. I'm a cleaner. This afternoon, when you picked me up in Streatham, I'd been cleaning someone's house. The woman in the café recognised me even though I looked so different to when we'd worked together. But I couldn't respond as though I knew her without making you suspicious. It would've meant admitting to the lie I'd told.'

Jack's grip on my face has tightened. His body is leaning away from mine, his weight on his haunches; if I kicked my legs up hard enough now, I might be able to knock him over. But he might have a knife in his pocket. It isn't worth the risk. I need to bide my time; get him onside while I work out how the hell I'm going to get myself out of here.

'I know you believe me. You might not want to, but you do. And I know where Siobhan is. She's not far from here, at her mother's house. I can give you the address.'

'You're lying,' he says coldly.

'I'm not. I wish I was. Come on,' I urge him. 'Let me give you the address. If you find her, bring her back here. If you don't, I'll still be here when you get back anyway.'

The address rolls from my tongue as Jack taps it into his phone. He believes me. He must feel such an idiot, to have wasted all this effort on the wrong person. If he wasn't so unhinged, it might be funny, only now he's even angrier than he was before.

'If I find out this is some bullshit story—' he starts.

'Then you can kill me,' I tell him. 'Do what you want. But don't let the person you wanted all along just walk away.'

He leans over and checks the knots that are binding my wrists and ankles. The pain in my hip has worsened. It can't be down to the bump I had earlier – that wasn't enough to cause the pain that now sears through my left side. It must have happened when Jack brought me here from the van, an injury I have no recollection of.

'You can scream if you like,' he says, 'but you'll just get a sore throat. No one comes near this place.'

Satisfied that I'm unable to free myself, he goes. I hear him leave the building; I hear his van start up on the lane outside. And then I'm left to the silence. For once, I'm grateful for it. It gives me the space and time to think. To plan. When they get back here, I'll be ready for them both.

THIRTY-EIGHT

SIOBHAN

As I leave my mother's street, I feel myself on the verge of tears I don't want to cry. There's a part of me that feels guilty that I'm about to inflict the most awful, unforgivable kind of suffering upon her. That I will take the last piece of her fragile self and shatter it into fragments. And then there's the other part of me: the voice in the back of my mind that nags away, as it has done for so many years now, that there's a secret only I'm ignorant of. That there's something she's never told me, something pivotal to the past that if let loose into the open would change the face and shape of everything I've thought I've known.

We are all capable of secrets. We are all capable of making bad decisions in the heat of an unprecedented moment. All of us can shy away from things we don't want to face up to. Truths we don't want to have to acknowledge as fact.

What if that's what I've been doing all these years?

In my suitcase, the baseball cap sent to me by Jack Lovell travels with me. I couldn't leave it at the flat in case Anna found it, because I know that in my absence she'll have been going through my things. I had to bring it with me, but now I need to find somewhere to discard it. The image of Alan Grove used in all the newspaper reports of his death and the subsequent police investigation has been ingrained on my memory for all these years. That sallow face. Those sunken cheekbones. The heavy, circled eyes and the Kappa baseball cap, identical to the one Jack Lovell somehow managed to get his hands on.

The train station is only a fifteen-minute walk from my mother's house, and I'm five minutes away when I start to sense I'm being followed. It's already dark, and when I look behind me, I see the headlights of a van stopped near the kerb. When I pick up my pace, I hear the van begin to move again, crawling behind me, its engine roaring into life when I break into a run. I shove the handle down on my suitcase and carry rather than drag it, though it's heavier than I expected it to be and it momentarily slows me down.

There's nowhere to break off from the street. There are houses either side of me, but there doesn't seem to be anyone around. I shout. I scream for help, making any noise I can to rouse the attention of anyone who might be out in their garden or close enough to an open window to hear my pleas. I let go of the suitcase, leaving it dumped on the pavement. It doesn't matter. Nothing is important any more.

I get my phone out to call my mother, but by the time I do, the van is already right behind me. I run faster, almost tripping over my own feet. As I find her number and call it, I veer right into a shortcut that goes through to a children's playground. The van can't follow me. But Jack can.

I hear my mother's voice at the other end of the line.

'Mum,' I splutter. 'I'm—' But the phone flips from my hand and bounces off the ground as I'm hit from behind. With the side of my face on the concrete, I hear her voice, tinny and distant, repeating my name, right before I see Jack smash the phone underfoot.

I try to fight him off. With my vision blurred and my head screaming with the pain of the blow, I claw at his face, I scratch at his eyes; anything to get him off me and get away from him. I feel sick. I try to scream again for help, but when something is held over my mouth, the words become strangled.

'Stop fighting me,' he says, and with the back of his hand, he hits me across the face, knocking from me the little strength that was left. A chemical smell fills my nostrils, sending waves of nausea through me. My eyelids flicker; the world around me starts to shift and sway. And then everything falls into blackness.

I don't remain unconscious for long. I can feel myself being dragged, carried, dropped. I am in the back of the van. I feel my body shaken and jolted as he drives too fast, and I'm aware when the roads change from long and straight to winding and narrow. But I can't move, and I can't speak. I can't cry out for help. It feels like the after-effects of two bottles of wine, or what I imagine it might be like to take an overdose. And then I remember the syringe in my jacket pocket. I mustn't forget it's there.

He doesn't take me very far; I'm not in the back of the van for long. When the doors are pulled open, I see trees and hedgerows, the darkened shapes blurred by the effects of what I think now must have been chloroform. My head is pounding and I feel sick. When he drops me onto the ground, I retch on the gravel beneath me.

'Up,' he says. 'Get up.'

But I can barely find the strength to sit. He drags me across the gravel, my palms ripped on the tiny stones as I try desperately to free myself from his grip. My vision is still too impaired to make out where we are. And then I see the gate swing shut behind us, and I know. He's brought me to the old cottage, back to where it all started.

How did he find out that Anna isn't me?

Inside the building, it's so dark I can barely make out the shapes around me. Unbelievably, some of the old furniture is still here, though it's now charred and ruined from the fire. Sickness churns in the pit of my stomach. I remember this place all too well, as though Lewis and I were here together just a few weeks ago.

Jack drags me into the middle of the room and I drop to the floor like a bag of cement. 'Planning on going somewhere, were you?' he asks.

When I look up, I see my passport in his hand. He's been through my suitcase. He must have my phone too, I think, although maybe not. Maybe he left it where it was, realising that the call had been connected to my mother and that regardless of the fact that he smashed it, it might still be used to track our location.

I hear a movement from the corner of the room, and for the first time I realise that Anna is with us. I hear her voice before I see her. 'You set me up, you bitch.'

THIRTY-NINE

ANNA

Before Jack came back with Siobhan, it was completely silent out here. It should be warmer – it's the start of May – but the dampness of the building, derelict for all this time, has seeped into the walls and lives here as a permanent feature, and now it's soaking into my skin, embedding itself in my flesh so that I can feel nothing but pain and cold. I know this is probably what I deserve. I know I'm bad, but I'm not one of those psychopaths you read about online – the type that get their own Netflix series after they've received multiple life sentences for heinous crimes that are then dramatised in the name of entertainment. Those people don't know they're bad. But I do. I get it. I've just never been able to do much to change it, and maybe I haven't wanted to.

I'm more of a vigilante, really. I see an injustice: I put it right. I act when others stand by and do nothing. Like Billy Chapman, who'd been getting away with his shit for far too long. Like Carrie, who was arrogant enough to think herself untouchable. Most of the things I've done, I've done for Siobhan. But I know she won't see it like that. She doesn't see things the way that I do.

Jack drags her over to where I'm sitting. He pulls her behind me so that we're sitting back to back and then starts to wind a rope around both our waists, tying us to one another.

'Don't do this,' I tell him. 'Please. You know I'm not Siobhan now. None of what happened was my fault. I wasn't responsible for your brother's death.'

In the darkness of the barely lit room, the slap comes from nowhere. I taste blood on my tongue; acrid, metallic. I've bitten through my lip.

'You didn't do anything to fucking stop it, either. You said nothing. If you'd told someone she'd been here that night, everything might have turned out differently.'

Behind me, Siobhan moans. It's like she's trying to say something, but she can't speak. I wonder what he did to her to get her here.

Did Sarah see anything? Perhaps she'll have alerted the police, though I'm not sure that would be the best outcome for any of us. Maybe she'll have followed Jack and Siobhan here, but I doubt it. My aunt doesn't really act upon things. She was always a passive type. One of life's victims.

She was over at our house the night of the fire. I was upstairs, reading in my room, when I heard her voice from the kitchen, high-pitched and fraught. They often bickered, my mother and her sister. I used to think that if that was what it was like to have a sibling, I was better off without one. At least with Siobhan we could separate off to our own homes when the day was over, to have a bit of space from each other. I had the best of both worlds, really.

'We can't keep doing this,' I heard my mother say as I crept along the landing, dodging the noisiest of the floorboards. 'We can't keep going over and over the same ground.'

'Just tell me then, Claire. Tell me I'm crazy for even thinking it might be possible.'

My mother said nothing, and her silence sounded worse than any words she might have spoken in response.

'She's my daughter,' she said eventually.

I descended the staircase quietly, taking my time with every step.

'Remember that time you told her she couldn't have those trainers?' Sarah said. 'And she reacted by trashing your bedroom. That temper—'

'I never want to speak about this again,' my mother snapped, cutting her sister short. 'If you really believed it, you should have done something about it at the time.'

'How could I?' Aunt Sarah retorted. 'I'd already lost enough.'

The silence that settled felt to me the same as the one that had descended on the evening of Uncle Garrett's death, a familiar and horrible weight pressing down on my shoulders as though an invisible pair of hands was clamped upon them, pinning my feet to the ground. I stood at the bottom of the staircase with my breath held, scared to make the slightest of movements in case either of them heard me there.

'Then you made your choice. So now you have to live with it.'

I looked down at my hand, drawn from their conversation by a pulsing pain at my palm. A thin trail of crimson blood trickled along my pale skin. I'd been clutching a hairbrush at the wrong end, so tightly that its bristles had punctured a series of holes in my hand. The throbbing was like a pulse. A heartbeat.

'She's just a child,' I heard my mother say.

There was silence for a while. Then I heard someone crying softly, while another voice, my mother's, tried to soothe and calm. I moved closer to the kitchen doorway, glancing through the crack to see them sitting at the tiny table in the corner, my mother stroking Aunt Sarah's hair as she sat with her head against her chest.

I knew how the conversation had started; I didn't need to have heard the words. The accusation. And all I could think in those moments was that if Aunt Sarah knew, there was a good chance Siobhan did too. I had to find her. I had to find out just how much either of our mothers might have told her. I knew where she'd be: at the old cottage with that boy from her year that she'd been seeing for a while. Lewis Handley: apparently more appealing than I now was. I'd been used and dumped when she'd found something more entertaining.

I'd been to the old cottage a couple of times before, once when there were other people there, but the other times just when it was Siobhan and Lewis. God, they talked some shit between themselves. They did other stuff too: things my Uncle Garrett would have turned purple over if he'd still been around to find out. I'd watched them kissing and touching each other, jealous that she was spending her time with him instead of me. Mad that where she'd once confided in me, now she preferred to tell her secrets to Lewis.

I had to speak to her. I had to find out everything she might know. What if she'd told Lewis? It would be just like her to spill someone else's secrets, too stupid to think of the consequences. I had to know if she'd said anything to him.

But by the time I found her at the old cottage, she had other things to worry about.

FORTY

SIOBHAN

As my senses begin to come back to me more clearly, I grow increasingly aware of the sights and sounds that surround me. I can make out enough of the shapes in the room to work out where we are: in what was once the dining room. This isn't the room where Lewis and I started the fire all those years ago. This is the room where Alan Grove was assaulted, and where he was later found dead.

'I won't be long,' Jack tells us, his voice somewhere near the door. 'When I get back, we're going to play a little game. You like a spot of pyrotechnics, don't you, Siobhan?'

Fire. He's going to start a fire. *Matilda, Who Told Lies and was Burned to Death.*

I feel heat rush through me as my body floods with panic. I try to free my hands, but they're tied too tightly.

'You knew, didn't you?' Anna's voice says right behind me. 'You knew all this time that he was coming for you.'

The noise she makes next doesn't sound human. It's the growl of an animal; the screech of a creature that's been hunted and trapped. It is visceral and deafening and desperate.

'All this time,' she says between gritted teeth. 'All this time

I've tried to do everything I could to help you, and this is how you repay me.'

'Fuck you,' I say, my voice a blade of ice. 'Nothing you've done was for me. It was all for yourself. I know you killed Carrie.'

I could kill her now, if I wanted to. And God, there's a bit of me that does. I think of the syringe, still in my pocket, because Jack only took my bag. Once he'd found my passport and he knew where my phone was, he must have thought I was devoid of anything else that might help me escape this place. He's got no idea that I was as prepared for Anna as I've been for him all these months.

I could inject her in the back, just about, if I twist myself around hard enough to reach her. She'd know I was up to something, but she'd have no idea what. I don't know how long the drugs would knock her out for, though, and I don't want to risk it. I've no way of getting myself free. Not without her. If we want to escape, we're going to have to work together – the last thing I want to do. The last thing I imagine she wants to do either.

'She was nothing to you,' she says. 'You thought she was your friend, but she didn't even like you.'

'I know. The police showed me a transcript of her text messages with Flynn.'

That shuts her up for a moment. She thinks she knows everything, that she has always had something on me. But I've been one step ahead of her this whole time. That meeting in the library didn't happen by chance. I'd known she was going to be there. Sad, pathetic little Anna. So desperate to please me. Willing to do anything for me. All I had to do was turn up and show her the way.

'She didn't deserve to die.'

'She didn't deserve her life,' Anna retorts. 'Everything I've done, Siobhan, I've done for you. She had your rightful place. It should have been you running that show, not her. It was you doing all the work. She wouldn't have even got that presenting post if it hadn't been for you, would she? And how did she repay you? By dragging your name through the dirt and belittling you to your colleagues. She was a jumped-up little rich bitch who nobody misses. The world's a better place without her.'

I hear her bitterness, the vitriol that pours from her mouth, and I see flashbacks I don't want to be exposed to. My childhood self, locked in a garden shed; Anna outside the door, taunting me with the key she'd removed from the lock. Another me, a little older this time, heartbroken at finding my pet hamster dead in its cage. Me, twelve years old, crying on my bed as I grieved for my dead father; Anna beside me, brushing my hair as she soothed me with words I now know were meaningless.

'Did you really think you'd be able to live my life, Anna? That you could remove yourself from all the people I've worked with, all my friends and family, and no one would think to come looking for me?'

'What about you?' she asks, turning the question back at me. 'Did you think you could just disappear? That everyone here would mourn you, believing you to be dead, while my body rotted in woodland somewhere, dumped there by that maniac? You left me with him knowing just how dangerous he was. You sacrificed me to save yourself.'

I think for a moment that she's faking it, that the tears are strained to force a sympathy I could never otherwise be made to feel. Then I realise they're real. I hear them in the darkness, heartfelt sobs that rack her body against mine, rocking us to the rhythm of the betrayal she finds herself a victim of. Tears for herself, all of them.

'I always wanted to be like you, but now I've no idea why. You're weak, Siobhan. You don't stand for anything. I've wasted all those years wishing I was more like you when really it should be you wanting to be more like me. I defend the people that matter. I get things done.'

'You hurt people, Anna. You killed a woman for no other reason than your own misguided obsession with me.'

'I'm not obsessed with you,' she snaps. 'You're nothing to me. Not any more. Not after this.' She inhales sharply, filling her lungs with the damp air of the room.

How long is Jack going to be? I wonder. What exactly does he have planned for us?

'What is it you think I have?' I ask her. 'Whatever it is, you're wrong. You seem to think I live some exciting, glamorous lifestyle, but it's nothing like that. You must have realised that by now. I wake up, I go to work, I get my shopping delivered, I watch television. I go to bed. Sleep, wake and repeat. You're deluded, Anna. You created a version of me you wanted to be real. The person *you* really wanted to be. It's a fantasy. None of what you believe is real.'

'I know I saved you,' she says. 'That's real. If fingers hadn't pointed at Lewis, it would have been only a matter of time before they turned to you. I could have told the police you were there. But I didn't. I saved you, and now you owe me everything. You owe me your life.'

'You didn't save me. Lewis did. He could have told them I was there – he could have implicated me if he'd wanted to. But he never did. He stood for something. Not like you, Anna. You just take what you want and hurt whoever gets in your way. Like poor Carrie.'

'Poor Carrie,' she repeats snidely, mocking my tone. 'I did it for you! So you could have what you deserved. And she was a real bitch beneath it all. Some of the things she said about you... she wasn't your friend.'

'She didn't deserve to die.'

'Who decides that, though? Who decides who gets to live or die?'

I see my mother's face in front of me, her expression when she asked me whether Anna had been involved in Carrie's murder. It never occurred to me at the time, but she didn't look surprised at the thought. If anything, if seemed there was an implication behind her words. Now, I think she may have been silently trying to tell me something.

Who decides who gets to live or die?

I don't want to ask the question, but I know I have no choice. I will never rest until I know the truth that's been hidden from me for all these years. It's going to hurt worse than any other kind of hell, but I'm braced for it. Almost as though I already know what's coming.

'The night my father died, Anna. Tell me what really happened.'

FORTY-ONE

ANNA

Siobhan's words echo around the empty room. I've always known that one day questions about that night might be raised in conversation, though I'd anticipated it would be Aunt Sarah who brought it up with me. I should have known that was wrong. Siobhan may be weak in so many ways, but Aunt Sarah is pathetic. She hides from things. Siobhan has always had something more about her.

'What do you want to know?' I ask her.

'The truth,' she says, the words forced from her between gritted teeth.

I don't know how long I've been here now, or how long it's been since Jack left us alone, but I don't think it's as long as it feels. It might still be the same day, but I've lost all sense of time. Daylight is long gone, I know that much. The gaps in the boards nailed over the windows were letting in little shards of sun earlier, but they disappeared a while ago, so I'm guessing it's maybe 9.30 or 10 p.m. Actually, it's probably later than that. I wonder where Jack has gone, and what he might bring with him when he returns.

I may not have been here for any great length of time, but

it's been long enough for the silence to do what it always does and play tricks on my mind. I don't deserve to be here. I had nothing to do with that night or with what happened to Lewis. And Jack seems to be forgetting something: Lewis did start that fire. He's acting as though his brother was innocent, but he wasn't. He may not have known that man was in the building with him, but he still struck the match. Sooner or later, I suppose, we all need to pay for our crimes.

It's this that concerns me. Here in the cold and the dark, I feel I could be in an oversized confessional booth, waiting for a priest to arrive to listen to my heart's secrets. There would be plenty I'd have to tell him. If I'm going to die at some point in the near future, which appears a likely prospect at the moment, it might be best to go out with a clean conscience. Not because I believe in heaven or hell or anything like that. Just because it'd probably be quite nice to get it all off my chest.

My mouth feels dry. I'd never anticipated that when I was finally made to come clean, I'd be doing it to Siobhan.

'You were there, weren't you?' she says, and the calmness of her voice is almost unnerving.

Once a month, always on a Friday, my mother and Sarah would go out for the evening. They would never venture far, usually to the local pub for a few drinks or to the social club for a game of bingo. On those nights, I would have a sleepover at their house. Siobhan and I would share her bed, sleeping top and tail and telling each other ghost stories long after we were supposed to have gone to sleep. I would always take the stories too far, their contents darker and more disturbing, and when Siobhan would beg me to stop, I would keep going, terrifying her with tales of children possessed by demons and spirits that would linger over their beds in the dark of night-time. Usually at some point she would end up in tears, and then I would hold her hand beneath the duvet, soothing her with gentle words so that she'd always remember it was me who was there for her:

that although I'd created the problem, I was the only person who could make it go away. I needed her to know that she needed me more than she feared me.

That particular Friday evening occurred in late summer, when the weather was still warm enough for Uncle Garrett to do a barbecue for everyone before my mother and Sarah went out. I was nine at the time; Siobhan was twelve. After our mothers had left the house, Uncle Garrett let us stay out and play in the garden until it was nearly dark.

I loved being at Siobhan's house. It was a huge detached Victorian place with a garden so big that children could easily get lost in it. Garrett's parents had invested in property at a young age, and by the time they retired and sold everything off, they'd made enough money to give each of their three sons a few hundred thousand pounds each. That was back in the eighties, when thirty grand would buy a decent-sized house with enough change left over to renovate it. And Uncle Garrett was generous with his good fortune, I'll give him that. At times it felt like an open house, everyone welcome, and they were always throwing parties and inviting people over. He made sure my mother was all right financially too, though I've never found out just how much he gave her, and whatever it was, I'm sure she found a way to squander it within next to no time. My mother never had much common sense with anything, and certainly not enough to make investments and do something sensible with the little bit of good luck life had thrown in her direction.

'Time for bed now, girls,' I remember him saying.

'Aww, Dad.'

'Siobhan. It's time for bed.'

'You should let us watch the end of the film,' I told him. 'What's the point in watching a film and not seeing the end?'

Uncle Garrett's left ear used to go red when something had annoyed him, and it did then, spreading in a glow that stretched down to his neck. 'It's late enough now. You can watch the rest in the morning.'

He held my gaze in the way a grown man might only do with another grown man, challenging and prolonged, with the intention of putting a stop to a fight that hadn't yet broken out. It wasn't the first time I'd attracted this kind of expression, and I'd seen the way Aunt Sarah had started to look at me too, wary and disconcerted. I instilled some kind of unease in them, yet I was never sure why.

'My mother would let us watch the end.'

'I'm not your mother, Anna. So if you want to stay here again, you'll listen now and do as you're told.'

It must have been nearly 10 p.m. by the time we'd put on our pyjamas and brushed our teeth. Uncle Garrett stayed downstairs; I could hear the television back on and, when I went out onto the landing, the hiss of another beer bottle being opened. Aunt Sarah would be back within a couple of hours. I would stay for breakfast and then Mum would come to pick me up.

Only that night wasn't going to be like all the others.

Siobhan fell asleep quickly, exhausted by the long evening and, for the first time, refusing to be drawn into the storytelling that had previously brought our sleepovers to a close. I watched her breathing as she slept, the gentle rise and fall of her chest, and I wondered at the unfairness of her life's simplicity. I kept thinking about the way Uncle Garrett had spoken to me. He wasn't my father. He couldn't tell me what to do, no matter how much he liked to think he could. My cheeks flared with the resentment I carried. He'd made me look stupid in front of Siobhan. He'd spoken to me like I was a little kid.

I was still lying awake over an hour later, too riled up to be able to drop off. I'd listened to the sounds of Uncle Garrett moving around downstairs: the living room door creaking when he left the room to go to the kitchen, the bang of the fridge door as it was shoved closed; the noise of the film that was playing on the television, one with gunfire and shouting and explosions. The type of film he thought Siobhan and I were too young to watch, because he still treated us both like little kids.

I heard him come upstairs to use the bathroom. When he emerged, I was standing on the landing in my nightdress.

'Go back to bed, Anna.' His words were slurred.

'I need a drink.'

'Then I'll bring you up some water. Go back into the bedroom, please.'

I did as I was told. I went back into the room, though I didn't get back into bed. Instead, I stood just behind the door, waiting for him to walk past. When he neared the top of the stairs, I went back out onto the landing. He sensed me there too late, stumbling as he turned, inebriated. I put a hand out. I shoved him. And in his drunken state, that was all it took.

There was a corner at the bottom of the staircase where Uncle Garrett's head hit the wall. He bounced off it, just like one of those crash-test dummies I'd seen in educational videos reminding people of the importance of wearing seat belts. There was a groan before he stirred. Then I heard him calling her name in a voice that was weakened by injury and fear.

Siobhan.

It was barely more than a whisper. There was blood on the wall, a single long smear where his head had made contact before sliding down the paintwork.

Siobhan.

For a long time afterwards, I convinced myself I couldn't remember the split seconds that had preceded that moment. It was like seeing myself from outside my body, the kind of experience people claim to have when their heart has stopped for a few seconds before they've been jolted back to life. It wasn't really me who raised that hand. It wasn't me who listened to the crack of his skull and then stood there doing nothing. Just watching. And it wasn't me who went back into the bedroom and got back beneath the duvet, curled up against Siobhan's sleeping body until I heard my mother and Aunt Sarah arrive home.

I knew afterwards that there was something wrong with me, and I realised even then, at my young age, that it was something no one would ever be able to put right. I lived with the knowledge for the rest of my childhood, managing to conceal my real self from most of the people around me. But not all of them. Aunt Sarah saw something in me; I've always known that. I saw the way she used to look at me when I was playing with Siobhan, long before the night Uncle Garrett died. She sensed something in me that no one else had noticed, and I know she was always wary of me.

In the here and now, in the burned-out former dining room of the old cottage where Alan Grove met his death, I can't share this level of detail with Siobhan. Like I said, I'm not a psychopath. I like to right wrongs, and Uncle Garrett was wrong to speak to me the way he did that night. Siobhan only wants to hear what she's come to suspect, which is that I may have played some part in her father's death.

'I was nine years old,' is all I say, which gives her no kind of answer to anything.

I feel her body tense behind me, her back rigid as she straightens. She must want to kill me. She deserves to feel that way, I suppose. But I was just a kid at the time. If Aunt Sarah had spoken to someone about those feelings she'd had about me before that night, perhaps Uncle Garrett would still be here now. She was the adult. It was her duty to look out for me. To make sure she kept me safe, even if that meant from myself.

'What are you saying, Anna – that I'm crazy to think a child that age could be capable of something like that? Or are you suggesting you were too young to take responsibility?'

But she's not going to get what she wants from me. It's not her place to judge me.

'You held my hand,' she says through gritted teeth, every word punctuated by the bluntness of her anger. 'We went downstairs, and you held my hand.'

'I wanted to look after you,' I tell her. And it's the truth. I did. In some strange kind of way, despite everything, I still do. That's all I ever wanted to do.

'All through our childhood, you did horrible things to me so that you could be the one to make me feel better. You told me stories that scared the life out of me, then spent hours brushing my hair when I was too frightened to turn the light off. That time I got locked in the garden shed, you spent ages pretending to search for the key when you'd had it the whole time. It was you who locked me in there.'

This isn't the time or place for a post-mortem of the past. I am who I am; Siobhan is who she's always been. And she's never going to change. She's never going to want to accept the fact that I love her more than anyone else ever can or will. Or at least I did once.

'How are we going to get out of this?' I ask her. Because no matter how she must feel about me in this moment, I am her only chance of survival. And she's the only hope I have too.

'There's a syringe in my pocket,' she tells me. 'I took it from the stash you were hiding in the back of the wardrobe. Were you planning to use it on me?'

'Maybe,' I tell her. 'One day.'

She laughs bitterly, but there's no humour in the sound. She hates me. And this is good, because we need her anger to fuel her strength: the only thing that's got a chance of getting us both out of this building alive. After that... God knows what happens.

'You stole it from the hospital?' she asks, but I don't offer an answer. I don't need to. Instead, I ask whether she's able to reach it. I feel her twist behind me as she gropes about in the darkness. 'I think so.'

'Give it to me,' I instruct her.

But then there's a noise from somewhere down the hallway. A door creaking and banging as it's shut. We're too late. Jack is already back.

FORTY-TWO

SIOBHAN

Jack moves about in the middle of the room, not far from where Anna is sitting. I can't see him, but I hear every sound: rustling; what sounds like a piece of furniture being dragged; the gentle hiss of a cap being unscrewed. Against my back, Anna's spine straightens as she inhales sharply. She can see all the things I'm only able to hear. Then comes the liquid, slopped over the floor. The smell of petrol as it fills the dampened air.

He moves around us quickly, shaking the petrol can once it's emptied. Then he stops in front of me, his figure outlined against the darkness.

'Get up,' he says.

With my ankles and hands tied, it's an almost impossible task. He untethers me from Anna before grabbing me beneath the arms, yanking me upright. His hand moves to his pocket and I see a flash of silver as he pulls out a knife. 'Don't try anything smart,' he warns.

I press my elbow to my body, aware of the shape of the filled syringe within the fabric of my jacket. It's not enough. It could take minutes – longer, even – for the drugs to flood his system and take effect, and I'm not even sure whether the dose is enough to knock him unconscious. Even if it does, there'll be plenty of time for him to use the knife that's in his hand before that happens.

He moves towards me and guides me to the centre of the room.

'I'm not a killer,' he tells me. 'But you are. So you're going to start it.'

'Jack,' Anna cries pleadingly. 'Let me go. Please. I'm not responsible for any of this – you know that now.'

Because underneath it all, this is what Anna is. A coward. Willing to sacrifice anyone to save her own skin.

'She murdered Carrie Adams,' I tell him calmly. 'Did she tell you that?'

'I didn't,' she argues. 'Jack, don't listen to her. The police have got the CCTV footage – they know it was Siobhan.'

'Shut the fuck up!'

And we do, because Jack is the one with the empty petrol can in his hand and presumably a lighter in the pocket in which his other hand is hidden.

'I don't care about Carrie fucking Adams. I care about my brother – about what you did to him. He loved you, did you know that? I mean, you must have. Why else would he have kept quiet for you. But you let him. What sort of person does that?'

'I had no idea what had happened,' I tell him, because it's the truth. 'It was only Lewis and Alan Grove here. The assault... there was no one else who could have been guilty.'

My body tenses as he steps closer, the knife still gripped in his fist. 'He didn't fucking touch him.'

I take a breath. Try to steady my nerves. 'So why did he confess to it?'

'Because he was set up,' he yells. 'He told me everything they'd done to him in that interview room, for hours and hours on end, relentless interrogation that terrified the shit out of him.

He was sixteen years old. Still a kid. He'd never been in any trouble in his life – he'd never seen the inside of a police station. They told him that if he confessed, he'd get a lesser sentence. They told him what would happen to him if he didn't. The offenders he'd get put away with. He did it because he trusted the police to be telling the truth, and we all know how that ends, don't we?'

'But if he didn't do it, then who did?'

'You tell me, Siobhan,' he says, jabbing the knife near my chest. 'You were the only other person there.'

'You think I hit him?' I ask quietly.

'I know it wasn't Jack.' He steps close to me. 'Do it,' he says, shoving the lighter into my tied hands. 'Do the last decent thing you'll ever do.'

I look at Anna. If she's scared, her face does nothing to betray it. She seems too composed, despite her earlier shock at the sight of the petrol. Perhaps she's accepted what's about to happen.

'Do it,' Jack says again.

My hands fumble with the lighter. I drop it. It hits the cold stone floor with a metallic ting that bounces around the empty room. Jack mumbles something beneath his breath and moves towards me, but I bend my knees over the lighter, pretending to pick it up. My tied hands move to my jacket. It's awkward to manoeuvre them into my pocket, but I manage it, and when I right myself to stand again, I lunge for Jack's arm.

Everything happens so quickly. I'm not sure whether the needle even pierces his skin, or if I manage to administer the drug. But he stops, stunned for a moment, his eyes scanning my body, looking to my hands. I drop the syringe to the floor.

'What the fuck was that?'

'Siobhan!'

Anna sees his hand around the knife before I do. I stagger back, but with my feet and hands still tied, all I manage to do is stumble. Jack grabs me before I fall. He has his hand around my back, his fingers curved at the side of my waist. He looks at me, his face just inches from mine: two dancers paused in a chilling pre-finale pose. And then he plunges the knife into my stomach.

Time seems to slow. He doesn't move at first; there's just a flicker behind his eyes, something that silently speaks a disbelief at what he's just done. At what he's found himself capable of, despite these months in the planning. I don't move either. I can't. The pain doesn't come at first, the shock managing to mask it. Then Jack steps away from me. I look to his hand, expecting to see my blood dripping from the blade. But it isn't there. Then I realise the knife is still embedded in me.

'Siobhan!' Anna cries again. And then to Jack, 'What have you done?'

It seems ironic, really. Only a couple of weeks ago, I sat across from her and watched her do nothing while I choked on an olive. I'm pretty sure now that at some point she planned to kill me. Maybe that's what she's now so outraged about: that Jack has taken the opportunity away from her.

I move my hands to my side, flinching when I accidentally knock the knife handle. Now the pain begins to come, rising like heat, making my already cloudy head feel fuzzier. But I'm not the only one. Jack is scrabbling at the floor, looking for the lighter I dropped just moments ago. His movements are clumsy; the drugs are already taking effect.

'Siobhan.' Anna's voice calls to me. 'Come to me. I can help you.'

I can't trust her, but I have no choice. I can feel my blood pumping out onto my arm, and when I look at the T-shirt I'm wearing beneath my jacket, it's stained with a dark flower that has spread across my stomach. I inch towards her, every movement deliberate and painful.

Then I hear a click. Jack has found the lighter. As I watch, he throws it across the room.

No one makes a sound as the tiny flicker of light catches the petrol and bursts into flame. Jack turns to us, face illuminated, eyes hazy as they search out first Anna's and then mine.

'Enjoy each other's company,' he says.

As the fire crackles and blazes, catching quickly in a rope of flame that snakes around the room, we watch him leave.

'Quickly,' Anna says. 'I need that knife.'

But I stall, sickened; too horrified to think. I can only be certain of one thing: I would rather die here than owe Anna my life.

FORTY-THREE

ANNA

'Siobhan,' I say again, repeating her name over and over. 'Stay with me. I need you to get closer to me.'

She isn't moving, rooted to the spot, the fire dancing circles around us. Why the fuck is she just standing there doing nothing?

I can see the blood that covers her T-shirt. I know you're not supposed to pull a knife out of someone who's been stabbed, but it's the only hope I've got of getting us both out of here. Jack Lovell doesn't get to decide how this ends.

Siobhan finally moves. She edges slowly towards me, shunting her body with her tied ankles. She is just feet away when she slumps to the ground, so close that our legs are touching. The knife is embedded in her side. I can't see any sign of the blade, just the handle, so I'm guessing Jack must have plunged it in as far as it would go. Around us, the fire is already blazing. History is repeating itself. 'I've got to pull it out,' I tell her. 'It's the only way we're going to get out of here.' I reach with my tied hands for the handle. 'On the count of three, okay? Once it's gone, I need you to put your arm over the wound and press it there. Okay?'

She manages a nod.

'One, two... three.'

I pull the blade swiftly from her body. The sound that leaves her isn't human. It tears through the cracking of the flames and the snapping of the old wooden furniture as it starts to disintegrate around us. The smell of the petrol and the smoke is now overpowering. If we don't get out of here soon, the smoke alone will kill us.

Siobhan hasn't listened to my instructions. She writhes on the floor, her back arched, her feet moving like a drunk cyclist's as she tries to push through the pain. I work quickly, holding the handle of the knife so that the blade points down. I cut through the first twist of rope quickly, but the second is thicker and tighter, and my wrists begin to burn with the effort of working the knife back and forth.

'Fuck!'

The blade slices through the inside of my wrist, blood sputtering like tiny jets. I keep working, painting the air blue with my words until the last circle of rope is near breaking point. Siobhan has fallen silent. I say her name, again and again, over and over, as I free my hands and then begin to work on the ropes that bind my ankles – a much quicker job with my hands untied. I nudge her with my knee, begging her to stay awake. To stay with me. The fire has circled us now. There's only one way to get out of here. We're going to have to go through it.

Siobhan is unconscious. I don't know whether it's blood loss or the shock of the pain, or perhaps it's smoke inhalation. Whichever way, we are running out of time. She can't die here. Ignoring the pain that flares up my arm, I stand and feel the blood run back through my numb limbs. I stoop and lift her, fighting the pain in my hip and in my head as I heave her up and over my shoulder.

I literally walk through fire. This must be what it means to go out in a blaze of glory. I hold my breath for as long as I can, grateful for all that swimming practice as a kid; all that time beating Siobhan at games of hide-and-seek; all those hours spent hiding under Carrie Adams' bed. It was all training for this, like this evening was meant for me.

My cut wrist pulses as I hold Siobhan, slumped like a sports bag over my shoulder. I smell burning fabric. And then something else. Flesh. My own.

When we get outside, the air is cold. I lower Siobhan to the ground and then take off my sweater, using it to smoother the flames that have caught at her clothes. I drop to the ground and roll on the damp grass, extinguishing the remaining flames from my own body, too fuelled with adrenaline to yet feel the pain I know will come later. Kneeling beside Siobhan, I use the sweater to staunch the flow of blood that still runs from her open wound.

'Anna,' she says, her voice weak.

'Don't try to speak. Just stay there.'

Jack's van hasn't moved. He didn't make it that far. When I get to the window, I see him inside, slumped at the wheel, the engine running. I open the driver's door and search his pockets for his phone. When I find it, I call 999.

'Ambulance, please. My cousin's been stabbed. There's a fire, too.'

I give them the address before returning to Siobhan. 'Help is on its way,' I tell her. 'Hang in there... you're going to be okay.'

Because she is. Somehow, I feel it, like this is what was meant to happen. The universe was never on my side. All of it was meant for Siobhan, and though I was never okay with that before, perhaps I've come to accept it.

And now I can see another way out.

'There's something I need to tell you. It was me, Siobhan. I assaulted Alan Grove. He was a fucking pervert. I'd seen him watching you with Lewis – it was disgusting. He'd been getting off on it.'

Her eyes look up at mine, glazed and exhausted. 'But you were outside,' she manages. 'When I saw you...'

'I'd already been in there and left. I was waiting for you.'

Alan Grove had scared the shit out of me, to be honest. There I'd been, listening in on Siobhan and Lewis, wondering how she could want to spend her time with him instead of me, when I'd heard a noise somewhere in the corner. He emerged from the shadows like some skinny Halloween ghoul – the type that looks more comical than scary when you see them up close. The zip on his trousers was undone, his hand still lingering. He looked as shocked to see me there as I was to see him, neither of us moving for a moment. And then that red mist descended, the same one that had fuelled what had happened to Uncle Garrett that night. For a moment, I wasn't myself. Or maybe that's exactly who I was.

Siobhan tries to speak again, but I cut her off. 'You can't say anything I don't already know. I know what I am.'

And for once, this is true. Maybe I didn't, before all this. But I accept it now. And with the acceptance comes a weird kind of peace.

Her eyes fall closed again. I can't do anything for her now. She will or she won't.

Nothing good can come after this. I should have taken my chance while I had it; maybe let her die at the dinner table that evening. I should have acted sooner instead of getting caught up in the joy ride that living her life became. Now, it's too late. Even if she dies, she hasn't done it quietly. I'll never live her life, not here, and perhaps I've always known that. It was fun while it lasted.

I don't want to go back to being Anna. The strange one. The obsessive one. The girl in the shadows. Yet I suppose that after tonight, I won't be that any more. For once, everyone will know me. Everyone will remember my name. And as I walk away from Siobhan, knowing we'll never see each other again, there's something comforting about that thought.

FORTY-FOUR

SIOBHAN

They say that when you're close to death, you see the people who have already left you. After Anna fades from my sight, my father replaces her. He appears hazy, only half here, as though I'm merging from my world into his, caught between the two.

'Hey, you,' he says, two little syllables that bring my childhood flooding back in a burst of light and colour.

'Hi, Dad.'

'You shouldn't be here.'

'Neither should you.'

There's a light that shines from behind him, blurring his edges so that it seems he might disappear if I don't hold on to him. I wonder if I can. I reach for his hand and he takes it, clasping my fingers between his. I am seven years old again. Protected. Safe.

'Was it Anna?' I ask. I don't need to say any more. There's a sadness in his eyes that I rarely saw when he was alive. He always had a boundless energy, and a face that wore a smile even when it was used as a disguise. This is how I want to continue to remember him. This is how he'll stay for ever.

I hear him say my name, yet his mouth doesn't move. My

eyes stay fixed on his, and there it is once more. *Siobhan*. But again, his lips didn't move. He hasn't spoken.

I feel myself rise from my skin. I am above my body, but I am no longer outside on the grass, alone in the darkness while I wait for an ambulance Anna may or may not have called. When I look down at myself, I am in bed. Not my bed in the flat in Greenwich, but my childhood bed, back in Hollybush House. I am sleeping beneath the duvet with the spots and stars, my bare arm arched above my head like a dancer taking flight.

Siobhan.

His voice is weak and distant. It comes through the open doorway of the bedroom, the landing light casting a glow on the carpet. He is downstairs. I am here. I am alone. Anna is no longer beside me.

Siobhan.

Years afterwards, as an adult, I went over and over what had happened that night, always coming back to the same thought: that I had heard his voice. It wasn't a dream, something I'd invented later to fill the gaps that had been missing that night. But it wasn't possible, either. If I'd heard him, I would have responded. I would have done something.

'You called for me,' I say to him now. 'I heard you and I didn't do anything. Why didn't I do anything?'

'It's not your fault, Siobhan. You were just a child.'

'So was Anna.'

'But she was different. Your mother said so herself, on more than one occasion. I should have listened to her.'

There is a movement at the bedroom door. The light is blocked for a second, then a shadow appears in the room. Anna. She is so small. Just a child. She moves to the foot of the bed like a ghost and stands there watching me as I sleep. She stays there, inert, her face expressionless. Then she moves and gets into the bed beside me. I watch her curl her body closer to my back before reaching across me to stroke the bare skin of my arm.

'It's okay,' she says, her voice gentle and soothing. 'Everything's going to be okay. It's for the best.'

My chest heaves. I can no longer feel the pain in my side. It has gone, evaporated into the air around me. *It's for the best.*

'I heard her say it,' I admit, my words catching on a sob. 'Those words... I knew that's what she'd said.'

I look desperately at my father, who is still there beside me, still as hazy as a summer cloud.

'I must have known it was her,' I tell him, my words desperate. 'All this time, at some level... but I never allowed the thought to stay with me.'

'Self-preservation,' he says with a shrug. 'We all do it.' My hand is still in his. He squeezes my fingers again, working the life back through them. 'There was nothing you could have done to change the outcome.' He smiles the smile he always wore, the one I still remember even after all these years, but it's a broken version of the one that lived before.

'I've got to leave you,' he tells me, his fingers loosening their grip on mine. 'It isn't your time yet.'

'Just a bit longer,' I tell him, reaching for his hand. 'Please.'

But he is blurring at the edges, his body melting as it fades into the air. 'Forgive your mother,' he says. 'Claire didn't want to believe her.' And then just as though he was never here, he's gone.

I gasp as a surge of pain floods through my side. There is noise and movement, something hard pressed against my back; a breeze against my skin as my body is lifted skywards.

'Have you got her?' I hear someone say.

And then another voice responds: 'She's back.'

I open my eyes to a flood of bright lights.

FORTY-FIVE

SIOBHAN

My mother is sitting beside my hospital bed, her hands clasped together on her knees. 'Oh thank God,' she says when she sees me wake, and she reaches for my hand, gripping it tightly in hers. 'How are you feeling?'

Disorientated, mostly. My mouth is dry, my lips sticking together when I try to respond to the question.

'Here,' she says, reaching to the little table at the end of the bed. 'Have some water.'

She takes the jug and fills a plastic cup before holding it to my lips. I sip a little, but even that seems to take an effort.

'Where's Anna?' I ask.

'Not now, Siobhan,' she says, putting the cup back on the table. 'You need to rest.'

'Where is she?' I insist. She walked away. I saw her. She looked as though she was heading back into the house. Back into the burning building. But would she really do that?

I should be relieved. I made a conscious decision to give her my own death, offering her up to Jack in place of me, and yet now that she's gone, nothing feels as I'd thought it would. I don't feel free. I just feel numb.

'Jack?' I ask, needing something in the way of information.

'He's in custody,' my mother tells me. She reaches across the bed for my hand. 'I can't begin to imagine what's been going on these past few weeks.'

'Anna killed Carrie,' I tell her quickly.

I watch her face for a reaction, but there's barely a flicker.

'I imagine it must have been easier the second time around,' I add.

Her mouth opens and closes soundlessly. 'I...' she finally manages, though it comes to nothing else.

'I know,' I tell her. 'She killed Dad, didn't she? She pushed him down those stairs.'

My mother's body heaves as a sob racks through her. 'Siobhan...'

But she can't say what she wants to. Is it guilt? Denial? Perhaps she didn't really know. Maybe there was always doubt. Yet there was suspicion too, no matter how crazy she might have thought it seemed.

When she looks at me again, her eyes are filled with tears. 'I'm so sorry, Siobhan. I should have done something at the time. I should have said something, but I wasn't sure of anything and there was no proof. She was nine years old. Nine. A child. I always suspected there was something different about her, and that night when Claire and I got back, something just didn't feel right. But no one else felt it. Only me. I never wanted to believe that there could be even the slightest possibility I might be right. It was just my overactive imagination – it was crazy to think she could be capable of something like that.'

She stops, too choked up to carry on with what she's saying.

No. *No.* Inside my head, an explosion erupts. I want to scream at her to stop. Stop talking. Stop saying these things. Stop finding excuses for what you didn't do. For what you should have done.

And then I hear my father's voice as I heard it earlier, the only thing to remain vivid as the rest of the world slipped away. *Forgive your mother.*

'But you told Claire you suspected something?'

My mother's eyebrows almost meet in the middle as she frowns. God, she looks so guilty. So broken. 'How do you—'

'It doesn't matter how I know,' I say quickly, because I can hardly tell her that the voice of my dead father spoke to me as I lay losing blood on the ground, waiting for someone to come and save me. I want to believe that to be true, but I know it's not. That's not what happened. I don't believe in ghosts or spirits or an afterlife. My dad is gone. But my own subconscious is real and alive, and I suspect it stores more than I'd ever imagined.

She begins to cry, silent tears that roll in fat splashes down her tired face. 'I am so sorry, Siobhan. I should have done something more. I should have tried to make Claire listen. But I could never be sure of anything. I was confused. I was grieving. My whole life had been ripped from beneath me. I didn't know what to think.'

Shame does that to a person. I know that better than anyone.

'How could I wreck my relationship with Claire like that?' she continues. 'I had no proof of anything. She's my sister. I couldn't accuse her child of murder based on an inkling. Just because I had a feeling that something wasn't right with her. Claire doted on Anna, you saw that. I know she had her problems, but she loved her child. She didn't see in her what I did, and I was scared for her. Anna was her world. And I needed them, Siobhan. I needed Claire. She'd always been my closest ally, my only real friend. Your dad was already gone. I'd have lost everyone.'

'Not everyone,' I remind her. 'You'd still have had me.'

There's a part of me that wants to hate her. There's a part of me that wants to walk away from all of this, blaming everyone else for the lies that have been told and the secrets that have been kept. But I can't. I think of the Invisible String. These were the people who made my mother feel safe. Hating her will mean having to hate myself too, because I think deep down I must always have known. I suppressed that night, burying it so deep it became obscured. I tried to explain away the things I'd heard by telling myself over and over that they had been a dream. Because sometimes the truth is too painful to accept, and lying to ourselves becomes a preferable alternative. It just needed to be peeled from beneath the layers under which I'd hidden it. It needed to be exposed when it was ready to fight its way to the surface. Perhaps that was why I'd been so ready to offer Anna my death, knowing it was what she deserved for everything she'd done all those years ago.

'Is this why you and Claire eventually stopped talking?'

My mother nods. 'I think as Anna got older, even Claire started to believe. She knows there's something off with her. She just doesn't want to accept it.'

I wince at the pain that shoots through my stomach. 'I need a break,' I tell her, and she shows enough self-awareness to realise what I mean: that I need a break from her.

'I'll be outside when you need me,' she says.

She leaves the room, but the silence doesn't last long. When the door opens again, I expect to see her back, returning with another apology and some late-thought excuse for all the things she didn't do. I'm relieved when it isn't her. Relieved, instead, to see Flynn standing in the doorway, a bag of chocolate chip muffins clutched to his chest. Remorse swells in my chest, that I could ever have thought this man guilty.

'Siobhan,' he says. 'Thank God you're all right.'

He puts the bag on the bedside table and sits next to me, his face etched with concern as his eyes roam from my cuts and grazes to the strips of gauze that hide my burns. 'Have the police been to see you yet?'

My heart sinks in my chest. I still have this to look forward to. 'No. Not yet.'

'They know you weren't involved with Carrie's death. They know it was Anna. One of the neighbours remembered a cleaner, and that it was possible she'd been given a key. They wanted to talk to you about her... that's why they came looking for you.'

Tears catch at the corners of my eyes as relief floods though me. I still believed that even after everything, she would manage to make me look guilty. I still feared I might spend the rest of my life paying for her crimes.

'But how did they know Anna and I were linked?'

'I don't know. I already know more than I'm supposed to. I'm sure they'll explain everything when they see you.'

'Do they know where she is?'

He shrugs. It's enough to give me an answer: Anna has managed to escape justice.

'You don't need to worry about anything,' he says, putting a hand over mine. 'She's gone. She won't come anywhere near you now, not with the police looking for her. And with Jack in custody, you're safe.' He squeezes my fingers. 'That's all that matters, isn't it?'

I close my eyes to find my dad's face looking back at me. I'm safe now. I suppose that should be enough. But there's no justice for Carrie. No justice for what Anna did to my family all those years ago.

Flynn is still looking at me when I open my eyes, still waiting for an answer. 'For now,' I tell him.

FORTY-SIX

ANNA

I stretch my legs out in the sunshine, my bare feet pushing into the soft pale-peach sand. Warmth beats down on me, heating my skin and filling me with a sense of hope. That anticipation you get at the start of a new and unknown beginning. The beach café is busy, filled with groups of young friends and older couples, everyone in swimwear, the women's sun-kissed bodies draped with beach cover-ups and kaftans. I sip the ice-cold lemonade that sits on the table beside me as I soak up the atmosphere, raising my dress a little to bare my knees to the sun. The three-quarter-length spring dress that was in Siobhan's suitcase is light enough, but I'll need to buy some clothing better suited to the Spanish climate.

The suitcase was in the back of Jack's van. With him slumped unconscious in the driver's seat, I was also able to search for her passport, because I knew she would have had it with her if she'd had the suitcase. She'd been planning to leave the country, knowing what Jack was going to do to me. I wonder where she is now; whether she made it to the hospital in time. Despite everything, there's a part of me that hopes she's alive. Once she finds out I'm gone, but that no one knows where...

what then? She'll still be in London, while I sit here in the sunshine, embracing the kind of anonymous escape she'd planned for herself. In this game of cat-and-mouse we created between us, I guess this makes me the winner.

I sense someone watching me, that heat that lands on the side of your face when you know there are eyes upon you. Among a group of men who look as though they might be suffering the morning after the night before, one has his attention on me. He smiles when our eyes meet. He's not bad looking: thirty-ish, dark-haired, clean-cut.

I'm glad I did my make-up in the back of the taxi: the one I called from Jack's phone not long after leaving the old cottage. I dumped the phone in the woods beyond the back of the garden, meeting the driver just down the road from a pub on the outskirts of town. Siobhan's cosmetics bag was in the suitcase. I used her make-up liberally, hiding my tired eyes with her black eyeliner and wearing a scarf to conceal the burn mark on my neck. Those on my arms are covered at the moment by a jacket that's too warm for this weather. I bought some Savlon at the airport, knowing I'll have to invent a story for how I came by the scars that will stain my skin.

When he catches my eye a second time, the man gets up from his chair and comes over.

'Just arrived?' he says, nodding at my suitcase. It still has the Heathrow to Palma tag on its handle.

'Yeah. Stag do?' I ask.

He nods and pulls a face. 'Went in too heavy on the first night.'

I laugh. 'Schoolboy error.'

'You here on your own then?'

'Yep. The best way to travel.'

He studies me with his eyes narrowed, a slight smirk on his face as though he finds me entertaining. If only you knew, I think. 'Fancy a drink tonight?' he asks.

'You're here with your friends.'

He shrugs. 'They won't miss me.'

'You think you can handle more alcohol after last night?'

'I'm always up for a challenge.'

I smile and reach for my lemonade. 'Then you've come to the right place.'

He asks for my phone number, but I don't have a phone, and even if I did, I wouldn't be sharing the number with him. Instead, I tell him he can meet me back here at 7.30 this evening. I took enough money from Siobhan's account to tide me over for a week or so. He'll serve a purpose for a night before I leave here, and then I can start making more permanent plans.

'Danny,' he says, offering his hand like I'm at a job interview.

I shake it, his fingers lingering on my skin. 'Siobhan,' I say, with my best Siobhan smile. I know this isn't for ever. This is just for today, for one last night. By the time the UK authorities start looking for me, I will have become someone else, someone with a different name. A different identity.

I finish my drink and leave him with his friends. The man who drove me from Palma airport to Portals Nous was helpful in advising where I could find the cheapest accommodation for the night, and I head there now, making my way first across the beach and then along the harbour front. It's then that I see her, standing near the railing at a row of moored fishing boats, a small dog waiting at her feet. She is beautiful: olive-skinned, with long dark hair swept over one shoulder, her bare arms toned and slender. I wonder how dark her eyes are, but they're hidden for the moment by sunglasses.

I rip the tag from my suitcase before walking towards her.

'Qué hermoso perro.'

She looks at me, surprised by my Spanish, because with my ghost-like complexion and the suitcase trailing behind me, I'm clearly not a local.

'*Gracias.*'

'I used to have one similar,' I say, leaning down to smooth the dog's soft fur. 'I miss him.' I can't gauge a reaction because of the sunglasses. It's hard to guess her age. She could be twenty-five; she could be forty. '*Cómo se llama?*'

'Lola.'

'Ah, a she. *Lo siento.*'

'You've just arrived here?' the woman asks, gesturing to my suitcase.

'I'm between homes. Still in the process of moving. My name's Siobhan, by the way.'

She smiles tightly, unsure what to make of the introduction. This isn't what people do any more. Friendliness is something to be wary of.

'I'd better get going,' I say.

'I have a salon in town,' she tells me. 'If you ever need a haircut...' She takes her phone from her pocket and slides something from its case. She passes it to me. A business card.

'Great. Thank you. Definitely. Anyway, nice to meet you. And you, Lola,' I add, reaching down to muss the fur at the back of the dog's neck.

As I walk away, I study the name on the business card. Catalina Perez. I speak it aloud once she's far enough away from me, the words tasting like chocolate on my tongue. It sounds like the name of a celebrity. It would suit me. And how difficult can cutting hair be anyway?

A LETTER FROM VICTORIA

Dear Reader,

I want to say a huge thank you for choosing to read *Your Perfect Life*. If you enjoyed it, and want to keep up to date with all my latest releases, just sign up at the following link. Your email address will never be shared, and you can unsubscribe at any time.

www.bookouture.com/victoria-jenkins

The idea for this book came from the premise of someone stealing another person's identity: a plot that has been often used as a basis for psychological thrillers and crime novels. Rather than have a stranger try to infiltrate another woman's life, I became fascinated by the idea of how this might be done – and how easily it might be achieved – by a relative: someone who knows the woman's life and can use her secrets to manipulate situations to her advantage. The idea that both women might simultaneously be trying to manipulate the other for their own gain – or in the case of Siobhan, to save her own life - came after I'd started writing the book, and I loved developing Siobhan's and Anna's characters. Anna in particular has a kind of unhinged psychopathic personality I've never written before, and I had a lot of fun bringing her to life.

As in most of the stories I write, there's a strong focus in the book on female relationships: cousins/mothers/friends/sisters/colleagues. I love writing female characters – the strong, the flawed and the vulnerable – female bonds, female feuds, revenge, rivalry and jealousy, and in *Your Perfect Life* I've hope there's been a blend of all these things.

I hope you loved *Your Perfect Life* and if you did, I would be very grateful if you could write a review. I'd love to hear what you think, and it makes such a difference helping new readers to discover one of my books for the first time.

I love hearing from my readers – you can get in touch through social media.

Thanks,

Victoria

facebook.com/victoriajenkinswriter

x.com/vicwritescrime

instagram.com/vicwritescrime

ACKNOWLEDGMENTS

Thank you to my editor, Claire Simmonds, who championed this book from the first read and brought it to life with her razor-sharp editing skills. It has been a pleasure working with you on this book.

Thank you, also, to Helen Jenner, for the first premise of the idea for this story: 'what if someone stole someone else's life, but they ended up regretting it?'

Thank you to everyone at Bookouture – to Jenny Geras, Noelle Holten, and all the brilliant team: you have supported my writing even when I've doubted it, and I continue to be grateful for this incredible opportunity you have given me.

To my family, as always, thank you for not blocking me from communications when I have been in one of my six-monthly panic modes. As you know by now, they will pass... so please continue to ignore my neuroticism.

This is a story about cousins, and so it's only right that it be dedicated to the loveliest three little cousins I know, collectively – and affectionately – known as 'the Kray triplets'. To Mia, Emily and Hettie: may you forever be the very best of friends (and not try to sabotage each other's lives, as demonstrated here).